BLUFF

MICHAEL KARDOS is the Pushcart
Prize-winning author of the novel
The Three-Day Affair and the story
collection *One Last Good Time*.
Originally from the Jersey Shore, he
currently lives in Starkville, Mississippi,
where he teaches creative writing.

BLUFF

MICHAEL KARDOS

A Mysterious Press book for
Head of Zeus

First published in the US in 2018 by Mysterious Press,
an imprint of Grove/Atlantic, New York

First published in the UK by Head of Zeus in 2018
This paperback edition published in the UK in 2019 by Head of Zeus Ltd

9 7 5 3 1 2 4 6 8

A catalogue record for this book is available from the British Library.

ISBN (PB): 9781788543743
ISBN (E): 9781788543712

This book was designed by Norman Tuttle at Alpha Design & Composition
This book was set in 12.5 pt. Dante MT
by Alpha Design & Composition of Pittsfield, NH.

for Katie

Trust everybody, but always cut the cards.

—American proverb

PART ONE

A

It started with that most basic of requests: *Pick a card*.

Though really it started before that, when I asked the woman at the nearest table, "Give me a hand, will you, please?"

She looked a little like me—long brown hair, narrow face, younger than most of the women in the room. Maybe that's why I'd approached her. Also because she'd seemed engrossed in the show. But when I spoke to her, she threw her hands up as if to prove she wasn't carrying a weapon.

"Oh . . . not me," she said. "I couldn't."

"Of course you can," I said. "You'll do great!" Usually, that was all it took—a little prodding, followed by some scattered, encouraging applause from the audience.

"No, no," she said. "I'm *way* too wasted."

I scanned the room for another woman to help out. (Women, I'd learned over the years, were better volunteers—they generally followed directions and didn't try to show off.) But I was too slow. A man at the same table was already springing up from his chair, saying, "I'll do it!"

Had my wits been more about me, his overeagerness would have put me on alert. But halfway through the show at this point, I just wanted to be done and go home. Close the door on what had been a trying day. Besides, the weather was only getting worse, and my car was half hopeless even on clear roads.

So I said, "Sure, come on up."

Immediately, people across the ballroom started in with *Oooh* and *Oh, damn* and the anxious laughter that told me now I had a problem.

Corporate shows around the holidays were usually plum gigs—good pay, good food, good spirit. And tonight's event, a holiday party for Great Nation Physical Therapy, in the Hyatt in downtown Newark, had seemed especially promising when I booked it. Who needed to be entertained more than a roomful of medical professionals during the holidays, glad to be away from illness and injury for a night?

But when I arrived, I learned that the party being thrown by the physical therapists wasn't *for* them. Rather, the purpose was to wine and dine the hundred or so personal injury attorneys who held the key to an endless supply of injured people in need of rehabilitation. Door prizes included a home theater system and a vacation in Aruba.

My volunteer followed me to the front of the room and stood teetering a little. Definitely dined and wined. But I was determined to push through the routine. It was the finale of the card portion of the show. Then on to the linking rings. I asked my volunteer his name.

"I'm Lou!" he said, beaming. I could picture his face, those white teeth, grinning at me from a highway billboard beneath an aggressive font. SOMEONE MUST PAY FOR YOUR INJURIES!

Within the hour, I'd learn that Lou Husk, though not yet thirty-five, was already a legend among his peers in the room—extreme climber, extreme skier, extremely not someone you want opposing you in court. But right then, standing beside him in the Grand Ballroom, I knew him only as the man who would help my show along, usher me a few minutes closer to collecting my check and going home.

I put on a smile and gave him a warm, two-handed *so-glad-to-meet-you* handshake. When I went to let go, he surprised me by raising my hand to his lips and kissing it.

Then he licked my knuckles.

It threw me. This wasn't some bachelor party or frat gig. And even then. In a decade of supporting myself as a working magician, I had been patted, grabbed, groped, and kissed. Even punched once . . . but never licked.

No one else seemed to notice. I wiped my hand on my pants and reminded myself that on my feet were a new pair of four-inch leopard print stilettos that replaced the red leather heels I'd lovingly worn into the ground. The rest of my outfit was less flashy: pencil pants, white tuxedo shirt left open at the collar, well-tailored black jacket. But even simple clothes cost money, and tonight's show paid for a new pair of shoes and half a month's rent.

I took a breath and got the deck of cards from the table behind me. Shuffled them a few times, fanned them out.

"Pick a card, Lou," I said, predicting he would select the very top or bottom card on the off chance it would mess me up.

He chose the top card.

Not that it mattered. In fact, the trick itself was the epitome of simple: card selected, shown to the audience, returned to the deck, vanished from the deck. (In that regard, I'll admit it was a lazy trick. Five years ago, I would've been more artful with the setup, if only for my own entertainment.) But this trick was all about the reveal. I went over to my duffel bag of gear and removed a circular target made of Styrofoam, eight inches in diameter.

Handed it to Lou and told him to hold the target high above his head with both hands.

I asked him to choose a number between twenty and forty.

"One hundred," he said.

This was why I preferred women volunteers. They did what I asked them to do. They understood that if they played along for a while, they might just get to see something amazing.

"You're gonna ruin the fun here, Lou," I said.

"Okay, fine," he said begrudgingly. "Twenty."

I removed a tape measure from my pocket and unspooled it until it measured twenty feet. Returned the tape measure to my pocket.

"Keep the target up high," I said. "Both hands. That's right." Then I asked him for another number between ten and twenty.

He watched me a moment. "Twenty."

I counted off cards from the deck, letting each card float to the floor. I dropped the rest of the deck. Now I was holding only the twentieth card. Slowly, I turned over the card and showed it to Lou and the audience, not looking at it myself, making a big deal out of saying, "Is this your card?"

"We both know you didn't really mess up," he said.

Right, I thought. *It's called playing along. It's called a performance.*

"You're saying it isn't your card?" I asked.

"I'm saying you already know it isn't."

In a moment, I was supposed to whip the card into the center of the target above his head. The card would travel fast enough to lodge in the Styrofoam, at which point my volunteer would pluck it out and show everyone that it had transformed into the selected card.

"Just hold very still, please," I said.

Lou grinned and jerked the target a full foot to the left.

"And . . . that would be the opposite of holding still," I said, trying to keep things light, though I felt dampness in my armpits and along the backs of my knees.

He centered the target again.

"Much better," I said.

He jerked it to the right.

The eight-inch target was an effective stage prop, but I could've hit a target half the size from twice the distance . . . provided that my volunteer stopped fucking moving it.

"Stillness, Lou," I said, struggling to remain calm. "Stillness is everything."

"You must be a real delight in the sack," he said.

A collective intake of breath from the room. They were amused, though, not aghast. This was classic Lou! They were witnessing the story they would tell tomorrow. I understood the impulse to want a story, to claim it. Still, I didn't want this diversion to be all they walked away remembering.

"Too bad *you'll* never know," I stage-whispered. Banter, I reminded myself. That's all this was. "Now just tell me your card," I said.

That was all Lou had to do. Then I would reconfirm that the lone card in my hand wasn't his. Then I would hurl it at the Styrofoam target and the magic would happen and we could all move on.

"Ace of spades," he said.

A lie. He had selected the three of diamonds. I knew because I had forced it on him at the start of the trick.

The audience tittered uncomfortably. They'd seen the card just after he selected it. They knew he was lying to me—they knew it wasn't banter, that he was genuinely trying to ruin my trick—but they were keeping his secret, either because I was the stranger in the room or because he'd beaten enough of them in court and they were relieved, now, not to be his adversary.

"How about you try again," I told him.

My voice must have lost any last trace of amusement, because he said, *"What? What did I do?"* If his two hands hadn't been holding the target over his head, one of them would have covered his heart.

I sighed. "Just try again. What was your card?"

"Okay. How about . . ." More grinning. "The ace of spades?"

I knew it was my fault for letting it get this far. It was something an amateur would do, getting into it with a volunteer who wanted exactly this—to show off, to perform a little impromptu theater for the audience.

But I was off my game, and had been since before the show even began. It had started with the email I received that afternoon: *You were not selected to perform at this year's World of Magic convention in New York City.* Rejection is a part of life, I knew that, but as a former grand prize winner in their international close-up magic competition I had counted on being given a show. More important, it was part of the plan—hell, it *was* the plan—to begin rejoining the wider community of magicians after almost a decade of going it alone. Swallow my pride, let bygones be bygones, and get back in the game, was my thinking. So the rejection had cut especially deep.

And right on the heels of that, I had to drive to Newark on icy roads to perform. Of course, that's what a professional does: performs. The show must go on and all that. (In fact, I was hoping this holiday party might lift my spirits.) Except, just as I'd finished setting up and was about to switch on my lapel mic, the overeager kitchen staff had burst into the ballroom with their buffet carts nearly an hour ahead of schedule. Once the first few lawyers stood and started serving themselves, the stampede was inevitable.

So I waited, pretending to be interested in my phone but becoming increasingly irritated, minute by minute, as the sleet fell and the roads froze over. Meanwhile, the attorneys made trip after trip to the raw bar, the carving station, the sushi station. I kept glancing at all that expensive food and thinking, These aren't even the top lawyers! I could tell from their suits, the way none of them hung right. Jackets too tight in the shoulders, too long in the cuff. Trousers with front pockets so loose I could've had my pick for the stolen cell phone routine I performed only when I was certain I could get away with a clean grab.

"Actually, your card wasn't the ace of spades," I said to Lou. "If you'll remember all the way back to two minutes ago, it was the three of diamonds."

His eyes narrowed. "Are you accusing me of lying?" Mock outrage, a performance—unless I had screwed up my force at the beginning of the trick. (I hadn't.)

"Either you're lying," I said, "or your eyes aren't so good."

"My eyes are perfect, honey," he said. "I think it's your magic act that's on life support."

And that, ladies and gents, is what did it. I suppose his words hit so hard because they happened to be true. What had once, long ago, been infinite potential was now, yes, on life support. But that didn't mean I was ready for that kind of appraisal. Especially today. Especially during the act. And worst of all was hearing it from a pickled show-stealer who had read me so easily I might as well have been blinking neon.

What I'm saying is, his jab caught me at the worst possible moment. I was desperate to be done with this trick, this show, this whole day of frustration and disappointment and self-doubt, and I felt all of it harden at that exact instant into a white-hot hunk of fury.

What I'm saying is, I let the card fly.

Once, I was clocked throwing a playing card at 72 miles per hour. No, that won't get me into the Guinness Book. Still, a card flying 72 mph travels twenty feet in a fifth of a second, which isn't enough time for a volunteer to react. No time to move out of the way, or even to flinch.

So it seemed like no time at all, when really it was one-fifth of a second later, that Lou Husk dropped the target, covered his left eye with his hands, and began to howl.

2

♦

What happened next happened quickly and is a bit hazy in my memory. Someone ran to the stage, then a few someones. Lou Husk's friends, or rivals, or whatever they were, started pooling their extensive knowledge of the city's urgent care clinics. Soon they were leaving the ballroom with the patient (who was still groaning, his palm shoved against his eye).

With my thinking pretty much limited to *holy shit, holy shit*, I hurriedly packed my gear with trembly hands. I wanted to get out of there as fast as possible and was doing my best to avoid looking at anyone (well aware that everyone was peering at me) when a representative from Great Nation Physical Therapy approached. She stopped several feet away from me as if I were feral and might decide to attack her, too. Not that I blamed her.

"You were scheduled for an hour," she said, "but you performed for less than thirty minutes and injured a guest."

I knew this already—I'd been there—and didn't know what to say. Anyway, I couldn't have said much. My mouth was dry and I felt shaky all over.

Did I just blind a man? Was I about to get arrested?

"We're going to have to hold on to your payment," she said.

"Of course," I told her. "I'm so sorry . . ." But she was already walking away again.

I carried my bag and fold-up table into the elevator. As the doors were shutting, a lawyer's thick arm shot forward, causing them to fly open again. The man stepped into the elevator and flashed a close-mouthed smile as we waited for the doors to shut.

My face must have revealed my terror, because he said, "Relax. I'm not in a suing mood."

We descended to the lobby, and when the doors opened again I started to hurry away. Before I could get anywhere he blurted out, "His nickname is Lucifer."

I stopped. "Excuse me?"

"Lou? He's not a well-liked individual. I thought you should know that."

The lawyer beside me had an ill-fitting suit, jowly cheeks, and a glistening forehead. He certainly had the look down.

"What does that possibly matter?" I asked.

He shrugged. "Maybe it doesn't. Are you looking for legal representation, Natalie?"

"I have to get out of here."

But it was a bluff, and he called me on it.

"In the middle of an ice storm? No, I don't advise that." And that was without him knowing about my bald tires and screeching brakes. "Come on," he said, taking the handle of my fold-up table from me. "Let's step into my office." He scanned the lobby. "Just as soon as I can find one."

The lobby bar was bright and close to the elevators, not crowded but moderately bustling, people coming and going. But across the large lobby, in a dimly lit corner, was a much smaller spillover bar, just long enough to accommodate four bar stools.

The area was closed, roped off. It was as good a place as any to hide and wait.

So that's where we sat, folded table and bag of gear beside me, while the ice continued to fall over Newark.

"I just want to say," he began, "that what you do with those cards . . ." He whistled. "Not the throwing. The other stuff. Like where the queens all ended up together? It's truly amazing."

"I don't know why you're telling me this," I said.

"What? You're a hell of a magician, Natalie. That's all I'm saying. It's a compliment."

"I just blinded a man!"

"*Maybe* you blinded a man. It was a playing card, not a knife."

"I can pierce the rind of a watermelon with a playing card."

He winced. "Well, then, all the more important you and I are talking." He offered me a meaty hand with black hairs sprouting out from the tops of his fingers. "Brock McKnight." I was relieved when his handshake didn't crush my bones.

We were by a window, and I could see across the road to another hotel where outside, beneath the overhang, a doorman stood alone and hugged himself for warmth. I shivered. "I feel sick," I said. It was true. Long ago I had decided that nothing was worse, nothing less forgivable, than to be the cause of someone else's physical harm. In all the years since, I had subscribed to very few creeds, but always that. "I didn't really mean to hurt him."

I was relieved that the words tasted mostly true.

"Of course you didn't," Brock said. "Why would you want to sabotage your career?"

Yes, exactly, I thought. An eye is very small. My aim was good, but was it *that* good? I didn't remember taking aim. I had been irate and embarrassed, true, but the throw had felt automatic.

Like with classical pianists, how the fingers do the thinking, not the brain. Otherwise, they could never do those lightning-fast runs up and down the keys.

But even if my hand had gone rogue, doing what my mind wouldn't have allowed it to do, did that make it any better? My hand was still part of me, wasn't it? That snapping wrist, those quick fingers, were mine.

"What's going to happen?" I asked.

"It depends," Brock said. "Do you carry liability insurance?" When I didn't answer right away, he sighed and began to relate highlights from The Legend of Lou Husk. The man with a plan. And that plan was evidently to make his adversaries wish they had never heard the name Lou Husk.

"If he goes to the police," Brock said, "it's conceivable the prosecutor could charge you with aggravated assault. But maybe not in Newark, where actual crimes are being committed and taking up police time. You'd probably be looking at misdemeanor endangerment."

"Which means?"

"The fine caps at a thousand dollars and a year in prison."

That word, "prison," echoed like profanity in a language I could barely identify. "For a *playing card*?"

"You said yourself it cuts watermelons."

"I guess a thousand dollars could be worse," I said.

"Oh, don't worry—it will be, since he'll almost certainly file a civil lawsuit, too. That's where the real money is. But that's a ways down the road." My eyes welling up didn't seem to faze Brock at all. He didn't bother to look out the window or pick imaginary fuzz off his suit in order to give me a moment to collect myself. He must have been used to people hitting rock bottom in his presence. "I'd like to be your lawyer, Natalie," he said.

"I can't afford one," I said, wiping my eyes with shaky hands.

"And now I'm supposed to say, 'There's no way you can't afford one.' And it's true. If he ends up blind in one eye . . ." He didn't need to finish. "Instead, I'll tell you I'm really good, and I work on a sliding scale."

But just how far would it slide? I dropped my head into my hands. "Why the hell would I let him get to me like that?" I muttered.

Over the years I'd faced some nasty characters, been in actual threatening situations. Yet I'd always kept my composure.

"Yeah, but lawyers," Brock said. "We're *professional* assholes. We have it all down to a science." He didn't totally mask his pride in saying so. "Look, I can tell you need a drink. What's your poison?"

If I knew my poison I'd be able to avoid it. And anyway, the bar where we were sitting was closed. I looked out the window again. It was only November. God knew what December would bring. "I can't believe I have to drive home in this."

"Where do you live?" he asked.

"Too far away for a cab," I said.

"And you're telling me there's no hotel rider in your contract?"

"I have birds," I said.

"Huh?"

"Doves. To feed. They need food and fresh water."

"She has birds." The lawyer shook his head and pried himself off the bar stool. "Come on, what's your drink? I'll get it from the other bar."

Outside, the ice was falling harder. "Just get me something I can't afford."

"That's just what I'll do"—he held a finger in the air as if testing the wind—"the moment I'm done taking a leak."

Alone with nothing but a promise. My stomach growled, and I saw my refrigerator at home—plenty of condiments, little to put them on—and wondered who exactly I had been spiting earlier by refusing to invite myself to the buffet. Maybe a stomach full of peel-and-eat shrimp would have made me more patient with my volunteer.

I checked my phone. No missed calls. I'd been hoping to hear from my mother today. As I was returning the phone to the side pocket of the duffel bag, Brock came back empty-handed. "I didn't feel like waiting," he said. But rather than sit down again, he went behind our private, closed-down bar and knelt down until only the top of his head was bobbing around.

"And . . . bingo." He stood up again. "I'm very surprised they have this." He came back around carrying a bottle and two rocks glasses. "This is like two hundred a bottle." He poured us each a generous drink. "No way should they be letting us do this." He shook his head. "It's a shame what America's become." Then he said, "To my newest client," and we drank, and the Scotch felt nourishing going down my throat.

Brock laid a reassuring or maybe possessive hand on my arm. "I think it's vitally important," he said, "that I pour us refills. This Scotch sat alone in a barrel for twenty years just so you and I could drink it and cement our new relationship."

It was the most sense anyone had made all night. He poured, and we drank.

"So now that I'm your lawyer," he said, "I would like to give you a piece of advice. May I do that?"

The Scotch had steadied me a little. I was now a woman with a lawyer who gave her advice. "Sure," I said.

"You should be working with larger objects," he said.

"Huh?"

"I mean cards? Coins? Who can see any of that from across a conference room?"

The ubiquitous criticism of the close-up magician. Brock McKnight might have been unique among the lawyers—he alone had followed me, the perpetrator, into the elevator. Still, he was a typical layperson, and despite myself I felt my hackles rise. "It's called sleight of hand," I said. "It's what I do."

"Still . . ." He finished his drink. "You do bigger stuff, it might go over better."

The ice storm was keeping me here. My lawyer's critique of my show was repelling me to the car. The Scotch was keeping me here. Two against one. "Trust me, I know what I'm doing," I said. "I'm a professional performer."

When he laughed, I assumed it was because I had hardly demonstrated my professionalism tonight. But that wasn't it. "Darling," he said, "everybody in that ballroom is a professional performer. We're litigators!" He shifted in his bar stool and got his wallet from his pants pocket. The business card he offered me was curved to the shape of his ass, like a little canoe on the river You're Fucked.

"Come by my office tomorrow afternoon," he said. "By then I'll have something on our pal Lou and we'll get the paperwork squared away." He saw me looking at the card. "Sliding scale," he said, "I promise," and I took it. Then, almost as if it were an afterthought: "By the way, that trick with the queens? I mean, I've seen a lot of card tricks in my day, but with you it's like another thing entirely. So come on—how'd you do it?"

The Four Queens is very straightforward to watch. I show the queens and lay them on the table, facedown, in a square. Then I lay three additional cards on top of each of the queens, so there are four stacks of four cards. One by one, the queens migrate to a single stack.

How did I do it? I did it by studying with a magician named Jack Clarion. I did it by learning the palms and passes and false shuffles in dozens of books on card manipulation, slowly, over many years and thousands of hours. I did it by developing my own routines with original patter to counterpoint the physical technique, until the moves were so undetectable you'd be fooled from a foot away, and until the routine was so well rehearsed that you could smash a lamp over my head and it wouldn't affect my timing.

"Sorry," I said. "It would violate the magician's oath."

Brock burst out laughing. "Are you for real?" He made himself stop laughing. "It's not like you're giving up the launch codes."

"Sorry," I said.

He reached into his wallet again and removed a bill. A hundred dollars. "I assume the physical therapists are withholding payment?"

"I'm not gonna take your money," I said.

"What, you don't take tips?"

I was immediately ready with my crude response, the result of too many bachelor parties—

Honey, I take the whole thing.

—but it was late, and I was exhausted and worried and had no taste for posturing.

"Yeah, I take tips," I said.

"Well then?" He waited until my fingertips were touching the bill. "By the way, how'd you do that trick with the four queens?"

I let go of the bill.

"A hundred isn't enough?"

"It's not that."

"The oath?" he asked, eyebrow cocked.

"The oath."

It wasn't the oath. In truth, I didn't especially care anymore about a couple of sentences uttered a million years ago in front of a handful of middle-aged men. But I did care about the shred of dignity I might still have at the end of the night. Then again, wasn't paying my heating bill dignified?

As if reading my mind, Brock set the bill on the bar. "Take it," he said.

I was about to stuff the hundred dollars into my pants pocket when instead I held it up in front of him. Slowly, I tore the bill in half, then in half again. I crushed the four pieces into a small wad, tighter and tighter, until there was nothing at all left between my fingertips. I showed the lawyer my empty hands, front and back.

My hands were still shaking a little, something that would persist for the next eleven days (until in a cold, windswept parking lot they would suddenly become still again). I took a drink as a bit of misdirection.

"You know, it's a shame," Brock said, "a woman with your talents stuck performing for people like us."

"It's an honest living," I said lamely.

"Maybe that's your problem," he said.

"What is?"

"I know a guy. Another magician of a sort. He does very well playing poker against people like me. I'm talking world-class."

"If he told you he's a card cheat, then he isn't world-class."

"I said guys *like* me. I'm his lawyer. There's confidentiality between us."

"You obviously consider it a sacred trust."

"Natalie, I'm trying to help you," he said. "You could earn real money if you're even half as good as my guy."

I looked him in the eye and said, "Webbs aren't criminals."

I had meant it, but my words sounded even to me like Scotch-influenced melodrama. And then there was the matter of the playing card I'd thrown, and how the question of whether or not I was a criminal was very much up in the air.

"Duly noted," Brock said, and slid off his bar stool again. "Come by tomorrow. Two o'clock?"

"All right," I said.

He shook my hand again. "You be careful getting home to those birds. I'm going upstairs to see if the zoo animals left me any petit fours. I'm a big fan of those."

He returned to his brethren, leaving me alone at the closed-down bar by the window. Outside, a steady rain had begun to fall, washing away the ice. I chose to attribute this to my attorney's vast influence.

3

♣

I braved the slow, white-knuckle drive south on Route 9, a caval-cade of trucks and SUVs whipping past me in the left lane, splashing a blinding slurry of ice and mud onto my windshield. I was intensely aware of statistics: how on this road, this night, *someone* was ending up in the back of an ambulance.

The terrifying conditions kept me focused on the road, yet halfway home I remembered that Lou Husk's wristwatch was still in my pocket. At the end of the trick, once the card had been transformed into the three of diamonds and the audience had finished applauding, I was supposed to say, "I have a prize for you, for being such a good volunteer." I would then give him back his watch, which I had stolen from his wrist while shaking hands at the beginning of the trick. If my volunteer happened to be wearing a watch, and it was a kind I could pinch—Lou's had been easy, the band made of spring segments—then producing it at the end of the trick made for a fine, surprising coda.

I rolled down my window and tossed out the watch.

By the time I parked along the road in front of my apartment, the rain had softened to a light drizzle, lifting a curtain on the raw night. There were a few bars within walking distance, and I probably would've been able to wangle free drinks because earlier, while sitting at the bar with Brock McKnight, I had become twenty-seven.

But at this hour the bars would be closing in on last call and turning on their rude, despairing lights. I removed my gear from the trunk and lugged it all up the three steps to the landing.

The apartment was only a small house with an upstairs and downstairs unit and a common entrance. Half a dozen of these houses stood in a line on my side of the street, bookended by a tattoo parlor and a mini-mart. I'd forgotten to leave the outside light on, and I fumbled for the keyhole while trying to prevent the table from unfolding or falling over. On the landing I tried to be quiet for Harley, the upstairs tenant, though I could already hear my birds cooing steadily.

I finally got the door open and stowed my gear under the bed. Back in the living room, I tossed my coat onto the loveseat, removed my new shoes, and checked on the birds. Their water bowl was mostly full but the food bowl was empty, so I took care of that. Unless you're a stage illusionist who's married to your assistant, coming home after a gig is the world's loneliest experience. I was glad to have the birds.

While they pecked at their food, I went in search of mine. The leftover spaghetti in the refrigerator had absorbed all the sauce and looked alarmingly wormlike, so I settled on a glass of adequate cabernet. I heard somewhere that drinking alone was only sad if the booze was too cheap or too expensive. I sat down on the loveseat and pulled an afghan over my legs.

I opened my laptop and touched a key to wake it up. Did some fast Google searches: *aggravated assault, misdemeanor endangerment*. Google's unblemished record of only fueling my anxieties remained intact.

I was about to shut the computer again when I found myself opening my email to reread the message that had come in that afternoon. I couldn't help myself, like picking at a scab.

Subject: WOM Application

Dear Natalie Webb,

I'm writing to let you know that the selection committee has decided to stand by its original decision. Unfortunately, you were not selected to perform at this year's World of Magic convention in New York City. Due to the number of magicians who applied to perform (we set an all-time record this year!) competition was especially stiff. As mentioned in my original email, the selection committee had a very difficult job, but they did it with the utmost care. To revisit those decisions now is simply not practicable.

Thank you for your understanding.

Yours in magic,
Brad Corzo
Chair, Panel Selection Committee, World of Magic

After reading the first rejection two weeks earlier, I had gone to Brad Corzo's website. I'd never heard of him, and, as I'd suspected, he didn't look like much of a magician—one of those people whose administrative credits overshadowed his professional ones. Did he not know that I had once been a Spotlight Guest, one of only four such magicians that year? That I'd performed on the main stage to a packed room?

I hadn't attended a World of Magic convention since I was eighteen, since my lightning-fast transformation from *Big Deal* to

Embarrassing Spectacle. But the self-imposed exile felt long enough, and I thought this would be the year to get back into the game. Ten years after my first WOM convention. The symmetry felt right. So I'd emailed back, asking if the committee might reconsider my application in light of my past professional accomplishments.

That email had been highly respectful and diplomatic and not at all pushy. But tonight had me feeling panicky and impulsive. I clicked the reply key.

> Dear Brad,
>
> Please review my bio one more time.
>
> Sincerely,
> Natalie Webb
> Grand Prize Winner, WOM international close-up competition

Then I couldn't help myself.

> P.S. I saw on your website that you performed for three different Boy Scout troops last year. Well done.

I clicked "send" before I could second-guess it and shut the browser. I was riled up all over again, thinking about this second-rate talent wielding his authority. *Yours in magic.* Give me a break. Then again, what use was talent anyway? The truth was, you didn't need much talent to fool a Scout troop or even a roomful of drunk attorneys. And all of my experience and technique hadn't prevented my show from going horribly awry tonight, so I supposed that understanding your audience was a talent, too. Then again, some audiences didn't merit being understood. Then again, what the hell was I even talking about?

Twenty-seven, man. It felt old. And on a dreary, drippy night like tonight it wasn't lost on me how many people never made it out of that year, people whose talents far exceeded my own: Jimi Hendrix. Jim Morrison. Janis Joplin. Kurt Cobain. Amy Winehouse.

Otis Redding, I'd always thought—but I was wrong. He didn't even make it past twenty-six.

Tonight could hardly have gone worse. And yet I'd made it home again without going down in a plane crash or overdosing on heroin or meeting any of a thousand tragic ends.

Call it a win, girl. Go to bed.

I awoke to sunlight. I got out of bed and made a real breakfast, a couple of over-hard eggs and a slice of toast.

In the living room, Ethel was preening. Julius, the fatter bird, jumped down from his wooden bar with a thud to peck at his food. There's nothing exotic about doves, they're just white pigeons, but they're gentle, steadfast creatures, the avian version of Labrador retrievers. When I was done with breakfast, I dug through the junk drawer for Scotch tape to restore Brock McKnight's hundred-dollar bill. (Fact: currency that's been taped together remains legal tender.)

After taping half of the bill together, I put on some Chopin. The "Fantaisie-Impromptu." Talk about technique. Hell, talk about magic. If I were ever to be granted three wishes, two of them would be to have the fingers for a piece like that. I tore off some more Scotch tape and reattached the third piece of the bill. Sunlight streamed soothingly through the half-open shades, and I let myself imagine that somewhere in New Jersey all that serotonin and vitamin D were having a similarly back-from-the-dead effect on my volunteer from last night. Maybe Lou Husk's eye was better this morning. Maybe it would all be okay.

Then came the knocking on my door.

It was the police. That overconfident *thump-thump-thump* on the outer door sounded like every cop show, the officers smug with their warrant.

I'd never been arrested before. My pajamas were still on. Would they let me get dressed before parading me, handcuffed, to their squad car?

I went out to the small entranceway. The door lacked a peephole, so I opened it and got blasted by frigid air.

It was just some kid. Thirteen, fourteen. Spiky blue Mohawk, and those earlobe expanders. Whatever they're called.

"Why do you do that to your ears?" I asked him.

The kid was short and I was up a step. He tilted his head up toward me and said, "Forget my ears."

"I'm just asking."

"So you asked." He coughed, and spat onto the cement beside him. "You want me to shovel your car out of the snow?"

The morning was intensely bright. I made a visor with my hand. "What're you talking about? There's no snow."

"Yeah, but when there is."

The kid was all points. Pointy hair, pointy chin, pointy nose. Pointy elbows sticking out from his arms, which were crossed in front of him. He hugged himself. It was too cold for the Public Enemy T-shirt he had on, and he was hopping from foot to foot. Any closer to him and I probably would've heard the wind whistling through his earlobes.

"Explain this scam to me again?" I asked.

"Ain't a scam. I'll make sure your car is always ready to roll," he said. "Fifty dollars for the whole winter."

"But you're not going to do that," I told him. "You'll take my money and that'll be the last time I ever see you."

"That's not true. You have my word as a Christian." He pointed across the street at the brick apartment building. "I live right there. First floor."

I distinctly remembered seeing a very old woman watering the flowers in front of that unit. He was probably lying. Then again, when had I last seen that woman? There were no flowers out front anymore. A lot of people came and went in ten years. Babies grew up. Kids became teenagers and moved away. People died all the time.

"So what do you think?" he asked.

"I think this is such a stupid idea I'm almost willing to do it as a sociological experiment." I was still feeling a little giddy that it wasn't the cops.

"Huh?"

"Forget it," I said, though now it was bugging me that I couldn't remember the last time I'd seen the woman from across the street. I never even knew her name.

"If it snows," I told him, "then come back and I'll pay you a few bucks to help get me out. Deal?"

"No, no deal." He watched the sky. "Man, I hope it snows *tonight*. I hope you get *stuck*."

"Hey, look, don't get all mad at me."

"Well, I am mad. You're calling me a liar and a thief."

"I'm not calling you anything."

"Yes, you are. Lady, you need to trust people. Plus, my mother's really sick."

"Oh, my god." The kid really needed to work on his patter. "You're going with the *sick mother* routine? Oh, brother. Hold on. Wait here a minute." I went back into my apartment and returned with the unattached quarter of the hundred-dollar bill. "This is worth twenty-five dollars," I told him, "but it's of no use to either of us this way. Understand? Do a good job, and for Christmas I'll give you the next piece. And so on. And it's real, so don't lose it."

Fact: three-quarters of a bill is still legal tender. So I wasn't giving up anything. But the kid didn't know it. He eyed the quarter of a bill and jammed it into his pants pocket.

"Who lives upstairs?" he asked.

"Why?"

His blue eyes were full of hope. "I could do his car, too."

"It's a her," I told him, "and she takes the bus."

"Figures," he muttered, his renewed entrepreneurial spirit dashed again. Without another word, he walked away from me.

"Hey," I called after him. When he turned around, I asked, "Want to see a really good coin trick?"

He studied me a moment. "Nah. Nobody wants to see that." He spat on the ground again and walked away.

4

♥

A few minutes past two that afternoon, I was sitting opposite Brock McKnight, a marble coffee table between us. His office looked like the movie set of *Serious Lawyer, Esq.*—large (and surprisingly tidy) desk of dark wood, leather chairs, abstract artwork in muted tones, bookshelves filled with legal volumes that I hoped were more than props. I had just signed Brock's one-page engagement letter authorizing him to be my attorney, and he was showing me that he was on the case.

"Lou ended up at University Hospital last night, not a clinic," Brock said. "That projectile of yours made an impressive gash in his cornea."

I winced.

"That's the good news," he said, glancing down at the legal pad in front of him. "The bad news is the hyphema." And before I could ask: "Bleeding between the iris and cornea."

"I feel terrible," I said.

"And remorse might come in handy at some point," he said, "but first the facts. He's sensitive to light and still in considerable pain. We won't know about any long-term vision damage for a while. Often a hyphema will heal, but it's too soon to tell. And Lou of all people knows not to file a lawsuit until he reaches

MMI—that's maximum medical improvement. So it could be weeks until he files. Could be months."

My head was throbbing. I asked him what it all meant.

"Besides the medical bills, there's the driver he's hired, there's going to be lost wages, and pain and suffering—definitely he'll want pain and suffering, given all the witnesses who saw him in pain, suffering."

"What do I do?"

"You? If you have a rich uncle, now would be a good time to reach out."

I thought about my upcoming December gigs, my Reasonable Rates, and knew I was in big trouble. There was no house to mortgage, no savings account to deplete, nothing to cash in. No rich uncle.

"I'm broke," I told my lawyer.

"Then get unbroke," he said.

That's when I asked him if he still had that card cheat's name handy.

"For real?" His eyes widened. "Because that was just some late-night bullshitting. And anyway, you said last night—"

"I have something else in mind," I told him. And without getting too much into the details (I'd only come up with the idea on the drive over), I mentioned the magazine article I thought I could get paid to write for some decent money—at least a couple of gigs' worth—comparing card magicians to cardsharps.

"I'd read that article," he said. "And the two of you would hit it off. You speak the same language." He went over to his desk. "How'd you get into all that anyway? Magic."

I skipped the part about my father's old boss giving me my first magic kit when I was eight. It wasn't a memory I liked to dwell on. "A man named Jack Clarion taught me," I said. "And when I was eighteen I won an international sleight of hand competition. I was the youngest winner they ever had."

"A prodigy."

"David Copperfield gave me my medal."

"No cash prize?"

"Five hundred dollars," I told him, "and a booking agent." I didn't bother to clarify that my agent had dropped me years ago.

"Here's what I'm thinking," Brock said, pulling a deck of cards from the top drawer. He tossed the deck, still in its seal, onto the coffee table. "You have duplicate queens, obviously. But how do you get rid of the duplicates before the final reveal? That's the part I don't understand. But I'm right about the extra queens, aren't I?"

I watched his face watching mine. He was used to getting what he wanted. "What?" he said. "My grandfather was a lawyer in Maryville, Tennessee. Sometimes he got paid in chickens, and I'm sure the farmers were attached to their birds, too."

I sighed. "Write it down first, please. The name and contact information of your cheat." I said this while picking up the pack and slitting the seal with my thumbnail. While he went to his computer and jotted down the information on a slip of paper, I opened the card case, removed the cards, and fanned them out to remove the four queens, which I set on the tabletop beside the rest of the deck.

"He's a particular fellow," Brock said, handing me the slip of paper. "A little curmudgeonly. Not charming like me. But damned if he isn't in a league all his own."

I glanced at the slip of paper. "You don't trust me with his full name?"

"That's what he goes by," Brock said with a shrug. "Now come on, your turn."

I pocketed the paper. "And you swear you'll keep this a secret?"

"Scout's honor," he said.

Laypeople always assume that an elegant trick must have an equally elegant method. But one of the true secrets of magic is that this is rarely the case. And with sleight of hand the secret is never a mirror or harness or contraption but rather five- or ten- or twenty thousand hours of practice. The artistry is in the execution, not the secret. It's in learning to hide what ought to be in plain sight.

I could have told him right then how to do the Four Queens, magician's oath be damned. But then he would know. He'd think: *Oh.* A vague disappointment, and then he'd be on to the next thing he wanted.

Better, always, to leave them full of wonder. Then at least you know you're still needed.

I picked up the stack of queens. "These ladies," I said, counting off one card at a time, "are very close, practically sisters, on account of having to live in a world created by the kings and jacks."

The lawyer's eyes narrowed.

"You can't imagine the pressure on them, with the demands of royalty, not to mention all that pomp and forced propriety."

He sighed.

I continued: "That's why, whenever they can, the queens always—"

"Stop." He raised his hands in surrender. "Enough."

"Hey, you asked. That's how that trick is done. The ladies find each other." I stood. "Now remember, you're sworn to secrecy."

Jack Clarion's magic shop was on Route 1 in Edison, in a strip mall between a nail salon and an unrented storefront. As I stepped inside, the door closed behind me, sleigh bells jangling. I stood in the entrance a moment while my eyes adjusted to the gloom.

At the other end of the store, Jack barely glanced up. He stood behind the glass countertop demo-ing a trick to a woman and her kid. I walked farther into the narrow store. Instead of watching Jack, the kid was smearing the countertop with his palms. I could tell he'd never paid attention to anything in his life. He'd take whatever trick his mother bought him today and try it once without reading the instructions before shoving it under his bed forever.

I waited off to the side while Jack rang up the lady's order and she and the kid left and the door jangled shut. Then I restocked a few supplies—borderless playing cards, flash paper, twenty yards of green magician's rope—screwing up my courage to tell Jack what had happened last night at the Hyatt.

I decided to ease into it. "So remember that magazine editor I met over the summer?"

"You mighta mentioned it two or three hundred times," Jack said.

After a show, a man had come up to me with his kid and introduced himself as Bruce Steadman, deputy editor for *Men's Quarterly*. He'd described himself as "an amateur but very serious magician" and raved about my performance. I was beyond flattered. Then he said, "I also really enjoy your writing in *Magician's Forum*," and I was flattered all over again.

Magician's Forum was a newsletter Jack had started up eons ago: for years a mailer, now a quarterly email. I was an occasional contributor—I would teach a trick, coins or cards or rope or whatever. Always a household object. Always sleight of hand. Writing for Jack didn't pay anything, but the deadlines made me keep coming up with new ideas, and I felt I owed Jack for introducing me to magic.

The magazine editor had handed me his business card and said, "If you have any magic-related stories you think could work, feel free to pitch me."

Guys handing me their cards was nothing new. They like the magic, and I'm five-eleven barefoot, and my dark brown hair is almost down to my ass, and sometimes I feel like a giraffe at a dog show. Usually men's business cards end up in the nearest trash can but: *Deputy editor. Men's Quarterly. Pitch me.* I felt I could do it. But I'd been waiting for the right idea. Or the right motivation. Now I had both.

"I think I finally have a pitch," I told Jack.

Jack sighed, or maybe wheezed. "What exactly is this idea of yours?" He was seventy-two and looked ten years older. His face was saggy and gray, and probably his opinion shouldn't have mattered to me anymore, but we went back a long way and I had learned plenty from him. And *he* had learned from the best: Cardini, Slydini—that whole greatest generation of -inis who'd performed in an age long before camera tricks and CGI, back when our eyes weren't accustomed to being deceived.

"I want to profile a professional card cheat," I said. The moment the words left my mouth I realized they would go over about as well as my card-in-the-eye news would. I braced myself and forged ahead. "I was thinking about how card magicians and card cheats have a lot in common, except that a card cheat has more at stake. Because if he gets caught he could end up at the bottom of a lake or something. I want to see what a magician might be able to learn from someone like that." I watched his eyes, hoping for agreement or understanding. "I think people might be interested in that. Magicians, but also regular readers. It's interesting, you know?"

"Remind me exactly what part is interesting?"

"You know—the whole thing. What? What's the matter, Jack?"

But I knew.

"Let me make sure I'm getting this right," he said. "You have a chance to tell a million readers about the art of conjuring and you're gonna spotlight a fucking cheat?"

What he meant was, nothing is more honest than a magic trick. It was a point of serious pride for Jack. Over the years I'd heard various iterations of the same lecture: how you know a magician is going to make you see something that isn't possible, believe something that isn't true. How the deception is fair because of the pact between magician and audience. How we're in it together. How done right it's a game we can both win.

Cheats, though (and here Jack would fake spit), *they ruin it for everyone. With a cheat there's no pact, and there's only one winner, and it won't be you.*

I didn't disagree. And yet: we admire the professional cardsharp, don't we? Even though it's only a thief thieving. We admire the cheat's skill because it's based in refinement. This was nothing I could ever say to Jack, but I wasn't alone in thinking it. Other magicians felt this way, too, about cardsharps—even the greatest sleight of hand artist who ever lived.

"What about Dai Vernon?" I asked Jack now. "He spent years chasing down the best cheats."

"You, with all due respect, are no Dai Vernon." With a rag he started wiping down the glass counter where the kid had greased it up. "And don't go falling for that center-deal nonsense."

"He learned it," I said.

"It's lore," he said. "It's patter."

"It's documented. Go online."

He shook his head. "Dai Vernon was a master, but cheats and con men were his whiskey and hookers. It was a big weakness. Don't let it become yours."

And that, right there, was Jack—a purist with a mortgage, a dwindling client base, an ex, and grown kids who didn't talk to him anymore. Jack's best trick was making other people disappear.

"You still gonna have a trick for me by Monday?" he asked.

Shit. I'd totally forgotten.

When I didn't answer right away, he said, "So no charity work anymore, is that it?"

"Give me a break, Jack." Fifteen years ago, my mother used to drop me off for lessons with Jack so she could steal an hour with a man who wasn't my father. Jack knew it, and so did I, and maybe that's why the two of us had worked so hard on the magic.

I wanted to tell him why my mind was elsewhere. Wished I could explain that money had suddenly become very important. *I blinded a man last night, and I'm terrified*, I would've blurted out if I weren't a coward, and if Jack weren't the one magician—the one human being—I didn't want to disappoint more than I felt I already had.

"No, I understand," he said, scrunching up the rag in his hands. "Go ahead, make some scumbag with a decent bottom deal look like Houdini and Jesse James and Sigmund Freud all rolled into one."

"I thought it would be interesting, is all," I said.

"Pornography is *interesting*," he said. "A dead dog in the street is *interesting*." He frowned. "You of all people ought to be aiming a little higher."

"Pardon me?"

"Come on, Natalie. You have the chops of a top magician." He shook his head. "Or at least you used to. You owe the profession."

"*I* owe the—?" My laughter was sucked away by the carpeted floor and the dark velvet curtains behind the display cases.

Magicians with far less technique than mine made DVDs. They did steady corporate gigs for real money. They played Caribbean resorts, not Newark hotels. They landed the prime performances at conventions. They made a living. Not many, but some.

"Just do me a favor—do *yourself* a favor—and don't spotlight some cheat," Jack said.

"Thanks for the vote of confidence," I said.

He was already back to wiping down the countertop, so I headed for the door, thinking that he was right about one thing. I was a real magician, and a real magician furthered her craft however she could, learning from anyone and everyone. In that way, I was a purist, too.

I had almost reached the door when Jack couldn't help himself. "I swear," he said, "you're getting to be as bitter as your old man."

But Jack had never met my father in person and knew him only from my selfish teenage grumblings. And that was near the end, when my father was spiteful and self-defeating. "My father did the best he could," I said.

"Whatever you need to tell yourself to sleep at night," he said.

"Really not interested in your pop psychology, Jack."

"No, you never want to hear anything." As I opened the door, he added, "I happen to know a cheat or two, but you won't get their names from me."

"Don't need them!" I called out as the door jangled shut behind me.

5

♠

Sitting alone in my car outside the shop, the engine running. *You have the chops of a top magician. Or at least you used to.* Damn you, Jack.

Either I had missed the eight-inch Styrofoam target because my throw wasn't as sharp as it once was (because I'd been temporarily enraged; because Lou Husk had been tall) or I had *hit* my target—the lawyer's smug face—exactly as I had meant to. Either reason proved Jack right. I wasn't the magician I had once been.

I had tried to sound tough in front of Jack because he'd put me on the defensive, but I didn't feel tough. I felt the opposite of tough. I felt the irrational and pointless yearning for my parents to swoop in and bail me out.

I tilted the car's rearview mirror and examined my face. In not too many years, I would be the age my father would always stay. I looked more like my mother—I had her thick hair, thin nose, and sharp jawline—but I had my father's green eyes and, more and more, the bags under them. Lately, when I saw myself in mirrors, it was my father who looked back.

Get-rich-quick guys who never get rich are a dime a dozen, but my father had been a rarer breed: he actually got rich. But then he got poor again, which was worse than back to zero because loss carries its own burden. He lost $108,000 in a single night—in a single *instant*—despite never having been a gambler or risk taker before, proving that the risk-taking impulse can lie dormant until a sufficient stake comes along.

Before any of that, he had worked for the Flowers Corporation, putting his accounting training to use. Then, one sunny spring day, he got fired for the crimes of being honest and decent. I was only eight at the time, so it was a number of years before I thought to consider the resentment he must have felt. Yet I don't remember him ever complaining.

Needing money, he went back to delivering pianos, something he'd done to pay for his college courses. And for the next four years he worked hard and came home each night, and sometimes after dinner he would sit down to play our own piano, a used chestnut upright, courtesy of his employee discount. He lacked finesse, and his hands looked all wrong on the keys with his fat fingers and swollen knuckles, yet his touch was light. He'd play bits of Bach's "Minuet in G" and the beginning of Beethoven's "Moonlight Sonata" and the end part of "Layla." Sometimes, after a couple of beers, he would sound out something he had heard on the radio, and if he didn't remember the lyrics he'd make some up.

I tried to remember him that way, mucking around the keys and singing. But we don't get to choose all our recollections, and mine invariably drifted toward the accident and what came after.

I was with him the day he crushed his hands. I went with him sometimes to the warehouse—to help, I always assumed, though by now I realized it was so my mother could have me out of her hair for a while. On that day, the day that mattered, my father wasn't supposed to work, but another man had called in sick and we lived closest to the warehouse. It was a Saturday and a Rangers game was on TV—tied in the third period, I'd always remember, one more reason not to be pulled away from the house on his day off. By the time my father's shoes and coat were on and we were backing down the driveway, he was in a rotten mood, and I was in a rotten mood, too, though it had nothing to do with the hockey game and everything to do with being twelve.

At the warehouse he pushed the dolly with the black baby grand piano on it toward the elevator and asked me to carry the bench. "Don't even say it," I said. That was the common refrain at school that year. I didn't know where it came from, had never bothered to wonder. It was just what Lisa Morrow and Kim Duluth and Gina Kasem and all the girls were saying.

How'd you do on the test?

Don't even say it.

What about Andrew Wasserman? You think he's hot?

Don't even say it.

My father shook his head. "Then carry the toolbox—you're no weakling."

I was already a ridiculous five feet, eight inches. The junior high basketball coach kept stopping me in the hallway to remind me about school spirit. I weighed barely a hundred pounds but could channel all of them into being a brat.

"Don't even say it, Dad," I said without so much as a glance in his direction.

When we reached the freight elevator, he set down the piano bench and the toolbox so he could pull open the steel doors, which opened the opposite way from most elevators—one door went up, the other down. He carried the bench into the elevator and stepped out again.

"I need both hands free to get the piano over the gap and into the elevator. So please, Natalie, my dearest"—his voice was soft, his closed-mouth smile oozing sarcasm—"pick up the goddamn toolbox."

Here was the world's easiest request. I was standing three feet from the man and carrying nothing.

"Don't. Even. Say. It."

I stepped into the elevator, leaving him to fetch his own toolbox. Again he exited, leaned into the piano, and heaved it across the gap and into the elevator.

One thing I always liked doing was pulling the canvas loop that hung from the freight elevator's ceiling in order to shut the steel doors. I hadn't been tall enough to reach the loop until that year, and even then it was hard to pull. But I could hang from it and slowly float to the ground like Mary Poppins with her umbrella. As I did, the two parallel, horizontal doors would close—one coming down from the ceiling, the other rising out of the floor. The two steel doors met in the middle with a satisfying clang.

As I reached up for the loop, my father snapped, "No!" as if reprimanding a dog or a small child. Evidently, my punishment for being a brat was to be deprived of this simple pleasure.

Feeling wronged and disrespected, I kicked the piano leg.

Immediately I regretted it. The piano looked expensive and belonged to someone. What if I had dented it? What if it got my dad fired?

My father glared at me. "What the—" He didn't need to finish.

I almost said sorry. I *was* sorry, but I couldn't make my mouth form the word. Feeling regret was involuntary, like a sneeze. Voicing an apology took effort and would make my shame public.

Really, though, my decision not to apologize was barely a decision at all. It was split-second and, I assumed, inconsequential. Already my father was shaking his head again, clearing it of me, and reaching up for the canvas loop. He gave it a strong pull—too strong, because the loop tore and detached from the top of the elevator.

"Son of a—" He threw the canvas strap to the ground, then reached up, gripped the bottom of the upper door with both hands, and yanked, hard, with all of his 275 pounds.

He must have ridden this elevator hundreds of times. Surely he knew that as the upper door came down, the lower door was simultaneously rising out of the floor, and that the two doors would slam together in the middle. But I had angered and distracted him. His attention was directed toward me, and not the steel doors, which slammed together with his hands, palms up, still between them.

In the weeks and months that followed there would be surgeries and pins and rods and casts and heavy narcotics. When all that was over, my mother would remain his driver and his therapist and his hands in all things mundane and intimate. Can any marriage survive that? Maybe some. But not many. Not theirs.

Besides collecting workers' comp and disability, my father filed a lawsuit to cover medical bills and pain and suffering. By the time he received the settlement check, a whole year had passed. His crushed hands had been reconstructed but remained mostly useless—would always be mostly useless—and by then he was becoming a different man: bigger, for one thing. He had swelled to well over three hundred pounds. Once the physical therapy was over he rarely left the house during the day, and his eyes took on a permanent squint. He went out at night and started becoming familiar to the hospital ER staff and local police.

Nothing major in the grand scheme: a couple of drunk and disorderlies, a couple of bar fights he had no chance of winning. But it was enough to land him in the local police blotter. And I would read the blotter and know my role in it.

It was late afternoon the day my father called me downstairs to open the envelope containing the settlement check from his lawsuit. My mother was at work. I loathed being alone with him. I couldn't stand to see his hands. After a year, they didn't look so bad anymore—a stranger might not notice—but they still horrified me. And I couldn't look at his face, either, because in it I saw the simple understanding that on an ordinary hockey Saturday, I had ruined him.

"Set that check on the table," he said, "so we can both see it."

One hundred and eight thousand dollars wasn't an amount I could fathom. We were suddenly rich. But my father shook his head. "Jesus Aitch," he said, "that right there is all they think I'm worth?"

I didn't know what to say. I knew the *they* in his sentence referred to the company he used to work for, and to the insurance agent he was always yelling at over the phone, but I knew it also referred to the whole world that had conspired against him, and that included me.

"I'm gonna go back upstairs, okay?" I said.

By then my mother had started taking me to Jack Clarion's magic shop a couple of afternoons a week so she could spend a secret hour with the man who ran the secondhand furniture store at the end of the strip mall. When I was at home I would hide out in my bedroom for long stretches, listening to CDs and practicing card flourishes and coin drops. Some were the moves Jack showed me. Others came from the books he convinced my mother to buy for me—*Modern Coin Magic, The Royal Road to Card*

Magic—dense books that confused me but filled me with wonder over secrets that felt as deep as the earth. The books, like the practicing, took me someplace safer, someplace else. I would read and practice, practice and read, and hope that my parents had forgotten I was in the house. I would hear the rise and fall of their voices—commands, rebukes, apologies, the choked-back sounds that contained deeper truths—but I'd be afraid to raise the volume on my CD player, afraid to remind them that the root of all their troubles was one flight up the stairs. Sleight of hand is a quiet activity. Playing cards make a gentle riffle like birds taking flight. Sponge balls make no noise. Even a dropped coin lands softly on thick bedroom carpet. I balanced a small mirror on my bed and watched my hands learn new moves that I would repeat over and over, hundreds of times, and then it would be dinner and then it would be bedtime.

On the night my father's check came, I stayed up in my bedroom until the pizza arrived. In the kitchen, I put two slices onto a plate and carried it back upstairs with me. Then I remained in my room until after I heard my mother come home, when my father called me downstairs to see the limousine parked out front.

"Put your shoes on, Natalie," he said. And to my mother: "Just me and the kid."

"What is this?" my mother asked.

"It's a car," he said. "Natalie, get your coat."

"Where are you going?" she asked.

"Honey, please. I said just me and Natalie."

He took me to Atlantic City. By the time we arrived it was late but no part of me was sleepy. At the Showboat casino he told the security man, "She's my hands." He had me reach into his pocket for the check and show it.

"So what do you think of that check?" he asked once we were inside the casino.

"What do you mean?"

"I don't mean anything other than what I asked. What do you think about it?"

I knew I was supposed to say something, so I went with the obvious. "It's so much money."

He shook his head. "No. That's where you're wrong. It isn't nearly enough. But I'll bet my lawyer has a new summer home."

I followed my father to the chip counter, where, after speaking with several employees, he was allowed to exchange the check for chips. He told the attendant to put them into one of the white buckets stacked on the counter. "Carry this for me, Nat, will you? That's my girl." He smiled at me, a real smile, and my whole body warmed up. I didn't understand exactly why we were there, but his smile, so rare these days, was worth the whole trip.

In the middle of the vast room, where machines bleeped and buzzed and sang all around us, he bent down to my level—I was still several inches shorter than he was—and put his head so close to mine we were almost touching.

"Being a grown-up," he said to me, "means being willing to commit to a thing. Do you understand?"

I nodded. He waited a moment, maybe hoping for more, but I had no more.

"The way I figure it," he said, "I'm due at least twice this much."

Although I'd figured out by then that he drank too much and picked fights with other men because it was his way of hurting himself—even a thirteen-year-old could figure that out—I wouldn't fully understand until much later how badly he needed to prove to his only daughter that he remained a man of action and strength, a hero who fought on. I knew then only that his breath smelled like pepperoni pizza and his green eyes were pleading with me to agree with him.

"Definitely," I said, my heart beating almost as fast as it had a year earlier, in the moments after the steel doors had slammed home. "You're right, Dad," I said. "You're owed at least that."

I had no idea what the hell I was talking about, but my words must have been the right ones because my father's lips curved into a satisfied smile. "I'm glad you feel that way," he said, putting his arm around me. I felt the warm weight of his ruined hand on my shoulder, and I didn't even mind it. Together we walked up to a mostly empty roulette table. The woman standing by the wheel wore black pants, a tuxedo shirt, and a red bow tie. She smiled at us.

"Good evening," she said.

"Well, that's exactly why we're here," my father said, returning her smile. "For a good evening. I want to place the whole bucket of chips on . . ." He turned to me and winked. "So what's it gonna be, kid? Red or black?"

6

Back at the apartment, the birds were cooing. You can't tell a dove's mood by its vocalizations, if doves even have moods. But their paper needed changing. The mini-mart supplied me with free day-old newspapers, and as I started to clean the cage I came across this headline: ON THE CAMPAIGN TRAIL WITH VICTOR FLOWERS.

After a long and successful career—several of them—in the private sector, my father's old boss was now turning his attention to politics and running for the U.S. Senate. Until he declared his candidacy last month, I'd done an admirable job of not thinking too much about him over the years. Now that he was suddenly in the news, I was struck by how seeing his picture or even his name could still send a nasty jolt through my body. I stopped myself from reading the article, deciding it was better off underneath my birds.

I washed my hands and removed Bruce Steadman's business card from my wallet. It was already past four, and I figured I'd leave a message for him and hear back after the weekend or, more likely, never. But he picked up on the second ring. I told him who I was and why—I hoped—he would remember me. And then I laid out the article I wanted to write.

"I admire your pieces in the *Magician's Forum*," he said when I was done. "I think you're a good writer, and your way of explaining magic to a layperson is top-notch. I told you that when we met."

"You did."

"But this piece you're describing, you'd really have to bring out the people element. The personalities. The cardsharp's, and yours, too. That's just as important as the moves. Do you think you'd be able to do that?"

I told him I thought so, and then he told me what "on spec" meant. How I'd have to write the article first, before he could commit to publishing it. "It's just that you haven't written for a national magazine before," he said.

I looked around my apartment. Every bill was overdue. It was a wonder that the phone in my hand was still working.

"Natalie?" he said.

"Yeah?"

"I really like the idea. We'll do our best to make this work." Then he told me what he would pay for the article once it was done, and that lifted my spirits.

"Do you already have a cardsharp in mind?" he asked.

I told him I did. "And he's world-class," I said, hoping that Brock McKnight, attorney-at-law, wasn't snowing me.

The editor for a major New York magazine had answered after two rings, but it took three messages on the cardsharp's cell phone for him to call me back.

Meanwhile, I kept waiting to hear from Brock to find out how Lou Husk was recovering, and if he'd decided yet whether to press charges or simply go after my nonexistent assets in a civil suit. On Wednesday morning, with still no word, I left a message for Brock to call me. Then I got in my car and did what my cardsharp had asked, meeting him at ten a.m. at the City Diner in Montclair.

The place was mostly empty, but I spotted him right away in the rear section, sitting alone. He had on mirrored sunglasses and the green hoodie he said he'd be wearing. The drawstrings were missing. His hair was greasy and graying but his skin was unlined. Without seeing his eyes, I couldn't tell his age. Forty? Fifty? He wore a gold wedding band on his left hand.

I introduced myself, and when I went to shake his hand he said, "Grab a seat," without setting down his fork. "Order some pancakes." He whistled to the server—two thick fingers in the mouth, a coach's whistle. It was alarmingly rude, and I gave the server a solidarity eye roll. "Natalie here would like a stack of pancakes," he said.

I don't like people ordering for me, and I nearly corrected him on principle: eggs, bucket of rocks, anything. But I held my tongue.

The server went away and dropped a check on a table by the window, where a woman about my age was sitting across from an older version of herself. When the mother reached out for the check, the daughter placed her hand on top of her mother's, stopping her.

I asked, "Do you really go by Ace?"

"Isn't because of the cards. My older brother always said I was stupid. He came up with it to rag me. He's dead now. This is the best diner you'll ever eat at."

Ace went back to working on his pancakes. This late in the morning, the restaurant was sparsely populated, primarily tables-for-one, everybody checking cell phones, except for a couple of old men with newspapers. There was no music, only the sound of dishes clanking in the kitchen and the card cheat across from me chewing like a satisfied cow. I hadn't known

49

what to expect, but what struck me about Ace was his gracelessness—though I was willing to believe that his graceless-ness could have been its own carefully cultivated grace.

"Tell me," he said, finishing a pancake and setting his fork and knife down, "exactly what my well-intentioned lawyer has gotten me into this time."

Keeping my voice low, I said, "I want to write an article about a professional cardsharp."

He nodded. "You said that on the phone. But an article for what?"

"For *Men's Quarterly*."

He shook his head. "No. I mean, what *for*?"

I explained how I wanted to know what a magician might learn from a poker cheat. Moves, patter, misdirection—

"You couldn't photograph me," he said. "And you'd have to change my name."

I told him I already assumed as much.

"Good," he said. "How much are you getting paid to write this? Because I want half."

Are you nuts? I wanted to say. "I'm afraid I can't do that."

"And yet that's the price of admission," he said.

The server came over and set a plate of pancakes in front of me. I used the time it took to unwrap my silverware from the paper napkin to make a fast decision. "I can give you twenty-five percent of what I make on the article."

But he, too, had been using my napkin-unfolding time for his own calculation. "Let's call it a thousand dollars, and that's the end of the negotiation."

I felt like delivering a clever exit line followed by a clever exit. But I wanted the interview more. The money, of course, mattered but there was more to it, I was beginning to realize. I was so damn tired of myself. One day I would die, and my gravestone would read, *She did some magic tricks.* It wasn't enough. I wanted to know more, do more, jump-start something.

"You're *good*, right?" I said. "The real deal? Brock McKnight vouched for you."

He watched me a moment. "I took my classmates' money in grade school," he said. "By the time I was fifteen I was into a dozen regular games in A.C., in Trenton. I always looked older. My hands were always adept. That part came easy, you know? But to make it great, to make it undetectable from every angle . . ." He kept his gaze on me. "A grade-school kid gets caught cheating other kids, maybe he gets a black eye. But to cheat grown men, to take their money . . . do you see what I'm saying?"

I did. And yet I didn't know the way I wanted to know, didn't know it in my blood. That was precisely what drew me to writing this article. When your performance went beyond dollars and into the realm of life and limb, how do you prepare? How do you protect yourself? How do you conquer the fear? How flawless, exactly, must your technique be?

"You're telling me your moves are undetectable," I said.

"I'm telling you," he said, "there are maybe a dozen people in the world who can do what I do."

If he was right, look where it had gotten him—the City Diner on a Wednesday morning, talking to me. I studied his hands again. Stubby fingers, yellowed fingernails . . . ah, but those fingernails were beautifully filed. It was almost December and his fingers showed no signs of cracking or dryness. The man moisturized. It wasn't much to go on, but it was all I had.

"All right," I said. I never claimed to be a shrewd negotiator. "A thousand."

"Up front," he said.

"Impossible," I said. "I don't have it."

"Not my problem, love."

"I can give you *maybe* three hundred. The rest—I really don't have it."

"Then I'll take the three hundred, but know that I'm not pleased. And I want the rest soon."

So this was how it would be with my cardsharp. "You'll make this worth my while, right?" I told him. "You'll give me what I need for this interview?"

"*Interview*?" He shook his head. "No, I'm gonna take you to play some poker. How are you at Texas Hold'em?"

"I'm okay," I said, "but no expert."

"Perfect," he said. "Then you'll lose fast and get to watch the rest of the game without any distractions."

I ate some pancake to stall. "What's the buy-in?" I asked.

"The one on Sunday night is four hundred."

"Can I just watch?"

"Afraid not. These are intimate games at people's homes. Actually, the game on Sunday's at a bakery. But there won't be spectators." I was running through a list of pawnable items—old books I rarely used? My TV?—when he smiled. "Lighten up, will you?" He had smoker's teeth but his fingers weren't remotely fidgety. Meaning, he'd quit. Meaning, he probably had iron will-power and maybe fortitude. "You'll play, you'll lose, but you'll have your article and be privy to things most people never get to see. Okay? Isn't that what you want?" I didn't answer right away because the accountant in my head was still lecturing me. "The game on Sunday is in A.C., by the way."

Atlantic City was more than a two-hour drive, and my car was pushing two hundred thousand miles and had never once earned the moniker Old Reliable.

"Who do the other players think you are?" I asked.

"They think I'm me. I'm Ace, the grinder from North Jersey. Guys like them love playing grinders, because if they lose, they can console themselves with the fact that they were up against a pro anyway, and if they win or break even they feel like they just won the World Series of Poker. Of course, against me they don't win."

A.C. was a trek, but it wasn't as if I had another gig lined up for Sunday night.

"I still want to talk to you, though," I said. "I want to ask you questions, not just watch you play."

"Then aren't you lucky there's an ATM across the street where you can get me my money."

We ate our pancakes, Ace and I, like an elderly couple so used to each other's company that talk wasn't necessary. When the bill came, he pushed it toward me.

7

♣

Once Ace's wallet was bulging with three hundred of my dollars, we walked down the street to a small pedestrian square. People were beginning to emerge from the surrounding buildings, squinting in the sun, to eat their sandwiches. Pigeons, cousins to my doves, bobbed along the sidewalk.

My cheat and I sat together on a metal bench. The morning's chill was evaporating. I removed a notepad and pen from my purse and asked Ace about his training, his experience, his life that had led him to become a professional card cheater.

His answers:

Why would you possibly want to know that?

Why does that matter?

Not your business. (Said while massaging his temples.)

You're not really asking me that, are you?

I was learning that I was one hell of an interviewer. That, or my subject was one hell of an interview. Either way, I was expertly performing the trick called "vanishing *Men's Quarterly* article."

I put the notepad and pen away, hoping that might cause Ace's lips to loosen. Bruce Steadman had told me to focus on the people as well as the moves, but I couldn't help wondering if the moves were maybe the doorway that led to someplace deeper. And when it came to Ace's moves, I had all kinds of questions. I wanted to forget about myself for a while, about the man I'd hurt, the money I owed, and to lose myself in table angles and the logistics of cutting the cards and false shuffles and deals.

I asked him if he used the mechanic's grip. When he raised an eyebrow, I said, "You don't use the straddle grip, do you? That would be too obvious, right?"

False dealing from the bottom of the deck wasn't all that hard in principle, but to do it well you had to eliminate friction, your fingers against the cards. So the grip mattered. With a straddle grip your index finger and pinky were out of the way, but it hardly looked natural. Even a layperson might find it fishy. If you're a magician doing it, who cares? The audience knows a trick is about to happen. But at the poker table, fishy can't fly, can it? Surely, fishy could get you—

Ace's grin was higher on one side than the other. "You're such a fucking magician," he said.

"What?"

"*Mechanic's* grip, *straddle* grip . . ." He shook his head. "You have no idea what I do."

"Then what are you saying?"

"I'm saying you're missing the whole point."

"Considering the three hundred dollars I just paid you, perhaps you'd care to educate me?"

He stared at me a moment. "How many children do you think I have?"

"What?"

"You know. Kids. How many do I have? Get it right and I'll give you back fifty dollars."

"And if I'm wrong?"

"Then you'll owe me twenty more," he said. "Hell, I don't care, make it ten. That's practically a free bet. Come on, how many kids?"

"You?" With his sunglasses on, his age remained a mystery. Still, after a little thought I had my answer: "Four."

His smile revealed small, crooked teeth. Orthodontic work needed but never received. "Not too shabby," he said. "Tell me how you knew."

"Remind me again what this has to do with cards?"

"Come on, Einstein, you guessed four. You *knew*. So educate me."

Two teenage boys on skateboards raced past, having chosen the mild weather over school. They slalomed around the people eating lunch, rounded a corner, and were gone.

"The obvious choice was zero," I said, "so that was out. You wouldn't have asked me to guess if you had one or two, or maybe even three, because there's nothing unusual about that. Five or more and you'd be a strict Catholic or Mormon or whatever, and that seems unlikely. It was either four, or maybe three. Maybe five with the last kid being an accident."

"So . . ."

I shrugged. "So I guessed. I narrowed it down to a few choices and I took my best guess and got lucky."

"Bravo." He graced me with a quick, quiet clap. "That's what *we* do. And don't call me a card cheat or a cardsharp. The cards are the medium, not the method. The method is the con. Do you follow?"

I liked that phrase. *The medium, not the method.* I wouldn't dare pull my notebook out of my purse, but I would commit that to memory. "We narrow down our choices," he was saying, "and make the most logical guess. It isn't rocket science, though I'll bet you rocket science isn't rocket science, either."

"You mean if you're a rocket scientist."

"And that's just the poker-playing part. An expert con man at the poker table *must* be an expert poker player—or at least a damn good one. Because a lot of the night, you're just playing poker. And as long as you're playing poker, you might as well win some hands. Might as well come out ahead on the merits of the poker game. But then you create a couple of hands that swell the pot, and you make sure to win those, and that's when you make the real money. A few big hands. You read people, you figure out who's desperate to win, who's dicking around with their phones, who's the biggest natural-born loser in the room. You figure out who you can separate from their money, and then you do it. And you do your homework beforehand so there's no surprises. I've got files on everyone I play against. I go in ready."

It all made sense. "But what about the grip?"

"Natalie—"

"I'm just really curious about that."

"Natalie, forget the grip. Will you forget the grip? Just shut up about the grip. The grip isn't important."

"Okay, but I have a deck of cards in my bag, if you want—"

He waved me away. "You'll see everything on Sunday, in front of real players. I want you to see it the way *they* see it. When you see it how they see it, in action, it'll all make sense. Then, afterward, you and I will talk. We'll dissect everything. How's your car, by the way?"

"Terrible," I said.

"But will it get us to A.C.?"

Ace would be getting a free ride to his poker game. Fine. I told myself that the drive would be useful for the interview. Unless he ended up being dangerous. That was always possible. I wished I could see his eyes behind those sunglasses. I had plenty of experience reading male faces for the bluff and had gotten pretty good at it over the years, but sometimes you get it wrong. And the parkway in South Jersey would be a lousy place to get it wrong. Yes, I would travel with him, I would drive, but I would leave my itinerary with my upstairs neighbor.

"I guess we'll find out, won't we?" I said.

Ace smacked the metal bench with his hand. "Natalie, you're an angel! Pick me up right here. Five o'clock on Sunday."

"I was hoping we could meet again before then."

"Then it appears your hopes are dashed." He stood. "And wear something sexy." I must have given him the stink eye, because he rushed to say, "Not for me. But if the other players decide to stare a little at something other than the table, or bet a little higher to show off for the lady in the room, it'll only help us."

"Help you, you mean."

"Me, us. We're a team!" He gave me a thumbs-up. "Okay, Natalie, I'll see you Sunday at five. Bring the money you still owe me."

As he started to walk away, the strangest question came to me. Maybe it was the sunglasses, but I still couldn't get a bead on him and I wanted to. "Do you live with your kids and wife and everything?"

He stopped walking. "You mean am I a family man?"

"I guess. Yeah, a family man."

"Is that something you truly want to know?"

"It really is."

He removed the sunglasses. His eyes, I was shocked to learn, were beautiful. Light blue, large and expressive. I would even go so far as to say they were caring eyes, intelligent eyes.

He said, "You think if you knew that my oldest kid played first-chair violin, that my youngest went through chemo a couple of years back, that my wife is a cardiac care nurse at Robert Wood Johnson, it might give you a different impression of me? Show a different side?" Without the sunglasses, his voice had lost its edge. His tone now seemed born of something besides hostility, something more like pain, and for the first time since meeting him I imagined that the hours we were going to spend together might actually yield something meaningful.

Of course, I couldn't say any of this. "I was just curious, is all," I said.

Almost imperceptibly he shook his head.

"What?" I asked.

He held my gaze a moment longer. "Zero kids, Natalie. Keep the ten." He replaced his sunglasses, turned away from me, and walked in the direction of the sun.

8

A paralegal from Brock's office returned my message late Wednesday only to tell me in a bored, lock-of-hair-twisting voice that Brock would call me by the end of the week, which he didn't do. On Saturday night I did a bachelor party for some middle-age, second-marriage deal in Morristown. ("Would you believe the ex never even let me *have* a bachelor party?" the groom made a point of telling me twice.) I decided not to perform Target Practice. Otherwise, the set went unremarkably. My audience's only regret seemed to be that I wasn't a stripper.

Afterward, one of the men kept invading my personal space while I packed up and I got out of there quickly. *No, honestly, I'm really not hungry at all.*

I arrived home starving and walked the two blocks to a Chinese place that stayed open late.

It was almost one a.m. when I returned to the apartment with my carton of lo mein. I let myself into the narrow landing and shut the outer door behind me, thinking of dinner and bed. That's when I heard the low snarl.

From the shadows at the top of the narrow wooden stairway leading to the upstairs apartment, something was suddenly charging/skidding/falling down toward me, its nails clicking like a massive raccoon's or a wild boar's, something driven by hunger and rage.

The sound I made wasn't human either.

I dropped my carton of food, and having just shut and locked the outer door, I now slammed my body against it. The doorknob jabbed my spine, and I gasped as the animal—border collie mixed with dragon—catapulted itself from the bottom stairs. Instinct caused me to pivot to the side and crouch a millisecond before the dog sank its teeth into the calf of my pant leg.

"No no no no!"

The denial came from upstairs. Harley bounded down the staircase and grabbed the dog by its collar. The dog released my leg, and Harley knelt down to the brute's level, putting her face dangerously close. "No biting!"

The dog shook itself free, sniffed the lo mein carton, and clicked its way back upstairs and into Harley's apartment.

"Did he get you?" Still on her haunches, she examined my pant leg.

I unlocked my apartment door and limped inside. Harley followed with the lo mein. I shut and locked the door behind us, switched on the light, limped over to the loveseat, and fell into it.

My pencil pants were torn and bloody. "Why the hell would you open your door this late at night?"

"To tell you about the dog," she said. "In case you heard him upstairs."

I rolled up the pant leg. My face felt cold. Harley was headed toward the kitchen. She returned with a wet dish towel. "Hold this against your leg." She worked at an animal hospital as a vet tech and knew how to keep animals alive and maybe people. "Did you have a show tonight?"

"You can't have a dog here!" My leg throbbed.

"Mustard really isn't a biter."

My pain and anger worked against any attempt to control my breathing. If I got stuck in the hospital because of that damn dog and had to miss my trip with Ace tomorrow . . . My vision was getting swimmy, same as when my father would come home after getting beaten up and I'd have to see his angry, swollen face. "You can't have him," I said.

"You have birds," she said.

"The birds are in my lease."

"But the shelter was going to put him down."

"The shelter *should* have put him down."

Harley had moved in last summer, and until now I'd always thought of her as one of the saner tenants to occupy that apartment.

"Let me see," she said. "Move the towel." She knelt down. "It's a puncture wound." She stood. "I have a good first-aid kit upstairs. I'll get some gauze and antibacterial. You lie down and elevate the leg."

"Do I need stitches?"

"For that? I don't think so. But it's probably going to swell. And maybe turn a weird color."

As she left my apartment I called after her, "Shut my door before opening yours!"

I checked the dish towel again. Still bleeding.

Some barking upstairs. Then Harley was back in my apartment with her first-aid kit. She set it on the coffee table, went into the kitchen, and returned with a roll of paper towels and hand soap and a bowl of water. She squatted down beside me and dipped a paper towel into the water, squeezed out some soap, and gently washed the wound. It hurt.

"Stop moving," she said. "You're worse than the dogs."

She patted my leg dry with another paper towel, taped a bandage on, and rolled down my pant leg.

She looked around the place. She'd never been in here before. We'd only ever spoken on the landing or on the street. She was a couple of years out of college, and I knew I didn't need to impress her. Still, I didn't like seeing my place through someone else's eyes. "How long have you lived here?" she asked.

"A year or so." It'd been eight years. "I'm gonna decorate soon."

"You have a lot of books." There were two faux-wood bookshelves along one wall. "Are they all magic books?"

"Most of them."

"I thought magicians are supposed to keep their secrets."

"Books are okay," I said.

"Like a loophole?"

"Yeah, I guess. Damn, my leg hurts."

"Let me get you some ice." She went into my kitchen again. The freezer opened and closed. Then a couple of cabinets. "You have any liquor?" Through my ceiling I heard the *click click click* of the dog pacing. Probably plotting.

"Under the sink," I told her.

She opened and closed a cabinet. The sound of pouring.

She returned with the ice in another dish towel and two glasses. I took one: straight-up vodka. And I didn't buy the good stuff.

Harley took a sip and asked, "Who's that guy?"

She meant the guy hanging up across the room. Except for my calendar of bookings, the black-and-white poster was the only thing on the wall. I knew she was only asking about it because I had revealed myself to be squeamish and cowardly, and people probably blacked out less if they were in the middle of a conversation.

In the photo, the magician was about fifty. Tuxedo, top hat, cape. An old-time look, but then again he was old-time. Also: white gloves. *Gloves.*

"Richard Valentine Pitchford," I said, and groaned a little. "He went by Cardini."

"So card tricks?"

"He revolutionized card magic. And he wore gloves. You wouldn't believe how hard that is."

"Probably like doing surgery on a dog while wearing gloves. That's what the vets do."

She had it wrong, though. Card magic was one hundred percent touch. A doctor's form-fitting latex gloves were nothing compared with white dress gloves. But I wasn't going to argue with the person patching me up. On the day Harley moved in, I'd seen her lugging boxes from a U-Haul and didn't go outside to help. I couldn't bear the thought of helping her and then being forgotten forever.

"I should've helped you move in," I told her now.

"Huh?"

"When you moved in. I was at home. I should've helped."

She looked surprised for an instant. Then a shrug. "You didn't know me." She nodded toward the carton of lo mein. "Do you want that? I can get you a fork."

I shook my head and held the cold dish towel against my leg. Harley's pajamas had stars and moons on them, and the cuffs of the pajama pants were orange. She looked like a rocket ship.

She frowned. "Are you going to rat me out to Tony?" Our landlord.

I glanced down at my pants: the bleeding seemed to be slowing. "Just keep your dog away from me."

"He isn't mine," she said. "He needs a home." She took a drink. "Did you know him?"

"Know who?"

"Cardini."

I shook my head. "He died before I was born." Still, I'd spent more than a few hours over the years imagining such a meeting. He watches me do a few card flourishes, a trick or two, and he strokes his pointy white beard and flashes his winning smile and says something beautiful.

"He was a perfect magician," I said. "Absolutely pure in his movements. He developed his magic in the trenches during the First World War. That's why he wore the gloves."

"For real?"

"It was cold in the trenches."

She took another sip, squeezed her eyes shut, and opened them again. "Hey, are you gonna be okay?"

"Yeah. Do I need like a tetanus shot or something?"

"You should probably do that tomorrow."

"Because I really don't like needles."

"No, you really don't like tetanus." She finished her drink. "David Blaine—do you know him?"

Always with the David Blaine. "You mean personally?"

"Yeah."

I told her I didn't. "I don't really know anyone anymore except for Jack Clarion."

"Who's that?" she asked.

"Exactly," I said, and took another drink.

9

♠

"You call that distracting?" Ace said.

"Pardon me?"

He had just gotten into my car and was checking me out. "I thought I told you to wear . . ." He shook his head. "Never mind."

I had on a black cardigan over a simple black top. Jeans and black knee-high boots. Sorry, Ace: no skin. He'd have to create his own distraction.

I remained irked for a few miles, but by the time we were south of the Driscoll Bridge I was feeling the stirrings of an actual adventure, an American road trip where anything could happen, and even if it didn't all go our way I'd have the story afterward— and it was a story I was getting paid to write.

In the past 365 days our planet had raced completely around a medium-sized star, yet I hadn't traveled more than a hundred miles from my apartment. I'd performed some shows, doing the same routines by rote and coming home again to frozen dinners and the gut-gnawing awareness that eventually the word "rut" loses its meaning. I was like some former high school jock who had once thrown a few winning passes and now had only the memory of those long-ago games to keep him warm at night. But this trip with my cheat had my heart pumping a little harder. I felt—dare I say it?—energized.

"If ever there was a shithead who needed to be separated from his money," Ace was telling me while fidgeting with my radio dial, "it's Carlo Desoto." Desoto was a middle manager at Atlantic Insurance. "He's the swell guy who denies your grandmother's cancer treatment." Ace settled on a Rolling Stones song and began drumming on his knees. "That's why we're driving all this way. Because he's in it for real money. The other guys are run-of-the-mill suckers who think they're better than they are, but for them it's a pastime. They have money to lose."

"What kind of money? A bakery owner?"

"His wife is an orthopedic surgeon."

"Ah."

"Yeah, ah. Listen, I do my homework. This is their golf. Their whatever. It's something they enjoy doing. All except for this guy Desoto. He's in deep. I met him at the Tropicana couple of months ago, watched him win and then give it all back. He had on this terrific Gucci suit, and it was so obvious that his wife thought he was working late at the office, or maybe having an affair. Such a beautiful thing to see. Desperation has a glimmer to it, like diamonds. Took me all of ten minutes to talk my way into one of his regular home games. I've seen it before. These guys, these family men, they get to losing more than they ever imagined they could lose. And when it gets bad enough, it's like a switch gets flipped, and they realize they're in so deep they'll never get out except for a miracle, and then that becomes the goal: the miracle. But they know miracles don't happen, so then it's almost like losing becomes the goal. Losing big. Losing so big you can't even believe it."

But of course I could believe it.

Red or black?

I could hear my father's voice as clearly now as when I was twelve.

"Because when you're desperate enough," Ace was saying, "the feeling of losing big isn't so different from the feeling of winning big. And someone who can't tell the difference anymore? Who's in so deep he needs that feeling at whatever the cost? *That's* who you want at your table." He slapped his leg. "That's Carlo Desoto."

The others at the table would be typical of the men into whose card games Ace found his way: utterly forgettable, and with just enough success to believe they were smart and clever.

"So can we talk about your tactics a little?" I asked. I wanted to understand the details of Ace's technique, his mechanics, his grip, but he kept insisting I see—or, more precisely, fail to see—all that in action. But I also wanted to know how he worked as a solo player. How often did he false deal? What kind of deal was it? And what about the cut? Someone else would be cutting the cards, which makes it useless to stack the deck beforehand. An accomplice could false-cut for him, or cut the deck at exactly the right place . . . but Ace worked alone.

"First you watch," he answered. "Then on the drive home, we talk. I don't want to bias your eyes."

I drove on, letting prime interviewing time go to waste but unsure what to do about it. At least my car was cooperating, deciding to wait a while longer before coughing out its last breath.

When we got close to Atlantic City, my phone navigated us to the bakery, and I parked across the street. We were several blocks in from the ocean, on an inadequately lit street lined with darkened storefronts. The air was gustier than it was up north, and I wrapped my arms around myself as Ace and I crossed the road. You couldn't see inside the bakery because of the shelves of bread blocking the windows. The sign on the door said CLOSED, but the door was unlocked.

Ace gently touched my arm. "If you win a hand, don't lay your cards down extra slow to rub it in. It's bad etiquette."

"Slow rolling. I know."

"And protect your cards. Not everyone's as honest as you and me."

I smiled.

"Let's go get 'em, tiger," he said, and we went in.

I was hit by a blast of warm air and a smell that was yeasty and sweet. Shelves behind the counter were partially stocked with what I supposed were the day's leftovers. In the center of the room was a cheap metal poker table, the fold-up kind, and on a long table near it was a spread of bread, cheeses, and olives. Beside the food were several bottles of wine and liquor.

Three other people were in the room. A skinny, older man came right over, all smiles. "Welcome, welcome." He reached out to shake Ace's hand. He was maybe early sixties, with a long, kind face and a day's gray stubble. Bakers woke up early. His day must have already been sixteen, seventeen hours old.

"This is my friend Natalie," Ace said. We saw no reason for me to use a fake first name. "Natalie, meet Ethan Garret."

"It smells wonderful in here," I told Ethan, who beamed and pumped my hand.

"Thanks for coming all this way. You'll make five."

"Five?" Ace frowned.

A younger man came over. Well built. Black cashmere sweater, brown corduroys, polished black shoes. His hair was as dark as his sweater, and his eyes were as dark as his hair. I'd have singled him out at a casino, too, but not for his betting style.

"Good to see you again, Ace," he said.

"Likewise."

"I'm Natalie," I said.

I felt myself being assessed. His smile seemed real, if guarded. "Carlo Desoto." We shook hands.

"And this is my niece, Ellen," Ethan said.

I felt embarrassed, having assumed that the woman standing by the food table was an employee, here to serve drinks or pick up after us. Had she been a man, I would have assumed she was a last-minute player substitution. Shame on me.

"Hi." Ellen gave the room a smile but saved a special finger wave for me that seemed to say, *We're both female!*

She wore a loose sweater—gold, with white stars—blue jeans, and canvas Keds. She had on very little makeup, if any, and her brown hair was cut short and might have looked stylish on another woman's face. Ace had fooled me back at the park on Wednesday with his *How many kids do I have?* nonsense, but this time I was certain I was dealing with the parent of small children.

Still annoyed at myself for dismissing her so quickly, I went over and made a point of shaking her hand firmly, saying, "Nice to meet you, Ellen. I'm Natalie." She smiled politely.

"You said there'd be six," Ace said to Carlo. I knew what annoyed him. Fewer players meant smaller pots, and we had come a long way. "What about Hank and Roy?"

"Roy's sick," Ethan said. "And Hank forgot about some event at his kid's school."

Ace bit his lip. "Still, I would think . . ." But that was all we

70

would learn about what he thought, because he went over to the drink table and unscrewed the cap from a bottle of tonic.

"What do you do, Ellen?" I asked.

"I teach kindergarten in Flemington."

"I guess you like kids." I always felt uncomfortable talking to mothers, who seemed to belong to a tribe with laws I wasn't privy to and grievances I didn't understand.

"Actually, they're pretty gross a lot of the time." She smiled. "But they're sweet. They keep me young."

The opposite seemed true. Her eyes looked tired and her mouth had permanent frown lines. I'd have guessed she was only a few years older than me, but children had aged her face and wreaked havoc on her fashion sense.

"Flemington's what? A couple of hours away?" Ace asked, the vodka tonic in his cup fizzing.

"Thereabouts," she said. "But I hadn't seen Ethan and Margie in a while, and I like driving." Her smile came and went in a single second. "I'm going to visit the ladies' room, if you don't mind." She headed toward the rear of the shop.

Once she was out of earshot, Ethan said, "She's in the middle of an ugly divorce."

"I don't like people watching the game," Ace said.

I glanced over at the restroom. "Ugly how?"

"Oh, the usual nonsense," Ethan said. "Husband's an ass but wants custody. Just your typical awfulness. She needed a night away. Her mother's watching the kids."

"She's gonna play, though, right?" Ace asked.

"Yeah, I'm gonna cover her," Ethan said. "I taught her to play years ago. She isn't half bad." He smiled. "Okay, maybe half bad." He gestured toward the food and drink. "You guys help yourself. Natalie, what's your line of work?"

I told Ethan the story Ace and I came up with in the car. "I'm an events coordinator for a couple of hotels." I'd performed in enough venues over the years to talk coherently about this.

"She hired me for one of those one-night poker courses," Ace chimed in from the food table, "for a bunch of Merck executives. When she told me she had a regular game in college, I knew we'd be friends."

I wished he hadn't said "college." I wasn't ready to improvise a whole undergraduate experience. But no one asked. As we chatted and poured drinks and filled our small plates with cheese and bread, I couldn't help taking note of the diverse agendas at the card table: Carlo's need to recoup his losses; Ace's need to make the trip to A.C. worth his while; Ethan's desire for an entertaining night, to play host, and to take his niece's mind off her domestic problems; Ellen's need to escape her life, and her kids, for a few hours; my own need to see Ace in action, to gather the raw material for my magazine article. We had only one thing in common. We would all try to win.

But Ace would win, because the game would be rigged.

He was the first to sit down. I didn't want to sit immediately to his right, because then I'd be the one cutting his cards. I didn't want my presence to affect what he did—to make it harder or easier. So I sat down opposite him, where I could watch his play head-on.

Carlo sat to Ace's right, and then Ellen asked, "We just sit anywhere?" After being told by Ethan that anywhere was fine, she sat to my left. His guests situated, Ethan took the last spot at the table, between me and Ace.

Ellen's hands, I noticed, were dry and cracked, no doubt from being washed a hundred times a day. Her fingernails were ragged

72

and bitten down. She caught me watching her hands, and I looked away.

"Do you play euchre, Natalie?" she asked.

"Euchre? No."

"It's such a great game," she said. "If everyone gets tired of playing poker, we could switch to that." She glanced around at the other players. "I'll teach anyone who doesn't know how. It's not hard to learn."

"I think we're probably gonna stick with poker tonight," Ace said in a voice that I suspected was him trying not to sound utterly condescending.

Ellen's head lowered. She had come all this way, and now there'd be no euchre.

Fortunately, I knew how to make everything right again. "How old are your kids?" I asked.

They were three and five. *And such rascals!* She found a picture on her phone of the two of them and passed the phone around the table. We learned about Jenna's recent fear of earthquakes and Nathan's love of bugs.

"His favorite lately?" She lowered her voice as if telling the punch line of the world's crudest joke. "It's the *dung beetle.*"

Finally, the game got under way. We were playing $2/$4 no-limit Hold'em. A generation ago, the popular game was seven card stud. Now everyone played Hold'em. First you were dealt two cards, facedown. Then came three community cards—the "flop"—followed by another community card, the "turn card." The last community card was the "river card." You try to make the best five-card hand out of all seven cards.

Tonight's initial buy-in was four hundred dollars. My initial buy-in would also be my final buy-in. If I lost all my chips, I would nurse a drink and snack on good bread and olives and watch the game without the distraction of my own play.

The first hands played out with no one betting large and nothing remarkable at the table. Lots of calling, lots of folding. Then I got lucky on a turn card with a third queen and raised to come away with a nice pot of chips. Whenever the deal came around to Ace, I gave him no more than a casual glance. But unless I missed something, he was playing it straight.

Who was the best player at the table? Who was the best bluff? I didn't know. I was faring better than Ellen, whose chips were steadily dwindling. Ethan had fallen behind, too. The rest of us were all slightly ahead of where we'd started.

After about an hour, things got interesting. It was Ethan's deal, and Ace's cut. But Ace had gotten up to replenish his drink. When Ethan finished shuffling and set the deck down for Ace to cut, Ace quickly stepped over to the card table, holding his glass with ice in it. Instead of cutting the cards, he simply tapped the top of the deck and went back to making his drink.

It was very beautiful, what had just occurred, and I smiled inwardly and thought: *So maybe you are an ace after all.*

The key to taking Carlo Desoto's money, I now understood, was Ethan's hospitality. Ethan was a retailer with a desire to be a magnanimous host. Ace forgoes the cut, opting for a quick tap instead, under the guise of wanting to finish making his drink before the next hand starts. He's simply keeping the game moving along. Plus, forgoing the cut sends a subtle message of goodwill. *We're all friends here*, it implies. *There's no need for these anti-cheating formalities.*

It all happened so quickly and subtly, this deft bit of misdirection, that I could have imagined it. Yet the following hands proved me right. On my deal, I set the deck to my right, and Ethan, probably without even thinking about it, followed the pattern established by Ace. No cut—just a tap. The following hand, when it was my turn to cut, I continued the pattern.

And just like that—presto!—we had become a poker table where nobody was cutting the cards any longer. Which meant that next time Ace had the deal, he could control a couple of choice cards to wherever he wanted in the deck.

Three hands later, as he started to gather the cards from the table, I awaited the distraction I knew had to be coming.

"So Ethan," Ace said, "what exactly is sourdough anyway?"

Right on cue.

And with all eyes but mine now on our host, who was more than glad to hold forth about his bread-baking secrets, I watched Ace shuffle the two black aces from the previous hand straight to the bottom of the deck. The move was so unsubtle, it was barely a move at all. He more or less just stuck the cards where he wanted them. Then he did a couple of overhand cuts and riffle shuffles that left the bottom cards in place. He set the deck on the table to his right, never once looking at Carlo, whose turn it was to cut.

Carlo was intently listening to the merits of using filtered water to feed the sourdough starter. He tapped the deck.

Ace picked it up again with his right hand and transferred it to his left. As he prepared to deal, his left index and middle fingers curled around the front of the deck.

Two fingers in front?

Oh, Ace, I thought. *How could you?*

I was appalled that he would hold the deck this way. His two fingers were out front to reduce friction on the bottom card, but there was no reason to use this grip *unless you were bottom dealing.* Ace was holding up a giant sign that read: "I'm going to bottom deal now!"

Yet no one seemed to notice. They were learning about sourdough. Did people really put up their hard-earned dollars only to be this inattentive to the game?

". . . the key is to not *overwhelm*," Ethan was saying. "If you wait for peak rise, you'll overwhelm the palate, so I never wait for peak rise. That's my trick. Plus the yeast. You'd be surprised how many kinds of yeasts there are. But when we're talking sourdough . . ."

Ace started dealing: Card to Ethan. Card to me. Card to Ellen. Card to Carlo. Card to himself.

The second disappointment overshadowed the first. Watching Ace deal himself his first card, I saw my *Men's Quarterly* article going up in smoke. I had traveled to Atlantic City, put hundreds of miles on my decrepit car, and invested way too much money, and all for nothing.

Ace dealt a second card to Ethan, me, Ellen, Carlo, himself.

I could have written an entire book on the flaws in Ace's bottom deal. Here would be the chapter titles:

—His bottom-dealt cards made a noticeable scraping sound coming off the deck
—The bottom half of the deck wedged outward
—His left wrist visibly tightened whenever he dealt himself a card
—His deal to himself was a beat slower than his deal to everyone else
—Two fucking fingers stuck out from the front of the deck!

Fact was, I was witnessing one of the worst displays of card manipulation of my not-so-brief career. Bottom dealing wasn't even that hard. If there was one rule of legerdemain worth abiding, it was that you never do a move in public until it's ready. And

Ace? Not ready. And this was his livelihood? Maybe Brock McKnight was right. Maybe I had chosen the wrong career.

It took chutzpah for Ace to sit down at the poker table with such artless technique. And even more chutzpah to invite me to witness it. Maybe all this chutzpah, I briefly considered, could become the focus of my magazine article—how this cardsharp whose skills were dull, dull, dull was nonetheless able to come out on top with nothing but misdirection and nerve.

Still, he was swimming in unsafe waters. With a bottom deal that bad, someone was going to catch him. Maybe not tonight, but someday. And what then? It didn't matter if the buy-in was four hundred or four thousand. Nobody liked to be cheated.

This storm seemed to brew nowhere else but in my mind, however, because suddenly the deal was done, and Ace set the deck down, and we each peeked at our two hole cards, and Ellen, sitting left of the big blind, made the first raise, and everything was so damn ordinary.

My cards stank, which was just as well. I folded and sat in quiet disgust. I thought about the money I had already paid Ace. I thought about the hope I'd invested in this trip and how it was all for nothing. Even if Ace won some money tonight, my cardsharp was a disaster. Which made me a disaster by association.

I decided to get very drunk.

The booze was free, and I liked booze, and so I would drink some of my losses back, and the best part was that no one would notice how inebriated I became, because no matter what I did—shout incoherently, strip naked—my drunkenness would be less obvious than Ace's bottom deal.

I got up and poured myself a generous refill of whiskey, neat. By the time the river card was laid on the table, it was clear that Ace wasn't going to win big. He'd missed his three-of-a-kind, and the pot of chips on the table never got very large anyway. I laughed inwardly (and perhaps a little outwardly—the whiskey was hitting me just right) at the poetic justice.

Then came more poetic justice. He lost the hand to Ellen—*Ellen*—who'd stayed in the betting and taken the pot with two pairs: jacks and threes.

"Wow," she said. She seemed embarrassed by the attention. "That was . . . wow."

Watching her collect the chips, I wondered if Ethan had undersold his niece's "half bad" poker skills. I set down my drink and kept a closer eye on her. Not for any reason. I knew she was only a kindergarten teacher. Maybe I was hoping to be surprised by something, anything, now that my cheat had exposed himself as a fool at the card table.

When it was Ellen's deal three hands later, she shuffled the cards with the stiff hands of a beginner. Her fingers were small, and they strained on the riffle shuffle, the bottom card flashing a little. She squared up the deck and set it to her right. I tapped the deck, same as everyone had been doing for at least a dozen hands now.

She picked up the cards and began to deal, and everything changed forever.

10

♦

When did you first get interested in magic?

I'm often asked that. I was eight when Victor Flowers handed me my first magic kit, thirteen when Jack Clarion gave me my first sleight of hand lesson. Sometime between those two events I remember watching a magician turn a cobra into a duck on TV. I don't remember who the magician was, but I clearly recall the brain-twisting feeling of seeing something that simply could not be.

That was how it was now. I was seeing what I couldn't be seeing. Only this was so much better, so much more, because there was no TV and it happened two feet from my face.

Without the distraction of Ethan's sourdough lecture or the benefit of large hands, Ellen quietly dealt herself the ace and seven of spades while dealing Carlo the king and five of spades, while also dealing three additional spades to the board. They both had flushes, but hers was the winning hand.

Here's the thing. I never saw her cull the cards. The culling was so invisible, I would have thought she'd swapped in a cold deck, except if she'd used a cold deck then she wouldn't have needed a false deal. And the false deal was what I detected, and why I suspected Ellen's winning hand was more than big luck.

I *barely* detected it, though.

It was more a sense than a sighting. My position, on her immediate right, was the *easiest* place to catch a false deal, yet I saw nothing. Her deal was inaudible, the pacing perfect. I knew she wasn't dealing from the bottom, because I kept snatching glimpses of the bottom card. So what was it, then?

By the time the hand was done and she had collected the chips, I realized it wasn't the deal itself that had put me on alert. It was her face. How she wasn't watching the cards as she dealt. That was her error. Beginners watch the cards as they deal. Or maybe it wasn't her face. Or maybe I was imagining everything, though I didn't think so. I began to suspect that Carlo Desoto's financial woes weren't a well-kept secret. And that Ellen was specifically targeting him as she played, same as Ace was—only she was doing it a thousand times better.

She won the largest pot of the night, over three hundred. And the way she smiled awkwardly through it all, seemingly embarrassed to be gathering up so many chips—it was Oscar caliber. Her outfit—that sweater, those shoes—I now saw it for what it was: a costume. Even her posture at the table, hunched over, making herself small. And the bitten-down fingernails. I had driven to Atlantic City with an amateur, but sitting at my table was a pro.

She could act, she could play poker, she could control the cards, but the deal had my brain at war with itself. A cobra turns into a duck. Impossible. But it happened. So easy, so pure. I didn't see the move when Ellen dealt, and I *always* see the move.

She held the deck in her hand like an amateur would. And with this ordinary grip she dealt three regular tosses around the table followed by a flawless false deal (A center deal? Good lord, was she center dealing?) to Carlo and another flawless false deal to herself. And then, when she had my undivided attention, she somehow still dealt three more false deals, the other three spades, to the table for community cards. Hell, maybe she false dealt all five community cards. I just didn't know anymore. Understand, I was a master card handler. This was my area of expertise and life-long obsession. And yet. A cobra. And then a duck.

Was I obligated to tell Ace?

Should I tell him about the expert at the card table who was fleecing him right along with everyone else? My relationship to Ace went back all of four days, but we had come here together—on a less-than-honest mission, true—but we were a team, and maybe that meant something. Or maybe he of all people ought to have been on the lookout for people like him.

Except that Ellen (*Ellen!* What a name. I'd been so gullible) was nothing like him.

My dilemma didn't last long. Ace soon found himself low on chips and was becoming noticeably irritated. He made my decision for me.

"Get me a drink, Natalie," he said when it was his turn to deal. I understood he was asking me to be his misdirection. Still, I didn't appreciate the rudeness. His flush loss had stunned him and made him a passive bettor but an active asshole. I would get him the drink but let him lose his money.

He won that hand and took a small pot, but it mattered little, because soon Ellen was cleaning up. Her cheating was amazing, but her poker play was obviously very strong, too. Every time she won a hand, she glanced over at Ethan as if she were astonished by her luck. Was he in on it? I didn't think so, but I no longer trusted my instincts. I bet a little, won a hand or two, but all I really did was mark time until Ellen's next deal.

Once again her manipulations were undetectable. I kept my eyes on the deck while she dealt the cards, and Carlo went all in on two pairs, kings high, and soon everyone was out except for him and Ellen, who beat him with a straight, and suddenly Carlo's chips were gone.

"Jesus," he said under his breath, and cashed in for four hundred more dollars' worth of chips. Unfortunately for the cheaters in the room, he started cutting the deck again, which meant no more false deals.

By eleven o'clock most of Carlo's chips were gone again. Thanks to decent game play, a little luck, and the knowledge to stay out of Ellen's way, most of my chips were still in front of me. Ace was down to a small pile. He slumped in his chair and shot me glances. He was down maybe three, three fifty for the night, not a nightmare loss unless you'd traveled a long distance and supposedly had the game rigged.

"We have a big drive ahead of us," he said after yet another losing hand followed by a rude, theatrical yawn. I ignored him.

"It's getting late, Natalie," he said after the following hand. "We need to get going."

I told him I'd like to play a little longer.

Carlo had said almost nothing for the last hour, his face getting paler. He checked his phone. "Yeah, it's time for me to call it a night," he said with little inflection. He cashed out his few remaining chips and after perfunctory good-byes hurried out the door, presumably directly to one of the casinos.

The four of us played a final hand, and then we cashed out and helped Ethan carry the leftover food and drink to the back counter. By now Ellen, the big winner, was laughing and saying to all of us how this was just *so, so amazing* and *just crazy*, and then she was saying good-bye and telling us that it was so great to meet us, and that this was just what the doctor had ordered. She kissed Ethan on the cheek and thanked him again.

I needed to get her alone, and it had to be now. I felt certain that once she was out of sight I'd never see her again.

"I'm going out for a little air," I said to the room while Ellen went to get her coat. If I got outside first, it wouldn't seem as if I was following her.

Ace's hand was on my arm. "I need you a minute." Despite my quiet protest, he led me to the alcove near the bathrooms. "That was some bullshit luck," he whispered. "I'll explain exactly what happened in the car. But it was some serious bullshit luck."

"Okay. That's fine. Whatever." I walked back into the main room. The front door was already closing behind Ellen. "I really want to get some air."

"You're just drunk," Ace said, louder than I would have liked. "You don't need air, you need a cold shower."

I glared at him. My arm was sore from where he had gripped it. "I said I'll be right back." But when I went to leave, he reached out for my arm again. "Let go of me!" I yanked my arm free from him and headed for the door.

"Yep. Definitely drunk," I heard him say to Ethan. "Pardon us." He followed me outside.

When the door shut behind us he said, "Well? Here's your fucking shithole Atlantic City air, Natalie. How do you like it?" He shook his head. "I swear, I'm not gonna ride home with you if you're gonna act like this."

All the anger and frustration I'd felt from Ace's weeklong display of disrespect—feelings I'd suppressed in the hope that he might possibly be the skilled cardsharp I'd been promised, that *he'd* promised me he was—I could suppress no longer.

"Then find your own ride home, you fucking loser." I hurried away from him.

"What?" I heard from behind me. "What did you say to me?"

"Asshole."

I was halfway down the block when I heard a whiny, "Natalie?"

But I had no time for that.

Ellen was nowhere in sight. No cars had gone by. I rushed to the end of the block and turned onto the street running perpendicular. She was rounding the corner. I ran after her down the empty street, slower than I wanted, my left leg burning from the dog bite. When I caught up, I called out to her and she turned around.

"Natalie? I'm in kind of a hurry. I lost track of time and—"

"Please," I said her. "I have to talk to you."

"It's really late. I have a long drive home and I teach in the morning."

"Trust me. We have to talk."

She said, "You can give me your number if you want, and I'll call you."

I shook my head. "I know."

"Sorry?"

"I *know.*"

"You know what?" She raised her hands in the air. Feigned ignorance and impatience.

"I'd never tell anyone," I said. "But it was the greatest thing I ever saw."

Somewhere not far away came the sound of a window being smashed.

"This isn't a good neighborhood," she said, pulling her purple scarf tighter around her. "I don't like being out here at night."

"Please, Ellen—"

"I had a nice time playing with you tonight, but I don't know what you're talking about, and to be honest you're scaring me a little."

84

When she started to walk away from me, I blurted out, "Let me buy you a cup of coffee." Her walking slowed down. "Please. Will you please let me buy you a cup of coffee?" She stopped and faced me. "Ace is a cheater," I said, "and I know you know it, and I know why you didn't say anything."

She watched me a moment before speaking again. "Your friend?"

"No. We aren't friends. We aren't anything. But you. My god, Ellen. You can't just walk away."

She watched me a moment, then took her phone out of her purse, checked it, and put it away again. "I can meet you at the Last Call Tavern on North Covington Road," she said. "I don't want you following me. Wait fifteen minutes and meet me there."

She turned away and started walking again. Her footfalls were the only sound on the night street.

I walked the other way, back toward the bakery, wondering how the hell I was going to ditch Ace but determined to ditch Ace. I didn't want him in my car. I didn't ever want to see him again, but we were over a hundred miles from home and I wasn't cold enough to leave him stranded. I decided to take him to the bar of his choice, let him drink it off for an hour until I picked him up again. I'd even give him booze money. Or I'd take him to a casino. Or wherever he wanted. I didn't care.

When I got back to my car, the passenger window was smashed. Ace's backpack, gone. Then I noticed the side of my car had been keyed.

I guessed he must have decided that vandalizing my car was worth the price of a bus ticket home.

I used the flashlight on my phone to verify what the keyed writing said.

BITCH

But Ace had it wrong. I wasn't a bitch. I was an accomplished magician and hopeful journalist who'd come to Atlantic City and found her story. The dues I'd had to pay included too much cash and a vandalized car, but there was no denying that, finally, I had found her, I had found her, God damn, I had found her.

The car started. I pressed the home button on my phone and said, "Driving directions to Last Call Tavern in Atlantic City."

When the phone couldn't find it, I repeated the request. Then I asked for directions to North Covington Road.

Which, I learned, didn't exist.

PART TWO

A

I went to bed to the distant rumble and crash of garbage trucks moving through the predawn streets and woke up several hours later hungry and fog-brained. I trudged out to the kitchen and started a half pot of coffee with the last of a container of Folgers. While the coffee dripped I went into the living room, where Ethel was pecking at a small disco ball hanging from the cage top and Julius was sitting comfortably in his food dish. I had left my phone on the coffee table. I picked it up to check email. There was a new message from Brad Corzo.

Subject: Invitation

Dear Natalie,

The talent committee is pleased to invite you to participate in the upcoming convention. Because final convention details are still being arranged, all presenters will be receiving a separate email once the date (either 12/18 or 12/19), time, and venue for their performances are set.

Please remember to register online for the conference (as a presenter, your registration fee is waived), and upload a current bio and photo, which will appear on the conference website.

Yours in magic,

Brad Corzo

Chair, Panel Selection Committee, World of Magic

P.S. I'd be remiss if I didn't mention that the Boy Scouts of America is one of the nation's largest and most important values-based youth organizations. I myself was once a Scout. Performing for them is always an honor and a privilege.

I let out an excited shriek, causing Ethel to jump down from her wooden bar.

This was huge, especially in light of my correspondence the other day, which had been downright petulant. I reread the email to make sure I wasn't misunderstanding, but it couldn't be clearer. The committee had actually changed its mind. I would perform at the convention.

This was big enough news that I had no problem letting Brad Corzo's petty scolding slide.

Dear Brad,

I'm grateful for your invitation, and I gladly accept. I'll go ahead and register, and will await your further correspondence. Very much looking forward to the convention.

Thank you again,

Natalie

Today was December 5. That gave me just under two weeks to prepare—not long, not long at all. Not if the idea was to make my performance great.

I carried my coffee mug into the bathroom to start the shower. And as the water rained down on me I thought about the cups and balls routine I'd been working on. I could lead into it with the disappearing signed bill trick and have the bill reappear inside the lime produced at the end of the cups and balls. This was something I liked to do, embed one trick inside another, like magical nesting dolls. It's very satisfying to an audience.

When I got out of the shower I saw the pack of cards sitting on the bathroom countertop. My bathroom mirror was the largest in the apartment, and when I'd gotten home last night I'd spent a few minutes in the bathroom with the cards, trying to figure out what the hell that woman, Ellen, might have been doing. I didn't get far. And now it hit me again that the greatest card manipulator I'd ever seen had vanished right before my eyes.

Already it felt like a strange, frenzied dream.

After finding my car vandalized and realizing Ellen had ditched me, I'd gone back into the bakery with an excuse about wanting her advice—*for my sister, who has a daughter in kindergarten.*

Ethan had written down Ellen's cell phone number. He didn't strike me as a confederate. He seemed ignorant about who she really was and what she could do.

I'm sure she'd be glad to help, he'd said.

I wanted to call her now, but I thought, toweling off, that maybe I shouldn't. Brad Corzo's email felt like a sign that I ought to forget about my detour into card cheats and poker games and refocus my energies on magic, where, after nearly a decade at sea, I was finally being offered an olive branch.

I brushed my teeth thinking: the World of Magic crowd would go nuts for the Rings of Fire linking ring routine I'd been working on. I should close with it.

I put on my jeans and shirt thinking: I need to find her.

I put on my socks thinking: forget about the lime. More striking if an *egg* appeared at the end of the cups and balls trick, and then I cracked it.

I ran a brush through my hair thinking: no way is that really Ellen's phone number. But I have to find out.

To my surprise, the outgoing message began: *Hi, this is Ellen.*

I left a message, because what was the harm? *This is Natalie, from last night. Please call me when you get a moment.*

But I knew she wouldn't.

I gave the birds fresh water and returned to the loveseat, about to Google her. What was her last name? Had she ever said? I typed in "Ellen" and "kindergarten" and "Flemington" and got no useful results. I found the school district's website and searched for kindergarten teachers. No Ellen. Obviously. She wasn't a kindergarten teacher. She didn't live in Flemington.

I poured a bowl of cereal, and while I ate I poked around the school district websites of towns near Flemington—Rowland Mills, East Amwell—but again, there was no Ellen who taught kindergarten. In Franklin there was a first grade teacher named Ellen Sacks, but a subsequent search revealed that she had been teaching at Franklin Elementary School since 1979.

I Googled more combinations of words—*Ellen, poker, New Jersey, Atlantic City*—before giving up. Monday mornings always made me restless and vaguely unsettled, society beginning its workweek and me coming off a weekend performance or nothing at all. I dusted and vacuumed the apartment (the vacuuming sending Mustard, upstairs, into a barking frenzy), but my fingers needed a deck of cards in them. I did a few bottom deals, which I knew Ellen hadn't done, and then some second deals, which didn't seem right either. What then? What had it been? I was about to call her number again when I decided the hell with it: Flemington, here I come.

I worried about driving my car with "BITCH" scratched into the side and a trash bag taped over the passenger window frame. There was no money to pay a ticket, nor money for car repairs to prevent getting ticketed, since stupid me had gone frugal on car insurance and waived comprehensive coverage.

I went online for home remedies for a scratched car. I didn't own a power sander or polishing wheel. I did own toothpaste. "See you later, birds," I said, and got my keys from the hook by the door.

Outside with a hand towel and a tube of Colgate, I attempted what one enthusiastic car owner had called "the never-fail tooth-paste method," which failed utterly.

I'll deal with the scratch later, I thought, and got under way.

While driving, I toggled radio stations and came upon an interview with none other than U.S. Senate candidate Victor Flowers.

I tell you, Todd, he was saying to the host, *I still say we're a country of optimists. We the people, and we the government, must work together for our kids and grandkids . . .*

This was New Jersey talk radio, as light and fluffy as a well-made omelet. It nauseated me, but I couldn't stop listening. Soon he and the host were reminiscing about Victor's days singing for his band, the Eternals.

We were these clean-cut kids playing the same clubs as the Ramones, the Velvet Underground. He laughed. *We were so out of place!*

The Eternals recorded, what, three albums? the host asked.

Only two, Victor said. *Two was plenty!* Both men guffawed.

And then you moved over to the business side of the industry.

Where I belonged, Victor said. *Offstage.*

And that's where the money was.

I've been very fortunate.

Victor Flowers sounded totally at ease on the radio. He must have been in his sixties by now, but there was a youthful chirpiness to his voice.

I called my mother in Reno.

"I'm in the car," I said when she picked up. "Victor Flowers is on the radio."

"Politics is a cesspool," she replied. My mother thought many things were a cesspool.

"Do you think he could actually win?" I asked.

"Honey, if I could tell the future, do you think I'd still be flat broke?"

All conversations with my mother eventually funneled into the topic of her lack of money. Not to make light of it—older and poor is a terrible combination. And I didn't believe Chip had meant to con her all those years back with his talk of a better life in Nevada. He was retired military and had intended to start up some business making specialized parts for military aircraft. He had ideas and, supposedly, connections. He just couldn't do it. The right place at the right time ended up being the wrong place at the wrong time. Or the right place at the wrong time. Or maybe the timing never mattered at all, given his appetite for the casinos.

My mother asked where I was driving to.

"The supermarket," I said, and I asked her if she was exercising the way she was supposed to. She'd recently been diagnosed with diabetes. "Yeah," she said, "sure." And then like any good evader of the truth, she changed the topic. "Any good bookings lined up?"

I told her about this morning's invitation to perform at the World of Magic convention.

"What does it pay?" she asked.

"It doesn't," I said, the defensiveness already creeping into my voice.

"Oh. That doesn't sound very savvy."

"It is, Mom. It's potentially very good for my career."

Why? Why had I gone and told my mother the truth, when a lie was always better for our relationship?

"Hmm," she said. "Well, I'm sure you know best."

"I do, Mom." I clenched my teeth. "I do know best."

I hung up the phone feeling angry and hurt—and guilty, as well, for feeling hurt and angry, because I was way too old for teenage histrionics. On the radio a listener was asking Victor Flowers the vital political question of whether he'd seen *Jersey Boys*. I changed the station to music and continued westward under a ceiling of low clouds, the taped trash bag flapping in the wind like a sad flag. Over the next hour, the ubiquitous Union County traffic lessened. I began to pass large farms of hard, brown earth where someday something would grow.

Flemington had only one kindergarten, and at 1:45 p.m. my car was parked across the street (the "bitch" side facing away from the school), engine on, heater running. My stomach was reminding me about the one lesson I should have learned from watching TV cops on a stakeout. I should have packed a sandwich.

Around 2:15, yellow buses started to line up outside the front of the school. At a little past 2:30 the school doors opened, and kids—so many kids—poured out of the building, along with some teachers who guided the kids toward the right buses. The teacher I'd hoped to see was not among them, because Ellen, if that was even her name, was not a kindergarten teacher. And if by chance she was, then she didn't work here. Still, I waited, because it's easy to follow Plan A when Plan B doesn't exist. When all the buses had groaned away, I waited while more teachers emerged from the building over the next half hour.

This was a flat, wide street, where across from the school a row of humble wooden houses stood with leafless trees out front and Christmas lights strung over shrubs and on rooftops. I imagined what it would be like to live here, to work a regular job and come home again at the end of the day to a family. We would eat together and do homework and maybe watch a show. Light a fire in the fireplace, listen to its snap and pop. I knew I should call my mother again and apologize for being short with her on the phone. For always being short with her. For failing to think of ways to bring her a little happiness. I knew she didn't have it easy. She'd never had it easy. I wished I could do more for her, whatever the hell more was.

The holidays were an undertow of guilt, and I found myself being pulled into the deeper waters and forgetting where I was—which was why I almost missed the petite blond woman leaving the school.

She was dressed more like an administrator than a kindergarten teacher: stylish gray coat over a black dress, stockings, pumps. Her gait, though. The briskness of it. The erect posture. It was how she'd hurried away from me on the quiet Atlantic City street the night before.

My car was an eyesore, but she hadn't seen it the prior night and didn't pay it any mind now. I got out of the car, quietly shut the door, and followed her to the parking lot.

She approached her car, a Toyota Prius. Either she was environmentally conscious or she liked being able to drive in silence.

When I had closed the gap between us to maybe ten yards, I called out, *"Ellen?"*

Not only had her hair lightened a few shades since last night; it had grown longer, past her shoulders. Eyeliner, mascara, blush, lipstick, all were applied expertly. Her green eyes were large and inquisitive and wide awake. Quite possibly, the circles under them last night had themselves been the product of makeup, not the absence of it. She looked as out of place now in the primary school parking lot as she had last night, the fatigued mom-slash-teacher at the poker table.

"Natalie?" She squinted and looked around as if perhaps she, and not I, were in the wrong place. "What are you . . ."

"The Last Call Tavern?" I said. "Where you asked me to meet you? It must have shut down since the last time you were there." I glanced around. "I can't believe you're really a kindergarten teacher."

She unlocked her door.

"Is that the wig?" I asked. "Or did you wear the wig last night?"

She faced me full-on. "Is there something I can do for you?"

"Is your name really Ellen?"

"Is yours really Natalie?"

"My last name's Webb," I said. "I'm a professional close-up magician." We were alone in the parking lot. Still, I lowered my voice. "I promise I'm not here to cause you any trouble. I don't care if you cheat at poker. Or I do care, but not in a bad way. Listen, can't we just please go and sit someplace that actually exists?" She kept watching me impassively. "Come on. I've driven a long way, and I could really use a beer."

"If you want a beer, no one's stopping you. If there's something you want from me, then tell me what it is. I'm very busy."

Aware that I might have only this one shot, I launched into my fastest explanation of the *Men's Quarterly* article, and why I'd been with Ace the previous night in Atlantic City, what I'd hoped to learn from him, and how he'd been a disaster, but how excited I had been to witness her, Ellen, at the card table.

"A magazine article," she said when I stopped talking. I waited while she looked out at the brown fields, the empty playground. "I have no idea what you're talking about." She clicked her key and the car door unlocked. "It was nice seeing you again."

"Wait!" I said, louder than I meant to. Her door was open. "Please, just . . . forget the article for a minute, will you?" I had so many questions, but the one forced itself to my lips. "Was it a center deal? It wasn't, was it?"

When she didn't answer right away, I knew she was deliberating: keep playing dumb, or drop the act. But I wasn't being fooled by the act, and I was her only audience. She must have come to the same conclusion, because she said, "My god, why are all magicians so obsessed with the Kennedy deal? It isn't even useful."

"I just want to know—"

"So you can write your article. Yes, you've explained all this already."

"I said forget the article. I want to be able to do it."

"In your little magic show, you mean."

I let it slide. "You might not call yourself a magician," I said, "but I saw you perform last night. No way did you pick up everything on your own. You had teachers. People showed you what they do because you needed to know. Please. Ellen. I need to know."

A cold breeze whipped across the schoolyard. Ellen unzipped her shoulder bag, felt around, and withdrew a pack of playing cards. "Here." She tossed me the pack. "Show me something. Show me if you're any good."

2

The raw air of the school parking lot was lousy for card manipulation, but I'd performed in worse settings: poolside with a wet deck; frat parties in rooms too dark to see and for audiences too drunk to care; hotel suites where the air was choked with smoke and sweaty bodies.

After a few cuts and flourishes to warm my hands and give Ellen a glimpse of my card handling, I did an abridged version of a card change/disappearance/reappearance I'd been doing for years. I kept the patter to a minimum, because my patter mattered to her as much as my shoe size. It was my hands she was interested in, a fast showcase of what they could do. And they could do a lot, and they did it well, and they didn't shake at all despite the cold. My hands, my fingers, they were mine again. When I returned the deck to her, she said nothing but walked around to the passenger side and opened the door for me.

While we drove, I gave her the silence she seemed to want while she decided the parameters of our conversation. After a short journey she stopped in front of a place called Sixty-Two, which was the street number.

Whatever setting I might have imagined for the clandestine shoptalk between magician and cardsharp, this wasn't it. The venue was either a café that sold beer or a bar that sold coffee drinks, ice cream, and, inexplicably, glass vases. The floor was cement, the ceiling drop panel, the walls brick. The music was '80s pop, the kind no one ever seeks out but everyone knows. This time in the afternoon, a lone bartender/barista stood behind the counter looking at his phone. Two guys in their twenties were shooting pool near the back.

I paid for a bottle of beer. Ellen ordered some triple espresso, high-octane drink that would have kept me awake for a month. To the guy behind the bar she said, "Sorry, I keep forgetting your name."

"David."

"Right. David. Got it." She paid for her drink, stuffed a dollar into the tip jar, and led me to a high-backed booth near the restrooms. We sat opposite each other. "I want you to understand something," she said. "I don't do this—explain myself. It's no one's business what I do." Her voice had a lower, richer tone to it than the night before. At the poker game she had a thin, nasally voice. "You're a magician and a woman," she was saying, "and maybe you think that means I can trust you—"

"You *can* trust me."

"Maybe. Maybe I can. Or maybe you only need to know I'm a kindergarten teacher."

"Why a kindergarten teacher?" I asked.

"What do you mean?"

"I saw what you can do. Why are you a kindergarten teacher?"

"Because I'm certified to be one."

"But what's the angle?"

"Angle? The angle is I like being a productive member of society," she said, and sipped her drink. "Also, there's this thing called the IRS, and it has a real bias against citizens who are able to live in homes and pay bills with no reported income."

100

"Still, how do you work it with your poker schedule? What if you have to travel to a game?"

Ellen chewed her lip. I felt her reading me as if there were cards in my hand. "You said forget the article. I'm holding you to that. I don't tell you a damn thing if it's for an article."

Why had I gone and said that? But I knew I couldn't take those words back now. She'd be out of here in two seconds.

"You have my word," I told her, my need to know eclipsing my good sense.

"I'm a substitute teacher," she said. "They call me, I tell them if I can work that day or not. Sometimes, like now, when my schedule is relatively clear, I take a long-term sub position. A little stability." My face must have made me look like a layperson who's just been given the unimpressive secret to an impressive magic trick. "What do you want me to say? People are more than one thing. I'm a teacher, too, and I'm good at it, and it gives me pleasure as well as a W-2 each year to make Uncle Sam happy."

"It's just weird."

"I've been a teacher almost as long as I've played cards. Weird for you? Maybe. Not for me."

"And the part about your being a mom?" I thought back to the previous evening. "Your son's love of dung beetles? Your daughter's . . . whatever it was?"

"Yeah, that was all fiction."

"You had pictures on your phone." Hearing my own words made me feel like such a sucker.

She smiled. "Come on, you're a smart woman. Stressed-out mom? It's a winning persona at the card table, even if I were playing honest poker. People lower their guard."

"You were convincing."

"Wasn't hard," she said. "A little frazzled, a little naive. God, I love bringing up euchre. Euchre's a great touch. I do that and people don't believe I can play a hand of poker, let alone cheat at it. They don't believe it even after I've taken all their money."

"What about Ethan?" I asked. "Was he in on it?"

She shook her head. "He knew my parents ages ago, when I was a kid living in A.C. I only got back in touch lately. Far as he knows, I *am* a stressed-out mother and wife."

"Well, like I said. You were convincing."

"You just have to commit to the role," she said with a shrug. "It helps a lot that I'm a woman."

"Be glad you aren't a magician," I said.

"I'm glad every day of my life," she said.

One of the guys in the back must have made a shot or won a game, because he started *whoop-whooping* as if he had just felled a gazelle with his bare hands.

"I know you won't agree," I said, "but you really would be an ideal subject for the article."

"Breathe one more word about a magazine article," she said, "and I'm gone. I'm being straight with you. One professional to another. It isn't gonna happen."

"You want the next game?" someone called out. The pool player with the ball cap had come halfway across the bar.

"No," Ellen said.

"Wasn't asking you," he said.

I stared at him. Held his gaze long enough for him to say, "What?" Then he turned away. Then he turned back again. "What? Hello?"

When he finally realized that was all I was going to give him, he shook his head and muttered, "Freak," before going back to his friend. He said something under his breath and the two of them giggled.

"I won't mention the article again," I said to Ellen. "But what about the false deal? Can't you share it with me? One professional to another?"

She watched me a moment. "You were right before," she said. "I did have teachers. So I'm sensitive to what you said. I am. But there are some secrets you don't reveal to anyone. Even to another magician. You know that."

If no magicians ever passed along their methods, much of the art form would be lost in a generation. I shared my secrets regularly in the *Magician's Forum*. Still, innovative secrets, the real breakthroughs, were hard-won assets, and every great or good magician had a trick that was too valuable to risk depreciation.

"Unless," Ellen said, shuffling in her seat, "we could maybe . . ." She bit her lip. "Maybe make some kind of a deal?"

"How's that?"

"I show you the move and, in exchange, you help me do a thing."

"A thing?"

"What?" she asked. "Too vague?"

I smiled. "It's a little vague."

She squinted at me. The lighting in here was needlessly, fluorescently bright. "What are you doing on January first? At night?"

"Why?"

"That's when the thing is."

"Do you mean a card game?"

"No, my classroom. I'm looking for a new teacher's aide. Yes, a card game."

"I'm not a cheat, Ellen."

She raised an eyebrow. "Of course you are."

"Doing magic shows isn't the same thing."

"I'm not talking about magic shows."

"Then what? You mean Atlantic City? I was observing Ace for the article. That's all."

"Oh, that's all?" She finished her drink and set the mug down. "You *knew* Ace was trying to cheat us out of our money, and yet you sat there and let it happen. And you went along with not cutting the deck because you thought it would help him to cheat the rest of us. I hate to be the one to tell you this, but what you did is called cheating at cards. And someone who cheats at cards is called a card cheat. So I'm asking, as respectfully as possible, that you please drop the black-or-white, holier-than-thou bullshit." She let her words sink in. "And by the way, I don't believe for a minute you're here because of any magazine article, even if you think you are. It's not why you were in A.C., and it's not why you're here now."

When I started to protest, she shook her head.

"Come on, you're no journalist," she said. "You're a conjurer, and from what little I've observed, you might be at the top of that game, but you're nowhere near the top of mine, and you know it, and it's driving you fucking crazy." She stopped talking, and for several seconds it was all Duran Duran and the barista, David, laughing into his phone. Then one of the guys in the back must have made a shot, because he shouted, *"Yeah, bitch!"*

When Ellen spoke again, it was softer than before. "I'll show you what I did at the Atlantic City game, and you'll agree to sit at the table with me for one measly night. We're talking three, four hours, tops."

She had my heart beating faster, I'll give her that.

"Come on," she said. "There's a lot of money involved, and I'd rather work with another woman."

"What's the buy-in?" I asked. Information gathering. Knowledge. That's all it was.

"It's steep," she said, "but we'd go home with everything, guaranteed. It's not a typical cash game. It's no-limit Hold'em run as a freeze-out tournament."

"Which means?"

"It means you can't buy in again when you're out of chips. One buy-in, and the winner takes all. We would take it all. Your share would be twenty percent."

Twenty percent of what? she wanted me to ask. Not that it mattered. I could have used twenty percent of anything. But Webbs weren't criminals, and Jack Clarion's old student knew the difference between a magician and a cardsharp. Didn't hurt, either, to have the World of Magic gig in front of me, reminding me who I was and who I wasn't.

"I'm not a cheat," I said.

"I thought we just established that you are."

I shook my head. "No."

"Then what you are is a cheat with no guts."

"I'm a magician," I said.

"Right. I just said that."

I smiled and sipped my drink. "It *was* a center deal, though, wasn't it? I'm almost sure. It had to be, if it wasn't a second deal, and it wasn't a bottom deal. You flashed the bottom card on purpose, and then you dealt from the center. Am I right? Just tell me I'm right."

She stared at me, waited until I couldn't bear it any longer. "Incorrect."

"For real?"

She stood up. "I'm sorry you drove all this way for nothing."

It was actually less than nothing, because now I knew about her. I knew she had the knowledge I wanted, but I was being denied access.

She glanced toward the back of the bar. "Would you at least like something for your trouble?"

"How's that?"

"Those guys playing pool—would you like some of their money?"

My first thought was: you're a pool hustler, too? Then I realized, no, that's not where this was going, and any number of classic bar cons and proposition bets started cycling through my mind. Bar-bill scam? No, this place was too rinky-dink, the drinks too cheap. I knew she had the deck of cards in her bag. With the cards she could take their money any number of ways. But which way? How?

"Follow me," she said. The guy in the baseball cap was lining up to take a shot when Ellen approached them. He stood up straight again and said, "Hey."

Both men wore T-shirts and blue jeans. Closer up, I saw that they were older than I'd first thought, at least five or ten years older than me, with fleshy faces and expanding guts, the lankness and grace of youth having fully given way to reveal the men they were stuck being from here on out.

Ellen said, "My friend and I were hoping you could settle a bet for us."

"What kind of bet?" he said.

"Do you guys have four twenty-dollar bills?"

The baseball cap guy frowned and got his wallet out. "I have two."

"I have a twenty and a ten," said his friend.

"No," Ellen said, "the ten's no good."

The ten was perfectly good, I assumed. Saying it wasn't? Misdirection.

"So three twenties?" Ellen said, and tilted her head, as if deliberating. "Okay," she said. "Let me have them a second."

The guys looked at each other.

"Just for a second. I want to show you . . . well, you'll see."

They handed her the twenties, and the baseball cap guy said to his friend, "You wouldn't give *me* twenty bucks if I asked," and the second guy said to the first guy, "That's because you're an ugly fuck and your tits are too big."

When the twenties were in Ellen's hand, she smoothed them out and said, "Nat, come with me a sec."

I followed her over to the bar, still clueless as to what the con was.

"David, we'll be back in two seconds," Ellen said loudly enough for the two pool players to hear. She kept going toward the exit. I kept following her.

Suddenly, we were outside in the cold late-afternoon gloom, standing in front of Ellen's car.

"Get in," she said.

We drove away.

"What was that?" I said, trying to see behind us through the side-view mirror.

"Here." Ellen handed me the bills. "Sixty dollars for your trouble."

"Did we just rob those guys?"

"Don't worry, they won't do anything."

"Why not?"

Ellen kept driving. "Because they're men. Imagine them telling a cop, *We gave sixty dollars to a couple of women because they asked us to, and then they walked out of the bar.* Take a guess what any cop would tell them?" She shook her head. "People who say the best cons leave the victim ignorant of the con? That's non-sense. People watch too many movies. The truth is, the real suck-ers almost always know they've been conned, only they can't do anything about it because they're born to be suckers. What?"

"Nothing," I said, looking at the bills in my hand. "I was expecting something more . . . I don't know. *More*."

"Okay, then here's another truth. Most cons aren't elaborate. The shortest route from A to B. That's your best route. How did we take their money?"

"By taking it?" I said.

"Bingo."

"But now you can't ever go back there. Why would you do something like that in your own local bar?"

She laughed. "What are you talking about, *my* bar? I've lived in this town for ten years and I never set foot in there before today."

She made a few turns, and then we were approaching the road where my car was standing vigil over the empty school.

"Is that yours?" she said. "You gotta fix that. You're gonna get a ticket."

I couldn't take my eyes off the bills. "We just robbed those two men," I said.

"How does it feel?" she asked.

"I don't know. Kind of weird."

"Does it feel terrible? Do you want to go back and apologize to those men and return their money?"

I hadn't answered by the time she stopped her car behind mine.

"Congratulations," she said. "You're now a thief as well as a card cheat. Keep this up, and we just might become friends."

3

♣

Back at home, I parked along the curb in front of my apartment. The kid from across the way, my snow shoveler in chief, was sitting on my front stoop, head in hands. When I approached, he raised his head and asked, "You have any smokes?"

I told him I didn't.

"I could really use a smoke. That's why I asked." His hands were jammed in his pockets. He was like a cartoon depiction of down-and-out.

"Everything all right?" I asked.

"No, man, everything's total shit. You wanna hear what happened?"

Up and down Selden Avenue it was another lonely late winter afternoon, dusty and gray in the fading light. The mini-mart on the corner had as many customers as the boarded-up storefront beside it. "Don't you have a friend or a parent or someone to talk to?"

"So what happened was," he said, "I stole some records from Hits Vinyl for my girl Cheri because she *said* she was into old school hip-hop, but then I got busted and then she fucked Bruce."

"Bruce . . ."

"Bruce!" He stared at me as if I were being intentionally obtuse. I ran through my mental list of Bruces. *Springsteen, Willis, Lee.* "Bruce Metzger!" he shouted at me. "The dick who doesn't know shit about old school hip-hop even though he thinks he does."

I waited for more, but now he was picking at a patch of flaky skin on the back of his hand.

"You should use moisturizer," I told him, because shoplifting was out of my wheelhouse. "I'm a close-up magician, and the skin on my hands has to stay in good condition so I can feel the cards."

"What the hell's a close-up magician?"

I explained that I did magic, but not with big contraptions or anything. Instead, I mainly used ordinary objects like coins and cards. "I can tell you what brand of moisturizer to get."

"I got Cheri good, though," he said. "And Bruce."

"Do I want to know this?"

He lowered his voice. "You know how you can light dog shit on fire in front of somebody's door and it flames up and stinks?"

"I guess," I said.

"It works with people shit, too."

"That's disgusting," I said. "And you shouldn't be setting things on fire."

"I'm already on probation," he said. I wasn't going to ask him what for. I knew I wouldn't need to. "For weed," he said. "I wish I lived in Colorado. I'd climb to the top of a mountain and smoke up all the time." He shook his head. "There's not even any good mountains in New Jersey. Man, I gotta stop getting busted. I'm gonna end up in *jail*. I'm gonna end up like my old man."

"Is he in jail?"

"What? No, he's a fucking asshole."

How he had decided to brood on my stoop of all stoops I had no clue. Still, I knew something was probably required of me.

"Can I ask you a question?" I said.

"You just did." Then his whole face crunched in on itself. "See? See that? Now why did I just say that? That's my old man's joke. It's not even funny." He breathed angrily. "Man, what a stupid joke that is. I gotta stop that."

"What's your name?"

He looked up at me. "It's Cool Calvin."

I fought back an eye roll. "Calvin, we haven't had any snow yet."

He stared at me blankly. "You mean, like, ever?"

And the genius award goes to . . . not this kid.

"I mean since we made our deal."

More blank staring. I started to think it might be his default expression.

"Here," I said, "I want to show you something." I removed a quarter from my purse and knuckle rolled it a few times. My fingers were cold, but after a million or so knuckle rolls I knew I wouldn't drop the coin.

"Cool," he said perfunctorily. I tossed the coin in the air—high, like ten feet—and when it came down I clapped both hands on either side of it, and then the quarter was gone.

"Wait—" He squinted. "Where'd it go?"

No matter how cheesy it might sound, I knew what a magic trick could do. In this moment, Calvin wasn't thinking about his old man or his cheating girlfriend or anything other than the quarter, and how it had just contradicted everything he thought he knew about cause and effect and what was real and what was impossible.

"Show me how you did that," he said.

I sat down beside him on the stoop and I showed him. This wasn't breaking a code. It was teaching a kid. I broke down the moves and had him try it a few times. Lord, his hands were inept—little wonder his girlfriend had strayed—but then again he was a beginner. In the beginning, we were all beginners.

"Practice it," I said. "Then show it to me next week."

"A week?" He grinned. "I'll show you tomorrow."

"I don't want to see it tomorrow," I said. "Take the week. And practice in front of a mirror. That's important." My phone rang. I checked the number. "I gotta grab this. I'll see you later, Calvin."

"Wait—" He sounded panicky. "I don't have a mirror."

"There's no bathroom mirror in your apartment?"

"Oh, right." He shook his head. "Duh. I'm so stupid."

I quickly went into my apartment, shut the door, and answered the call.

"I don't think I was clear before," Ellen said, as if our conversation from before were still ongoing. "I'd be paying the buy-in for both of us. You wouldn't be putting anything up."

"Yeah. Still. No, I'm sorry."

"I think you're making a big mistake," she said.

"I might be," I told her truthfully, "but the answer's still no."

Without question, Ellen fascinated me. And maybe if I hadn't just cheered that kid up with a magic trick . . . And maybe if not for the convention . . . But I had just cheered that kid up with a magic trick, and I did have the convention to prepare for, which could lead to more shows, which could lead to more money. I knew I was running on fumes as a magician, but fumes can get you where you're going as long as you don't have too far to travel. At least that was my hope.

"Listen," I said, "I gotta run. Maybe we can stay in touch?"

112

"Yeah, it doesn't work that way." All the energy had left her voice. "All right, Natalie, you take care of yourself." The phone went silent.

I shouldn't have stormed out of your shop last week. You've always been there for me, and without you I would have nothing. You saw something worthwhile in a depressed and lonely kid and gave me confidence and were always on my side, and I'm sorry. And by the way, you were right. The whole idea of profiling a cheat—that was dumb. I've got better uses for my time.

I rehearsed several versions of an apology until the moment I entered the dark store, and then the jangle of the sleigh bells shook them all away. It was Tuesday morning. Jack sat on a stool behind the glass counter with a notebook in front of him. He often sat there with a pencil and notebook, I'd noticed over the years—checking and rechecking the math, I supposed, that proved his business was still tanking.

"I am becoming more like him," I said.

"Like who?"

"My dad."

He put down the pencil and shut the notebook. "Forget what I said."

"You were right. I'm becoming more like him. He cared about things. He was actually alive before he was dead."

"It was a cheap shot. I was aggravated. I'm an ass."

"No—you're a crotchety jerk. There's a big difference."

He slid the pencil into the spiral rings of the notebook and set it down. "You want a soda?"

"Actually, I was hoping we could talk through a routine I need to prepare. You know, for the World of Magic convention? Where I'll be performing in a couple of weeks?"

After a moment of confusion, he smiled, something I hadn't seen him do in a long time. I'd forgotten how bad his teeth were.

"Good for you," he said, and then his smile vanished. "You know the shithead is one of the directors of the conference now?"

No, I hadn't known. I shrugged. "I don't care one way or the other. It doesn't matter."

He nodded. "Atta girl."

I almost made it big. That's the truth. I was seventeen. My dad had been dead for two years, and during that time I had thrown myself into magic for the same reasons so many other kids do—to have control over something, to be mysterious, to avoid whatever needed avoiding. But unlike most kids who dabble for a few years before stuffing their gear into the back of their bedroom closet, I had Jack Clarion for a teacher. So all my practice happened to be the right kind of practice. It led somewhere. I shut myself in my room and woodshedded, and I got pretty good pretty fast. Then Jack goes and registers me for the WOM convention and enters me in the close-up contest without telling me about it first. One day I walk into his store for a lesson and he says, Guess what you're doing next month? I suppose he saw something in me. We rode the train together to the city and spent the day attending lectures and shows. I'd been to New York only a couple of times before that, and I was anxious about everything and certain I was going to get mugged. My mother had pretty much guaranteed I would. The only thing I wasn't nervous about was the time I'd be onstage. I was too young and naive to be worried about that.

I came in second that year. The guy who won, Mick Shane, deserved to win. His close-up performance was inventive and as smooth as silk. He isn't a household name, but who is, among laymen, except for David Copperfield and David Blaine and Criss Angel and Penn and Teller? And they all do stage acts. They might have started in close-up, but they moved on to bigger things: bigger props, bigger stages, bigger pay. But magicians all know Mick. He'd been around a long time and never changed his focus from close-up magic with everyday objects. He was an inspiring artist, and I was honored to have come in second to him.

And coming in second to Mick Shane was enough to earn me plenty of attention. I was young and clever and skilled, the girl who'd outperformed hundreds of grown men. Before the weekend was out, I had a booking agent. Before the month was out, that agency had lined me up with a dozen corporate and private gigs.

They were flying me places: Seattle, San Francisco, Cancún, even London. My mother couldn't believe it. They paid her way, too, since I was a minor. We traveled together that year. My mother liked to talk as if she were worldly and well traveled, but all her travels were to places like Dollywood and Ocean City, Maryland. So boarding a plane and heading abroad—this was new for both of us. It was wonderful. It began to seem impossible that my life could be otherwise.

Then the next WOM convention came along, and being eighteen, a full-fledged adult, I insisted on going alone. I won the close-up contest that year. Grand prize. And guess who came in second? Mick was a very gracious runner-up, paying me compliments and inviting me for coffee. We talked about magic in a way I'd never talked about it with anybody, not even with Jack. He told me which moves he—*he*—hadn't mastered yet, and he guessed how I did one of the tricks in my performance, where I passed a pencil through a glass of water. His guess was about half right, and I didn't mind telling him what he'd gotten wrong, because he was impressed, and I was flattered. He said he had a great balcony in his room. *Here's an idea*, he said. *Let's order room service.* He was very handsome—older, for sure, but not *old*—and a hero of mine, with the greatest hands I ever saw. He was a true master, though getting me into bed that afternoon had been one of his easier tricks.

For the remainder of the convention we were inseparable, sitting beside each other at performances and lectures and meals. I returned to my own hotel room only to retrieve and deposit outfits. For three days we were a couple, and then on the last day of the convention, at breakfast in the hotel restaurant, he told me that we couldn't be in contact anymore. I thought he was joking.

You know I'm married, he said.

What?

It's common knowledge, he said.

I became immediately aware of the packed restaurant, all the other magicians at all the other tables.

Where's your ring? I asked. His fingers were long and tan, even over the place where a ring would fit.

He shrugged. *I'm allergic to gold.*

I left him there at the table and returned to my room. If his marriage really was common knowledge, then so was our affair. I had thought people were glancing my way all weekend because I was a rising star at the convention. Grand prize winner, and just eighteen, and a woman! I had felt special, being seen with—being attached to—one of the great magicians of our time. But all I'd been doing was making an ass of myself. No one had told me. They were all probably enjoying it too much.

Then I did something I shouldn't have done. Mick had a performance later that morning, and I entered the theater just after it started. I watched him go through his first routine, and then I went to the front of the theater, stood right up by the stage so he couldn't miss me, and gave him the finger with both hands. And I stayed there, frozen, not saying a word yet trying to ruin his show—by throwing him off, by diverting the audience's attention. I stood there silently, arms extended, middle fingers in the air. Mick was doing one of his signature routines with five golf balls, and he carried on, glancing periodically at the exit, hoping maybe for security to bail him out, but he was on his own. At first, the audience might have thought I was part of the act. Then a couple of guys started whispering, *"Stop that,"* and, *"Sit down,"* but I ignored them. Then Mick dropped a golf ball. It made a satisfying clunk on the wooden stage. Mick soldiered on with the four remaining balls, but I knew he was sweating it. After a couple of excruciating minutes, I uttered a single "Fuck you!"—to him, to everyone—and walked out of the convention. I knew I could never go back but, I figured, who the hell cares? I didn't need the likes of Mick Shane or anyone else.

Soon after, I started reading online that Mick was performing *my* pencil-through-water-glass trick in his shows. That was his quiet, nasty revenge—doing my trick. Everyone assumed it'd been his all along, that he'd taught it to me for my show at the competition, since I was, you know, his little slut.

So I did what I had to. I exposed the method—to my best fucking trick—on every magic blog I could find. Now everyone could learn it, and the trick became worthless. On magic forums online, guys were calling me a bitch and a whore. They depicted in revolting detail exactly how I ought to be punished for revealing the great Mick Shane's trick—even while they were using it in their own shows.

I stopped going to conventions after that.

It was hard to believe all that was almost a decade in the past. When I let myself, I could still hear the explosion of applause after being announced as the grand prize winner. I could still feel the medallion being hung around my neck and could still smell Mick Shane's spicy cologne. That whole experience was a rabbit hole I tried not to go down anymore, though it was hard not to think about it with the convention just a couple of weeks away.

I reminded myself that the antidote to fear was practice. I would practice in front of the bathroom mirror until my reflection grew tired of seeing me. I would pace my apartment and fine-tune my patter until it shimmered. And when I walked into that convention two weeks from now, it wouldn't matter which ghosts were there with me.

4

Ellen called just once more, on Saturday afternoon. I was practicing at the time and let the call go to voicemail. An hour later I checked it.

> *Yeah . . . so . . . this thing we were talking about the other day? Turns out I really need you for it. I've tried like hell to find someone else, but I can't. I'm getting a little desperate here. We're running out of time. I'm just being honest, okay? And the thing is, it's so guaranteed, Natalie. And it's such a good . . . anyway, just call me back, okay? Just . . . all right? Call me.*

But I didn't. I'd already made my decision and didn't want Ellen's voice in my head. I had work to do.

When Brock McKnight called shortly after, however, I picked up. A weekend call from my lawyer felt like something I shouldn't ignore.

"You want the good news or the bad news?" he asked.

I braced myself and told him to go ahead with the bad.

I could almost hear his grin when he said, "There's no bad."

"For real?"

"I suppose I could tell you that Lou was ready to hit you with a civil suit so big it would stop your heart. But instead I'll tell you that he's decided, on second thought, *not* to do that."

He explained, to my amazed ears, that the criminal lawsuit was dead in the water. Lou Husk, like Brock, assumed that the police would be less than enthusiastic about investigating a playing-card incident. It just wasn't worth their time. Maybe in some Podunk town but not in Newark. "But the civil suit. That was real," Brock said. "And that's where *my* magic comes in. Did you know Lou and I live in the same town?"

They lived in South Montgomery, he told me, which sounded exactly right. South Montgomery was the epicenter of type-A Jersey suburbanites with means.

"A few years back," Brock said, "our kids were in the same soccer league. Lou's kid tripped my kid twice in the same quarter. Ref didn't even blow his damn whistle, because terrific players get away with murder, and Lou's kid was fast and athletic and big. But guess what he wasn't?"

"What?" I asked.

"He wasn't *eight*." Brock let me chew on that a moment. "Lou had lied to get his nine-year-old into the eight-year-old league. And let me tell you, a year makes a big difference at that age."

After the soccer game, Brock had acted on a hunch and cashed in a favor with a guy at the vital records office. Sure enough, Lou's son's birth certificate said September 30. Which happened to be the very last day of the year for school cutoff, league cutoff . . . basically, the kid was facing a lifetime of always being the youngest.

"Dear old dad must have seen this baby in his arms—future soccer star, baseball star, whatever—and realized how much better it would be if only his birthday were a couple of days later. So he decides, October 2—why not? And suddenly his kid goes from being the youngest to being the oldest. It's a lifelong edge," Brock said, "and Lou is all about edges. I mean, the kid himself thinks his birthday is October 2."

I tried to imagine what kind of man would lie to his own son about his birthday just to gain an edge in youth soccer. The answer, of course, was a man like Lou Husk.

"Is that illegal?" I asked.

"What, forging a duplicate birth certificate for schools and sports leagues? Yeah, it's illegal. But the bigger issue is that if the other parents were to find out, they'd kill him. His son would suffer. They'd be pariahs. You can't imagine what these people are like. And Lou knows it. If he ever found out that some neighborhood dad did that to give his kid an unfair edge, Lou would be the one leading the lynch mob."

I was still trying to get my head around it. "Soccer, huh?"

"I've been holding on to that little secret a long time," Brock said, "waiting to leverage it. And I have to be honest—I could probably get a lot more out of him. But I happen to like you."

"I'm glad."

"I was going to call Lou on Monday, but I was driving this morning and passed him on the road walking his dog. Some designer ball of hip dysplasia. Anyway, we had a chat about what it might mean to him and Junior if the original birth certificate from vital records were ever to make the rounds. And Lou's thinking about your lawsuit suddenly . . . *evolved*. Didn't hurt that his eye is healing well. He looks good. No more eye patch. He's driving again."

"I'm really glad," I said. "So does this mean . . ."

"It means you're a very lucky magician." And just as I was beginning to feel like one, he added, "We're settling for fifteen thousand."

"*What?*"

"With your approval, of course."

"Fifteen thousand dollars?"

"Yeah." He paused. "Wait. You aren't disappointed, are you?"

"That's a lot of money," I said.

"No." His voice hardened a little. "Two hundred thousand is a lot of money. That's how much he was going to sue you for. Don't forget, Lou is an ass, but this isn't a frivolous suit. You did fuck up the guy's eye. He's had expenses. This is a legitimate claim."

Brock was right—I knew that. But it was so much money. Money I didn't have. I told him so.

"We can work out a payment plan with Lou," Brock said. "Or if he insists on getting paid quickly, we could probably get you a loan. We'll work it out. But can I please tell him you're okay with this deal?"

What choice did I have? I told him yes, but evidently without sufficient enthusiasm, because Brock reminded me that this was "good news, an excellent outcome," and then we hung up and I told myself *You are lucky, you are lucky*, even though it felt less like luck than like drowning.

And I'd be lying if I didn't think of Ellen and her poker game. A cut of whatever she was planning would go a long way right now. Of course I thought that. Of course I was tempted. But to do it would be to cross over, that was how I saw it. I'd be betraying my art and my livelihood. I'd be betraying my father, who was not a criminal.

While I had my phone out I checked my email. I was hungry for the details about my convention performance. Not that the details mattered, but whatever they were, they would make everything feel more real. I needed that to look forward to. My fastest route to fifteen thousand dollars, I knew, was a string of solid bookings. That meant building from the ground up again, and the WOM convention was the ideal way to start—the way to remind all the people who mattered that I was still in the game.

No new emails.

Just as I set down the phone, it buzzed. I figured it was probably Brock calling again, having forgotten to relate some other bit of wonderful news, like maybe I had herpes. Turns out it wasn't a phone call at all: it was a reminder I'd set on my calendar.

Oh, shit. I'd been so focused on the convention I forgot I had a show tonight.

Kyle Horowitz was becoming a man.

5

♠

The bar mitzvah was a fancy evening affair at the Talmadge Inn in Metuchen. With formal dress and a six-piece band, it was just like a wedding except for the fifty kids plus the two high school girls in spandex whose job it was to keep them all corralled on the dance floor.

And me.

Maybe there was no shame in entertaining a room of spiffed-up thirteen-year-olds, but whenever I did a show for kids, even when it paid well, I couldn't shake the feeling that I was no different from anyone who'd ever floundered through a dozen off-the-shelf tricks for some six-year-old's birthday party, maybe twisting balloons into poodles for good measure.

Still, tonight's gig paid just over five percent of my settlement. And because kids always want what the other has, I knew I could count on a few referrals over the next year.

Money, right? It made the world go around. Unless you were Incan.

For real. The Incas didn't use currency. They were a unique empire, full of master architects and sophisticated farmers, constructing pyramids and irrigation systems, but never needing dollars or pesos or gold coins.

My mother told me this when I was fifteen. By then my father was vast and ruined, and my mother was explaining to me that she and Chip Dawkins were in love and wanted to get married, which meant finally filing for divorce.

I'd known about Chip for a while. My mother still dropped me off periodically at Jack's magic store, but she and Chip had gotten bolder, and my mother would go out at night with the flimsiest of excuses. My father said nothing. At least nothing I overheard.

I don't want to hurt him, she would say to me. *You know that.* I suppose I did. But I also knew she hadn't forgiven him for losing all that money and never would. The money wasn't the only thing, but it was the biggest thing. And now we were broke, and Chip Dawkins wasn't, and she must have decided that her life, and mine, would improve if she were to hitch her star to his.

She didn't say it like that. What she said, sitting at the foot of my bed one night, was, *We aren't Incas, you and I.* And I said something like, *Huh?* And she explained how the Incas didn't need money but we did. There were tremendous medical debts, still, and legal bills for dealing with the medical bills, plus all the ordinary expenses of being alive in America. But Chip had been selling her on his aircraft parts business and what it could do for them. I'd met Chip a few times by then. He had a smoker's cough and a voice like wet sand and, as far as I could tell, a personality to match his voice. He wanted to move to Nevada, where the air was dry and where he could build a manufacturing plant and warehouse. The opportunity was incredible, the way he explained it to my mother and my mother explained it to me. And there would be opportunities for her, too. She could get her real estate license. Housing prices out West were rising, rising, and you had to jump on an opportunity like that while it was red hot. The houses practically sold themselves to all those

Californians wanting to retire inland where their dollar went further.

Had we gone then, when I was fifteen, maybe we'd all be rich right now. But my father's reaction to receiving the divorce papers was to get himself killed in a bar fight, and my mother was so guilt-ridden that she dropped Chip cold turkey for a year. Then she picked him up again, but they delayed their move West for another year so I could finish high school. They put off staking their claim, and by the time they finally went to Reno they were too late. They bought a home at the peak of the market, and then the recession blew in, and Chip never did open his factory, but he did open his wallet and become a frequent patron of the Grand Sierra casino and the Gold Dust West casino and the Peppermill Resort Spa casino.

That's what my mother did. She married gamblers. My father had gambled once and lost everything; Chip spent more than two years going broke. In Reno, the Biggest Little City in the World, he and my mother became poor and stayed poor. But they stayed together.

I sometimes fantasized about sending my mother a big fat check, totally out of the blue. At my current savings rate I could do that in about ten thousand years.

I missed my father. I missed my mother. I missed the days when I never would have imagined that I could miss them.

The bar mitzvah kids were as attentive as one could expect for thirteen-year-olds hopped up on Shirley Temples and a chocolate fountain. When my show was over I packed my gear and collected my check. Then I nursed a glass of house Cab in the mostly empty hotel bar. I'd worn the top hat tonight—not the tall kind, more like a bowler—and the bartender complimented me on it. I caught him smiling at me a few times. He was tall, with floppy hair and a nice chin, and I kind of hoped he'd ask for my number but he never did.

When my drink was gone, I left a large tip and carried my gear outside and across the dark Talmadge Inn parking lot to my car. Loaded everything into the backseat and started the engine. Before pulling away, I checked email on my phone. And there it was: a new message from Brad Corzo.

> Subject: WOM Schedule of Events
>
> Dear participants:
> The conference schedule is now posted on the WOM website (link below). Please be sure to make it to your venue at least 15 minutes ahead of time. Stage magicians requiring longer setup should contact me individually.
> If you have not yet registered for the conference or uploaded your bio and photo, please do so at your earliest convenience.
> Looking forward to seeing everyone soon!
>
> Yours in magic,
> Brad Corzo
> Chair, Panel Selection Committee, World of Magic

The link opened a PDF grid that was hard to navigate on my phone, but I did my best. Some of the names I knew from years ago, though many were new to me—just as my name would be unfamiliar to the newer magicians attending.

I scanned the grid, scrolling, looking for my name. Finally, there it was.

Reading the event title, I felt my stomach twist.

Room: Exhibition Hall E
Event Title: Magic Safety with Cal Murrow
Event Type: Presentation/Discussion
Event Details: Working with flash paper? Knives? Firearms? Rope? Even magicians working with everyday objects can expose themselves and their audience to risk and injury. Renowned stage magician Cal Murrow, with the help of Sergeant Roy Sturgis, NYPD, and New Jersey native Natalie "Card-in-the-Eye" Webb (have no fear, folks, she'll only be talking!), will lead this discussion aimed at reducing the chance of accidents, injuries, and lawsuits.

I stared at my phone, thinking: What a sucker I am.

Thinking: I should have fucking known.

I should have known I wouldn't be forgiven. Not after ten years, not ever. Not as long as they could still remind me I didn't belong. Who exactly "they" were I could only wonder. The whole selection committee? Or just its chair? My email to Corzo should have been nicer, fine, I should've left out the Boy Scout stuff. But damn.

Mick Shane, it occurred to me, must be getting a good laugh.

The question of exactly how the selection committee had come to learn about my playing-card incident interested me for all of about two seconds. Then I realized one of the lawyers must have tweeted it, or posted about it, or blogged about it, or mentioned it in a discussion forum . . . all it would have taken was for the Venn diagram of personal injury attorneys and magic enthusiasts to have an overlap of one. One lawyer to get the magic community gossiping. The only real surprise was my own foolishness in assuming that somehow word *wouldn't* get out. That the story of my Newark mishap would have died quietly in the Hyatt ballroom on that icy night, or at worst been the subject of some water-cooler gossip the next day.

I screamed in my car. I wanted to hit someone and took it out on the steering wheel, which blared in the parking lot. How could I have been so naive as to think the magic fraternity, this *brotherhood*, would simply welcome me back?

I would think long and hard about the email I was going to send Brad Corzo.

Except: No, I wouldn't. I was done with all that. And there were far more pressing matters.

It was late, almost midnight. So what? I made the call. When it went to voicemail I hung up and, frustrated, furious, I stomped on the accelerator and pulled onto the road way too close to another car. His horn blared. I gave him the finger in my rearview—it wasn't his fault, but fuck him anyway—and then my phone buzzed and I took the call.

"Do you still need a partner?" I blurted out.

Ellen's pause, only a second or two, felt endless. "What's going on? Are you having a change of heart?"

"Yes or no. Do you still need a partner?"

"Yeah, I do."

"And you would teach me? Show me what you know?"

I sped through a yellow light.

"Natalie, if you agree to this, I'll teach you *everything*. Then we'll play one night of poker and walk away with a million dollars."

I almost drove off the road. "Say that again."

"Your take would be twenty percent."

My god, what was she involved in? What the hell was this? I had been hoping for maybe a couple of thousand dollars to jump-start things—some dollars into the Lou Husk fund, or maybe I could get my car repaired. But two hundred thousand?

"I can't do that," I said, cursing myself. I couldn't *believe* I was already reneging. But it was too much. Too criminal.

"What are you talking about?" she said. "Of course you can."

"For that kind of money. . . . it's too dangerous."

"I promise you it isn't," she said.

"You have to be straight with me."

"I'm *being* straight," she said. "The players are all business-men. They're really wealthy, but they're respectable. I'm telling you, this isn't some floating, high-stakes, backroom game."

Two hundred thousand dollars. To say no would be madness. To say yes would mean committing to being . . . what? A card-sharp? No. That was just some fancy word. A thief. A criminal. Webbs weren't criminals. When I told Brock that, I'd meant it.

"It's just a high-dollar home game," she was saying. "The guy hosting it has this mansion on the water. You even know him."

"Huh?"

"Not *know* him. I mean you know who he is. He's running for office. They have this monthly game at his home, and once a year—"

"Wait," I said.

Businessman. Mansion by the water.

"They do this special thing where—"

"*Wait. Stop.* Ellen, just stop talking." My fingers felt numb on the steering wheel. I tried to catch my breath. "Is it Victor Flow-ers?" Silence on the other end. I thought the call might have been disconnected. "Ellen?"

Then: "Am I allowed to talk now?"

"Yes. Talk."

"Victor Flowers. That's right. He's actually a huge gambler. Nobody knows it. But yeah."

"Your plan is to take Victor Flowers's money," I said.

"His and three other guys', yeah," Ellen said.

I wasn't in my car any longer. I was at a mansion by the water. "Victor Flowers takes a helicopter to work," I managed to say. It was the best I could do.

"Does he? Well, that makes sense. He's rich as fuck. I'm telling you, Natalie, for these guys it won't even be a big loss. We can do it. It'll work. But there's a lot to prepare, and not a lot of time. So Nat?"

I was still vaguely aware of hearing Ellen's voice on the phone, but my car's interior, the dashboard, the doors, the windshield, everything had dissolved around me, and I was smelling meat cooking on a grill and seeing the green lawn and the endless view off the bluff.

"Nat?"

I was inside Victor Flowers's mansion again, going from room to room, searching for musical instruments, a scavenger hunt, and through a closed door I heard a voice, and it was a voice I had never heard before. It was my father, afraid.

My father, who refused to be a criminal. My father, relentlessly honest even in the face of temptation and coercion. I had been clinging to that fact, that nugget of family history, as if it were itself a full credo, a complete thought, when in actuality, I now realized, there was an entire other half that I had always conveniently overlooked: *My father was no criminal—and look where it got him.*

My very honest, very dead father.

A New Jersey Transit train rumbled past in the opposite direction on tracks so close to the road that I felt the vibrations shake my whole body, and I was on Route 27 again in my shitty, busted car on a dark two-lane road at midnight, heading toward my empty Rahway apartment.

"Natalie?"

"What?" I said.

"So is this the part where you tell me you're in?"

6

It was true, by the way, about the helicopter. I still remember my father talking about his boss's aerial commute as if wealth had nothing to do with it. As if it were nothing more than a matter of shrewd time management.

"All that traffic on the Jersey Turnpike, at the tunnel. What a waste of time and money," my father would say. "Victor Flowers arrives at his office in fourteen minutes."

If you didn't fear flying and had enough money maybe it made sense. My father would have known. He was a numbers guy, even if he didn't look like one: six-foot-three and thick everywhere. He'd taken accounting courses at Union County and Fairleigh Dickinson, delivering those pianos to pay for it, and he wasn't far from a degree when debt and lower back pain finally got the better of him. He dropped the coursework and took a job at the Flowers Corporation as a bookkeeper, hoping to work his way up. And he did—far enough, some half a dozen years later, for us to receive an invitation to the Memorial Day party that Mr. Flowers threw each year at his waterfront home in the Highlands.

I was excited to go. At eight years old I believed that all mansions held secret rooms and hidden treasure. And my mother loved the shore, though when Memorial Day came, she said she wasn't feeling well. Too many hours on her feet, she said, doing inventory at the bookstore.

So it was just my father and me. Driving south on the parkway, he told me that Victor Flowers used to be a rock-and-roll singer before he went into business and made millions of dollars. And his foundation, Notes for Kids, donated musical instruments to schools that couldn't afford them.

"Is he nice?" I asked.

My father chewed on his lip before answering. "Victor Flowers is an impressive man." He must have realized his answer had little to do with my question, because he added, "He's been good to our family."

I let it drop and listened to the radio. I could tell my father had a lot on his mind, because he was muttering to himself. I thought about how I wouldn't know anyone at this party, and wished my mother had come. But once we arrived and got out of the car, my anxiety was quelled by all the amazing smells: grilling meat, salty air, freshly cut grass, and everything in bloom.

We walked toward the driveway, where the break in a line of high hedges gave me a view of the home where Mr. Flowers lived.

"Whoa," I said.

"Whoa is right," my father replied. I deigned to let him take my hand, and together we followed a path around the side of the stone mansion to an immense yard where kids were running and playing games like Frisbee and soccer and Wiffle ball.

I was hungry for everything—for whatever was sizzling on the grills, and the green grass, and the bay shimmering in the sunlight beyond the high bluff, and the trees along the perimeter of the property that were ideal for climbing, and the laughter. Our Plainfield apartment was dark and heavy by comparison. My parents often talked about moving to a house with a yard. *Soon,*

134

they told me. Which would have been fine. Even better would have been if our apartment could feel the way it used to. Lately, my parents either argued or avoided each other, and being at home felt like riding down a slide in cold weather and knowing that whatever you touched next would give you a shock.

Like today. Somehow I knew, not in my brain but in a deeper part where the guts were, that my mother wasn't actually sick. She was only pretending.

A thin, smallish man came our way. My father said, "Honey, I'd like you to meet Mr. Flowers."

Mr. Flowers was dressed like my father in khaki pants and a button-down shirt. His sleeves were rolled up to just below the elbows, and his forearms were tan. His hair was dark brown, almost black, and cut short, and his face was so smooth it appeared slippery. Mr. Flowers shook my hand and smiled and said it was a pleasure to meet me. His voice was as smooth as his face. I wanted to ask him to sing a song—I'd never met a professional singer before—but I knew I couldn't.

Mr. Flowers said to my father, "I was hoping you and I could talk in private."

My father's slow nod looked resigned, as if he'd been expecting this request. He watched the scene around us for a moment before saying, "You'll be okay here for a few minutes, won't you, Nat? There's plenty of kids."

Of course there were, but I didn't know any of them.

"*Dad.*"

"I promise I won't keep him long," Mr. Flowers said, and my father smiled and mussed my hair a little, and they went off toward the house.

I smoothed my hair and fixed the part, then walked across the lawn to get a better view of the bay far below. My mother would have gone crazy over this view, with the New York skyline across the water to the left and, straight ahead, the Atlantic Ocean going on and on. Not to England. That's what everyone always said, but I knew from the globe in my bedroom that if you went straight across the ocean from here you'd end up in Morocco.

From behind me, I heard: "You're Big Bird."

I turned around to face a sandy-haired boy with sun-peeled shoulders. He wasn't in my class, but I half recognized him from school. That's where kids had started calling me that. My hair wasn't yellow, it was brown, and long, but I was a head taller than most of the other kids. I hated being so tall, especially for a girl, and I could think of nothing worse than being compared to a huge, big-beaked bird—a *boy* bird—that acted like a three-year-old.

And the worst part? The name fit. I was exactly like a dumb big bird that could hardly balance on her own two legs.

The boy called out to some other kids. "Look"—he pointed at me—"it's Big Bird!"

It was bad enough hearing it at school. For the name to follow me here, now, was unbearable. My eyes filling with tears, I hurried toward the house in my stupid dress shoes to lose myself in the crowd standing on the wooden deck. But everyone's eyes felt heavy on me, so I let myself into the house.

I was standing in the largest kitchen I'd ever seen. I ignored some grown-ups holding tilted cups and laughing with each other and went deeper into the house until I was alone in a room with leather sofas and a black grand piano in the corner, its cover open. On a shelf attached to the wall lay an electric guitar that someone had written on in an illegible scrawl. On another shelf was a saxophone, and on other shelves I saw a clarinet, a trumpet, a trombone.

I wondered if any other instruments were hidden in the house, in other rooms. It started to feel like a treasure hunt, and I was ready to begin searching when I heard, through a door, a voice that sounded like my father's when he was explaining something important to me.

I approached the closed door and listened. Definitely my father. He had told me to wait outside, but I knew he'd probably let me stay with him if I promised to sit still and keep quiet. My hand was reaching for the doorknob when I heard another voice.

"Oh, Dan, if you can't even do to this one simple thing, then I don't know what."

And then came my father's voice again: "You know I haven't been comfortable with any of this. But *this*. It's . . . I mean no disrespect."

"You don't, huh?"

"No. I'm just being honest. It's—"

"It's nothing. It's accounting."

"Victor, we both know what it is."

"It's what I say it is. Less than nothing."

And then came the strangest part. I distinctly heard my father say: *It's laundry. It's laundry, and I'm not doing it.*

For years after, I believed the two of them had been arguing over who would do the laundry. After all, my father sometimes had that same argument with my mother. Even after I learned what money laundering was, it took me a while to paste that new information onto the old scene from my past and finally go: *Ah.*

"I'd be very careful, Dan," Mr. Flowers was telling my father. "This is way above your pay grade."

"It's criminal activity," my father said.

"*Watch it,*" Mr. Flowers said, and my eyes widened. My body stiffened. I knew from hearing my parents argue how easily a simple disagreement could explode into something larger.

My father started speaking slowly, softly, and I realized I was wrong about having heard him talk this way before. This was new. He was trying to keep his voice from shaking. This, I suddenly realized, was what my father sounded like scared.

"I gave you a career," Mr. Flowers said. "Are you that ungrateful? Are you that naive?"

Mr. Flowers wasn't shouting. His voice was like frozen water. I understood now why my father hadn't answered my question in the car. Mr. Flowers wasn't nice.

My father's reply was so soft I could barely hear it. "I have a family," he said. "I just can't."

I heard the unmistakable sound of a fist against a hard surface—a table, a desktop—but that was the extent of Mr. Flowers's outburst; his voice stayed under control. "I can make you do it. I don't have to ask."

"I'm sorry," my father said.

"I really wish you had any sense at all in that giant head of yours," he said, apparently done with back-and-forth conversation. "But you don't, do you? You're just a big dumb ape. I need to get something from the other room."

I heard footsteps coming and ducked around a corner just as Mr. Flowers came out of the room, shutting the door behind him. He turned and went the other way.

A moment later I heard, coming from inside the room, a sickening thud, followed by a grunt. Then it all repeated.

A man's deep voice—not my father's—said: "Get up."

I hadn't known anyone else was in the room with my father and didn't wait around to find out who it was. I found my feet and, heart pounding, I ran back through the kitchen and outside again, where bright sunlight assaulted me. I cut a path between adults on the deck and kept running to the cool grass, where my legs gave out and I spent the next few minutes trying to catch my breath and slow the beating of my heart.

I waited, terrified that my father would never return to me. But soon Mr. Flowers and my father emerged from the house, along with a third man, shorter than my father but thicker in the neck and in the arms and everywhere. He wore the same nonexpression my father did when he watched Westerns on Sunday afternoon TV.

Mr. Flowers and my father seemed to be talking calmly. At one point, Mr. Flowers touched my father's arm. None of it made any sense. I wished I'd never entered Mr. Flowers's house. It was an ugly, mean house. A horrible house. Bad things happened there.

Spotting me, my father waved me over. When I approached, he smiled but it was more like a grimace.

"Have you eaten?" Mr. Flowers asked.

"I'm not hungry," I said.

"Thirsty?" he asked.

I was so thirsty. But I didn't want anything from him. "No."

Mr. Flowers removed a large coin from his pocket and bent down. "Natalie, this is a silver dollar. Have you ever seen one before?"

The only dollars I'd ever seen were paper. I shook my head.

He held the dollar between his thumb and fingertips.

"Watch," he said, and reached over with his other hand to take the coin. He slowly opened up that other hand. The coin was gone. When he reached up toward my face, I stepped backward in fear. His hand followed me. "The dollar, Natalie—" I felt the hair covering my ear being tickled. "It's in your ear now."

He lowered his hand. The coin lay in his palm.

I knew I was supposed to say something, but his fingers in my hair had felt like worms. I glanced at my father, whose hand gently covered his ribs, and back at Mr. Flowers.

"Here," Mr. Flowers said, handing me the coin. "It's yours now."

I stared at him.

"What do you say, Natalie?" my father prompted automatically.

"Thank you," I mumbled.

"You're welcome," Mr. Flowers said. Then he turned to my father and, in his smooth tenor, he said, "I'm glad we had a chance to talk, Dan. It's good to know where a person stands." He smiled. "You two enjoy yourselves." Then he left us to greet some new arrivals.

My father touched my shoulder. "Are you having an okay time?" he asked.

I burst into tears.

"Honey." My father bent down to me, grimacing a little. "Honey, what is it?"

Past my father, I could see a couple of the other kids watching us. "I'm so thirsty," I said.

"Okay, sure, sweetie," he said. "Then let's get you a drink. And food, while we're at it. All right? Let's get you something to eat."

We filled a plate of food for me, and a cup of iced tea.

"Aren't you eating?" I asked my father, but he said he wasn't hungry.

We carried everything to a spot on the grass closer to the edge of the property, farther away from the shouts of kids, the smack of bocce balls hitting each other, the clang of horseshoes.

I ate, watching the water and saying little. He only touched his ribs a few times. I started to feel better. I knew no one would call me Big Bird as long as I was with my father. We walked a little, went to the edge of the bluff, and stood facing the water. I told my father about Morocco, but he just grunted. When the afternoon breeze shifted and the air began to cool, the first guests began to leave. "Okay, kid," my father said, "let's hit the road."

We waited for Mr. Flowers to finish saying good-bye to several guests. There was a tall stack of identical gift-wrapped boxes, and he was handing the boxes to kids as they were leaving. Mr. Flowers shook my father's hand. I looked around for that other man, the one who'd hurt my father, but he was gone.

Mr. Flowers turned to me. "This is a magic kit," he said, lifting one of the boxes from the stack. "If you work at it, you can learn to fool anyone. Would you like that?"

I nodded because I knew I was supposed to.

"Trust me," he said, "the world is full of endless possibilities." He smiled. "Can you say that to me?"

I glanced at my father, but he was watching something beyond us.

"The world is full of endless possibilities," I mumbled.

But I must have satisfied our host, because he said, "Good girl," and smiled. "You should always think big like that." He lowered his voice. "Your father, he doesn't think big. He doesn't want to give you all this." He gestured to his house, his whole property.

"Victor," my father began.

"He would rather you look out your window at a slum than at the sea. Isn't that right, Dan?"

My father's lips were locked tight.

Mr. Flowers offered me the wrapped box. It was large but surprisingly light.

"Thank him," my father muttered.

I thanked him.

"It's my pleasure, sweetheart," Mr. Flowers said. "And Natalie?" He waited until I was looking at him. "You take care of your dad?"

"Listen, Nat," my father began. "Mr. Flowers. He can . . ." He shook his head. "It's just how he is."

We had descended the bluff and were heading toward the parkway again. I'd waited as long as I could before unwrapping the gift and was now turning the box over in my hands, examining the pictures and reading the words that promised everything.

Change milk to water!

"Natalie?"

"Fine." I hated Mr. Flowers. That other man had done the hitting, but somehow I knew it was Mr. Flowers's fault. When he gave me this present, I should have told him I didn't want it. Now that I had it, I knew I should throw it into the kitchen trash can the moment we got home. The trouble was, I wanted it.

Read your friend's mind!

"Mr. Flowers didn't mean anything," said my father, who by the next day would be not only unemployed but unemployable, on account of Victor Flowers floating some well-placed rumors about my father's financial ethics and mental stability.

When we got home, I mumbled hello to my mother, who was paging through a magazine on the sofa, and rushed to my bedroom to open the magic kit. I touched the dice, the cards, the segments of rope and small plastic contraptions.

Do the impossible!

Down the hall, my mother and father began to speak quietly. It wasn't long before their talk turned to harsh whispers and then to arguing. All I knew about the nature of their argument was that it wouldn't end soon.

I opened the pack of cards. I played Crazy Eights with my mother sometimes, but I had never taken the time to inspect the intricate strangeness of the designs, nor had I paid attention to the feel of the cards' crisp edges against my fingertips.

When something downstairs smashed—a glass? a dish?—I gasped, because that was something new.

The world is full of endless possibilities, I whispered to myself, touching the cards, laying them on the carpet, turning them upside down, noticing they looked the same no matter which way they faced.

The world is full of endless possibilities. I said the words as if they were magic. I was desperate to believe, and so I did. The world was full of endless possibilities, and I vowed to be the one who did the impossible.

7

♣

As I got out of my car with a sack of groceries and lightbulbs, Harley was leaving the apartment building in her green scrubs and white canvas sneakers.

"It's freezing outside," I said. It was still technically the afternoon but the sun had already dipped below the apartment building across the street. "You want a ride to work?"

"I'm never cold," she said. "Thanks, though. Hey, guess what? I found a forever home for Mustard."

I assumed forever meant until the new owner realized the dog was a ruthless killer. But I didn't want to ruin Harley's good mood.

"That's great," I said.

"It is." Her smile faded. "Let's hope it goes as easy for Jasmine."

"Who?"

"Someone found her wandering on Route 1."

A new dog already? "Does she eat people, too?"

"What? No, Jasmine's sweet. She's great about letting me change her bandages."

"What's wrong with her?" I asked.

"Oh, it's just some pus-filled—"

"Never mind. Forget I asked."

Her face brightened again. "So how's magic these days? December must be a busy month."

I had a few shows lined up. I didn't care about any of them.

"I'm mostly thinking about the new year," I told her, and Harley went off to the bus stop and I went inside, where the birds seemed disconcerted, jumping off their perch to the cage floor and then jumping up again, over and over. I took them out and set them on top of the cage, changed their newspaper, and vacuumed up the birdseed that was always spilling onto the carpet. In the kitchen I downed a tall glass of water. Then I got to work, scrubbing the bathroom and kitchen. I dusted all the surfaces and ran a wet paper towel along the floorboards. I replaced some of the blown-out bulbs. I walked from room to room, frowning at the shabby carpet, the dusty curtains, the yard-sale furniture, the upside-down milk crates on which the TV still sat after all these years. Everything came up pathetically short. Money was always tight, but that was no excuse for refusing year after year to create a home rather than a way station.

Not sure what to do with myself, I went into the kitchen, shoved aside old mail and bills, and did some food prep. I sliced an onion and a green pepper to add to the canned sauce. I remembered that I ought to wash my hands so they wouldn't stink from the onions. Other people! They made you change your game.

At a little before five I returned the birds to their cage. No sooner had I shut the cage when there was a knock on my door. Ellen stood on my stoop in a beige wool trench coat, her breath visible in the cold.

"We barely know each other," she said, "but I need you to understand this is the most important thing I'll ever do. And your *yes* came on the heels of some pretty strong *no*s. I have to know you're really up for this."

145

As I often did, I thought about my father hobbled and demeaned, standing beside me at the Showboat's roulette table. Except that now, for the first time, I saw the hint of nobility and resoluteness in what I had always assumed was simply the impulsive, self-destructive act of a broken man.

"I'm all in," I told her.

"And you aren't gonna get cold feet in a week? Because that'll be too late for me to find somebody else."

Red or black.

I held her gaze. "I told you, I'm all in."

I wasn't used to cooking and talking. Wasn't used to making enough food for two. Wasn't used to the larger pots. I overcooked the garlic bread. I undercooked the spaghetti. At least I knew the pinot noir would be fine. I really knew my mid-priced wines.

I served the meal, and as we ate at my small bistro table Ellen told me about Victor Flowers: former musician turned record-business guy turned financial manager and real estate developer. I didn't tell her I already knew this. I let her talk. "He believes in the American dream," she said, "because he's the product of it. Self-made and all that. What else . . . he collects musical instruments. And art. He'll bore you to tears explaining the historical significance of every little thing in his house. He lives alone. Never married, no kids, no romantic relationships that I can tell. Evidently a guy who values making money over dating. He's private but sociable. Charming. Even at our poker games."

I had decided not to mention Victor Flowers's role in my family's past. That was my business, and it wasn't relevant. And it wasn't as if he would recognize me. I'd met him only that one time, and I had been a child.

"How long has he been a gambler?" I asked.

"Forever, I think, but he's very private about it. Which makes sense. His reputation was built on being smart with money— valuing a dollar and all that. Same with his foundation. It looks bad to donors if the head of the charity is known as a big gambler. And now that he's running for office he's doubling down on his image. He doesn't want any drama."

The way Victor avoided the casinos, she told me, was to host his own game. High-stakes Texas Hold'em. They met monthly, though once a year they played tournament-style for even higher stakes: $250,000 buy-in.

"One winner," Ellen explained. "No second or third place. Whoever wins gets the entire million and a half."

"Rich people are insane," I concluded.

She smiled. "These guys are very sane and predictable. That's why we can go in and take their money. It's why on January first you're gonna make two hundred thousand dollars."

I had a habit of always converting money into how much my father lost at the roulette wheel all those years ago. The busted car I drove had cost me two thousand dollars: just under two per- cent of my father's loss. Last year, I made twenty-six thousand dollars doing magic: about a quarter of my father's loss at the rou- lette wheel.

My take for one night of poker would be almost twice what my father had lost.

"I'm sure you have everything planned out," I said to Ellen.

"I do."

"But what if we get caught?"

She shook her head. "Can't happen."

"It can always happen."

"Not the way I'm planning it."

We were still seated at my bistro table, plates in front of us, in my lousy apartment. This talk of stealing a fortune felt very abstract, and I needed it to feel real.

"Show me the false deal," I said.

"I told you I would."

"Please. Show me now." I stood up to put my plate and silverware into the sink. I returned with a pack of cards and handed it to her.

"Natalie, the deal . . . it's a good move, but that's all it is. Don't lose the forest for the trees. What we have to do—it's a lot more than a single move."

Undoubtedly true. But all of this would only become real to me when she revealed her secret. I replied: *Show. The. Move.*"

She sighed, pushed her plate aside, and slid the cards out of the pack. "Have a seat," she said as she began to shuffle the cards. Her fingernails were still ragged, her hands were dry, but in her card handling she was nothing like the hesitant amateur I'd seen in Atlantic City. She made a few cuts, and then: she did it. She made everything real.

"Second from the bottom," she said. "I learned it as the Greek deal. Done right it's invisible, and you can flash the bottom card so the other players think they're gaining an advantage."

I remembered, during the game in Atlantic City, how she'd occasionally given us all an "accidental" peek at the bottom card before dealing from the top of the deck. Or so it had looked. In actuality, she was sliding the bottom card out of the way and false dealing from the card just above it.

"Learn the Greek deal," she said, "and you'll never need to bottom deal again."

"Do it," I said, and watched as Ellen—how did she handle the cards so well with such small hands?—fanned the deck to locate the four aces, which she set at the bottom of the deck. She placed another card underneath. Then she dealt out four hands of four cards each. She turned over her own pile to reveal the four aces.

I was glad not to have misremembered the level of her talent. Or maybe I had, because her deal tonight was better than it had been in Atlantic City. This time I was watching for it—no distractions, no misdirection—and yet I caught not a whiff of the false deal.

"In magicians' terminology," I said, "that is called fucking amazing. Teach it to me."

She was gathering up the cards. "We have a lot to do tonight."

"I know we do. But I gave up magic last night. So how about throwing me a bone?"

She squared up the stack of cards in front of her. "Get a second deck," she said.

By the time I had attained a halting, awkward grasp of the Greek deal the bottle of wine was long gone. The table was cleared and we had dug into a package of cookies I'd bought for the occasion. Julius and Ethel had both started cooing. Their concerts were unpredictable.

"You use the doves in your act, I assume," Ellen said.

"Actually, they're just pets."

"Yeah, birds freak me out. They're like rats with wings."

"Some people have rats for pets, too," I said.

"Yuck." She made a face. "No offense. By the way, Victor and his friends think my name is Emily Ross, wealthy descendant of Horace Smith."

"Who?"

"Of the Smith and Wesson company."

"Lucky for you."

"You said it. Victor ate up my own little piece of Americana, just like I knew he would. My great-great-great-granddad Horace started out inventing a new method for killing whales: an exploding bullet."

"How very disgusting."

"Victor was extremely interested in my entrepreneurial ancestry, which I happened to mention at a reception for Notes for Kids last winter. We had a lovely conversation. He was intrigued by my pro-gun-control stance even though it hurt my personal fortune." She smiled. "I left him knowing two things about me: I had money to donate, and I was a serious poker player who, like him, hated the public nature of casinos. Next day, I got the call."

While she spoke, I was dealing second-from-the-bottom cards over and over. "How'd you know he played poker?"

"Not everyone's as good at keeping secrets as we are."

Fair enough. "So you played in Victor Flowers's home game for a year. When did you first start thinking about a big take?"

"I figured just getting invited to their regular game was a major score. But the moment they started talking about their annual tournament, I knew. It's perfect, Natalie. There's no second buy-in. That makes planning easier. But there are other things, too, like Victor not hiring a dealer. He likes it to be a game among friends. I guess he thinks a hired dealer would take away from the friendly feel. It's always the same guys. They even have a name for their group: the Midnight Riders."

"Why?"

"Victor loves Paul Revere. He's got a big painting of him over the staircase. But also they're all businessmen who wake up early—so the game always finishes by midnight."

"And you can wake up to teach the next morning."

"It's a perk," she said. "But I knew I needed a partner. And I figured with almost a year, how hard could it be? I know a number of other card mechanics, but apparently not the right ones. Most of them have a few moves, and they seek out sloppy games with weak players. They pick over played cards and grab from the muck and control a couple of cards here and there, anything to get an edge. Even the good ones are pretty much just grinders at heart. I started to realize that guys like that—and I do mean *guys* like that—weren't up to this job."

I stopped dealing the cards. "Wait a minute. Do you want to work with me because I'm good or because I'm a woman?"

"Give yourself a little credit, will you? But it doesn't hurt that you're a woman. A woman at the card table can get away with more." She smiled. "Anyway, I trust a male cheat as far as I can throw him."

"You think women are more honest?"

"In life? No idea. But at a card table with all guys? Definitely. I'd rather work with a woman any day."

"Like Thelma and Louise," I said.

"That's a terrible example, Natalie."

"I just mean they worked well together."

"Yes, they drove off a cliff together very successfully. Let's not do that."

I started dealing the cards again. I knew that once Ellen left I'd be doing Greek deals in front of the bathroom mirror late into the night. "So you were having trouble finding a partner . . ."

"I was starting to get desperate," she said, "which is how I ended up in Atlantic City." Her eyes widened a moment, and she broke into a smile. "Meeting you," she said, "was a hell of a coincidence, but not as much as maybe you think. We were both in A.C. that night for the same reason: for Ace." For a moment I had the inane thought: *She's writing a magazine article?* Then I understood. "His name came up a couple of times, so I drove down to see him in action." She shrugged. "What can I tell you? It was a bad tip."

"His bottom deal was a little rough."

She cracked a smile. "When I saw how awful he was, I figured I might as well make some money so the night wouldn't be a total waste."

"No regrets about cheating your friend?"

"Hey," she said, "I'm going through a bad divorce, right? Ethan's probably glad I had a big night. And don't forget, he came out ahead, too."

"And then I ran after you on the street like a crazy person," I said.

"You were sort of keyed up." She smiled and took another cookie. "I don't blame you. I'm pretty terrific."

8

♥

I'd forgotten I was out of coffee, so we decided to stretch our legs and walk down the street to the mini-mart for a cup. It wasn't late, but there was no longer any hint of dusk, and the street was empty except for a stray cat with no tail. Seeing us, it darted across the road and into an alley.

By the time we got back to the apartment Ellen had almost stopped complaining about the mini-mart coffee. I apologized for not living next to a higher-quality mart, and we sat at the table again. But before we got down to the nitty-gritty, Ellen wanted me to understand just how unusual our situation was. "Your typical card mechanic spots a couple of good cards in the muck—an ace, a king—and controls them to the bottom of the deck. It's helpful but not a guaranteed win. Do you understand? It's cards. You could have a strong hand and still lose. But with a million dollars in play, plus our own combined half million in chips, we have to factor out all the luck. We need a winning hand that will make the other guys go all in."

"How?" I asked.

"Feel like taking a guess?"

"With the two of us in on it? I'm guessing we swap in a cold deck."

"No," she said. "We don't want any evidence. Cheating is supposed to be *low* risk. Even your friend Ace knew that."

"Ace isn't my friend," I reminded her.

"Whatever. His skills were atrocious but his strategy was sound. Poker players aren't generally out to spot a cheat. They're too caught up in playing each hand. So Ace gets the benefit of the doubt. And then imagine that the worst thing happens: someone calls him out for cheating. What do you suppose he does?"

"He denies it."

"Right. Vehemently. He acts offended and insulted. And then he immediately stops cheating. It's his word against his accuser's, and his accuser is never *sure*, just suspicious. There's no evidence, so that's the end of it." She sipped her coffee and made a face. "But if you sneak a cold deck into the game?"

"Evidence," I said.

"Not to mention you'd have to know the exact deck your host will be using—what brand, what color, if the cards are bordered or not. Then you have to pull the switch off. But what if you can't? Or what if you get caught? Imagine getting caught with a second deck." She shook her head. "Even a roomful of pacifists will turn mean if they catch you swapping in a deck. And I never once played poker with a roomful of pacifists."

"What, then?"

She turned toward my window, but the blinds were shut. I imagined she was seeing Victor Flowers's game room.

"Ideally," she said, "we get the game down from six players to four. That shouldn't be hard. Two of the guys aren't all that good, and I can throw myself a couple of aces along the way. So we do that, then we—actually, you—will start controlling cards to the bottom of the deck. We're going to create a hand, a perfect one, where the remaining guys will both go all in, but I'll

154

win the hand." She looked around. "Do you have a sheet of paper and a pen?"

I got them for her, and she began to write.

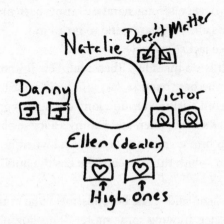

"That's everyone's initial deal," she said. "Victor bets first. He's gonna bet a lot with those two queens."

"How do you know?"

"Because that's what he *has* to do, if he's a decent player. And he is. I'll call. And Danny—Danny Squire, by the way. Recognize the name?"

I did, from all those TV commercials for Squire Lexus, Squire BMW, Squire Porsche, Squire every-car-I-could-never-afford.

"The car guy?" I asked.

"Yep. Total asshole. Anyway, either he'll call or, more likely, he'll raise with those jacks. You'll fold. Then comes the flop."

She wrote some more.

I assessed the hand. "Now Danny and Victor both have three of a kind."

"That's right. Three jacks for Danny, three queens for Victor. Those are two very strong hands. Danny bets first, and with those jacks he's almost guaranteed to go all in."

"With three jacks?"

"The math is on his side," Ellen said. "He'll know he almost certainly has the best hand so far, and he'll want to scare away anyone else from sticking around long enough to get lucky later in the hand. It's smart poker, and Danny's a loose player to begin with. I've seen him go all in with less. And when he does, Victor has to go all in—with three queens, he has the nuts."

"The who?"

"The nuts," she said. "The best possible hand at that point."

I looked at her drawing some more. "This doesn't seem guaranteed," I said.

Ellen looked, too, but she saw something else, something deeper. "They're gamblers, Natalie. They're gonna gamble. Except, really? To them? This hand isn't even gambling. One glance at their cards and it'll be automatic. Like an algorithm—they *have* to go with the odds when the odds are this much in their favor. I've seen Danny go all in when he shouldn't have, but he's never not gone all in when he should. And only an idiot folds when he has the nuts, and Victor is no idiot. But if for some reason neither one of them goes all in? Then I'll do it. And they'll *have* to follow, because they'll have the two best possible hands at that point, and they aren't going to give away their money for no reason."

"Why jacks and queens?" I asked. "Why not really high cards? Aces and kings?"

"It all has to be believable," she said. "When the dealing and betting are over and everyone lays down the cards, it has to look like an actual poker hand. The big hands you always see in movies, royal flushes beating out four aces . . . it's absurd. Real poker doesn't come down to billion-to-one hands. We're giving them very strong hands, the kind of hands that will get any decent player betting big and—this is important—betting *early* in the hand, because they'll want to scare away the other players before those final two community cards get dealt. That's *why* players go all in: it's an aggressive move, but it's also defense." I wasn't dubious, exactly, just a step or so behind. "I've studied these guys for a year," she said. "It's gonna work. Victor and Danny? Neither one would ever admit it but they can't stand each other. They're gonna be especially aggressive in a hand where they both think they can stick it to the other one. Trust me, this hand is gonna get them into a war. And when the hand is over, and they've both lost to my flush in hearts, there won't be anything suspicious about any of it."

I nodded, looking over the cards some more. "Okay," I said. "I think I get it."

"Good." She smiled. "Of course, the next card will be another heart, any heart, giving me my flush, so I'll beat them both."

Turn: any ♡

"As long as we make sure the final card isn't a jack or a queen," she said, "or a pair with the turn card, I'm guaranteed to win. Do you still follow?"

I thought I did. Still, there was a glaring problem with her plan. "You're talking about controlling a hell of a lot of cards: three jacks, three queens, plus three additional hearts . . . I can't control that many cards during a single shuffle." I was damn good at controlling cards, but that many? In a specific order? "There's just no way."

"Neither can I," she said. "No one can. So what you're gonna do is palm some cards off and collect the rest when the deck comes back around to your shuffle again."

To palm cards off the top would mean playing with less than a full deck. It would mean keeping those palmed cards on my body—pocketing them or sitting on them—until I had all of them, at which point I would have to add them back into the deck so Ellen could execute the false deal. If anything went wrong, if one of the guys were to count the cards and see the deck was short, it could mean me getting caught red-handed.

"This doesn't sound much better than using a cold deck," I said.

"Palming is a risk," she said, "but I'm gonna help you with that. I've palmed cards in game situations for years and never once been caught. Do you use the gambler's cop?"

This was a palm where you used the edge of the table to help conceal a card. I'd always assumed it was unnecessarily risky because part of the card is exposed beneath the table. "No."

"Why not? My god, you magicians." She shook her head. "It's perfect for me because my hands are small, but even with your big hands, it's a better move than the classic palm when you're seated at a table. Trust me. You're gonna be fine. And once you've returned the cards to the deck for dealing, the evidence disappears. That's why it's better than a cold deck."

"But what if I *do* get caught? What will these guys do to me?"

"They aren't mafiosi, Natalie. These are professional men with clients to think about and public images to uphold. They don't even want anyone knowing they're *in* the game. They can afford to lose a quarter million in a night. They'd never do anything to jeopardize their own lives. It would be illogical."

"Ellen." I was old enough to know how little logic explained why people did many of the things they did. "What could they *do* to me?"

"Worst case? And I mean *worst* case, like you sneeze and all the palmed cards go flying across the room? They kick you out the door and keep your buy-in. Which, if you'll remember, is really my buy-in. I'd be the one out of luck, not you. But that's not gonna happen. We're gonna work hard. We'll be ready. You'll be palming cards in your sleep. You're gonna earn your money."

"What if we switch jobs? You shuffle and I deal?"

She shook her head. "If you're a little slow palming off the cards, you can take some extra time. These guys play with two decks, and while you're shuffling the one, I'll be dealing the other and can slow the pace down a little. If you absolutely have to, you can wait for the deck to come around a third time to grab the rest. But if you're the dealer, there's only one chance to get it right." She shrugged. "Besides. This is my gig. I set it up, and I'm staking everything on it. I deal the cards."

I nodded.

"No one's gonna be watching the shuffler anyway," she said. "The dealer gets all the attention. And the Greek deal is a really hard move to get right. It's taken me years to perfect."

"Why not just bottom deal?" I asked.

"You saw why in Atlantic City. And here tonight. The Greek deal's just a better move when it's done right."

I had to agree. "All of this. It's . . . hard. This is really hard sleight of hand we're talking about."

"I know."

"If I hadn't gone running after you in Atlantic City, what were you going to do? Who were you going to find?"

She took another sip of coffee. "I don't know. I guess we both got lucky."

She gave me a lesson in the finer points of the gambler's cop. By the time she put her coat on and I walked her to the door it was past midnight. The birds were side by side on the perch with their eyes closed. Ellen and I made plans to meet up again on Tuesday when she was done teaching for the day. In the meantime, I had plenty of magic to practice. Ellen was almost out the door when I stopped her. "What about the cut?" I couldn't believe this hadn't occurred to me earlier. "Whoever's sitting between us is going to cut the cards."

"Of course," she said.

"But if I arrange the deck and then someone cuts the cards, it would undo everything. That's *why* cards get cut."

She smiled. "All taken care of."

"How?"

"It's late," she said. "You've had a big day. Sleep on it and tell me what you come up with." I was shutting the door when she turned around and said, "By the way, your name's Nora."

"Nora?"

"Nora Thompson. And don't just practice the Greek deal because I said it was hard. Work on controlling the cards. That's your job." She waved. "See you on Tuesday."

9
♠

The next morning, my eyes opened at the first light and I was fully awake. The air felt crisper, electric. In the bathroom, the blue tiles on the walls seemed brighter, as did the silver faucets. Everything seemed more. I knew things, amazing things, that I did not know yesterday, and I anticipated the busy hours and days ahead, when I would work to reduce and ultimately eliminate the friction between what I knew and what my hands could do.

There were a few shows on my December calendar. The money for those gigs, I knew, would help pay for Lou Husk's settlement, but if they took away from the time I would otherwise be practicing for the game with Victor Flowers, then they weren't worth keeping. Also, I couldn't bring myself to care one iota about coins or linking rings or silks or ropes or clever reveals inside citrus fruits. I didn't care about witty patter or making a crowd laugh or gasp or admire me for all my years of dedication to the art of close-up prestidigitation. All I cared about was January 1. Being ready. Being perfect.

My next show was on Saturday night in Hartford, Connecticut, the private holiday party of a retired Aetna executive. This was a referral from another retired Hartford exec, whose party I'd done a year ago. It was an easy gig, but at a home gig like that I couldn't just leave right after the show. I'd be expected to schmooze and laugh at all the right moments, as if their motive in inviting me was so that I could be their audience and bear witness to their success and energy and wit, to the ease with which they inhabited their white-haired years.

I was meeting with Ellen again in just a few days. I kept thinking about all that time driving up to Hartford and back, the obligatory traffic jam on the Cross Bronx Expressway, all those wasted hours. So I called Jack at the store and asked him to help me find a replacement.

"For this Saturday?" he asked. "December's a busy time. What's the matter? You don't sound so good."

"I think it's the flu," I said, making my voice rasp without overdoing it. "Or something like it."

"You have enough food at home?" he asked. "You have Gatorade? You have to drink Gatorade if it's the flu."

"Yeah, I have whatever I need. I just need a replacement."

"Why don't you give Milo Dunning a ring."

Magic Milo? "Milo's the worst," I said.

"Nah, he's all right." That was Jack's code for: he spends a lot of money in my shop. "And this is for retirees? Milo's your man."

Jack gave me Milo's number, and then we brainstormed a couple of other magicians in case Milo wasn't available.

"Drink at least three Gatorades a day," Jack said. "The big size. Otherwise, you aren't staying hydrated enough."

"Sure, Jack."

"You don't want to mess with the flu. You want to stay hydrated."

"All right."

"Your urine should be clear, not yellow."

"Thank you, Jack."

Magic Milo was also an endodontist. He was one of those guys who must've owned dozens of magic convention T-shirts, an enthusiastic amateur for whom the money from the occasional gig didn't matter because he made plenty doing root canals.

He was available. And as he thanked me again and again, I was thinking about my other December events—bachelor party in Hoboken, private holiday party in Far Hills, corporate event in New Brunswick. I was becoming nauseated thinking about having to paste on a smile and go through with all those shows.

"Hey, Milo," I said, cutting short his anecdote about having visited Hartford several years before, and touring Mark Twain's house, and how it really was worth seeing next time I went there.

"That *Connecticut Yankee in King Arthur's Court* . . ." He laughed, high-pitched and honking.

"Hey, Milo . . ." I cringed a little, knowing the bachelor party would not go well. But he would do all right with the other shows. "What does the rest of your December look like?"

Ellen arrived after school let out on Tuesday carrying a plastic bag, whose contents she dumped onto my bistro table. Eighteen sealed decks of playing cards.

"Victor always starts the night with two sealed decks. So you need to be practicing with fresh cards. Tomorrow, throw the first pack away and open a new one. Every day, a new pack, understand?"

"All right," I told her.

"You say that, but you have a trash bag for a car window," she said. "A fortune is riding on this game, and I've made it easy for you: eighteen days, eighteen decks. Don't be stingy with the cards." She turned to face the birds, which had started cooing—first one, then the other.

"They do that a lot," she said.

"I barely notice anymore," I told her.

"I don't get it," she said. "You're a magician with doves but you don't use them in your act? What's up with that?"

I told her about buying them when I was in high school, and how I hadn't given much thought to the tricks beforehand. "Once I learned how the tricks were done, I felt bad stuffing them into tiny pouches and into tight harnesses made of fishing line. And to make a bird stay quiet and still? You have to flip it over onto its back superfast. Basically, you're giving it lots of g-force to make it pass out."

"No kidding," she said.

"Yeah. It all seemed cruel." I vividly remembered all those years back, trying the move on Ethel, flipping the bird upside down but not fast enough, then doing it again, harder, and the frightened bird was suddenly, eerily motionless, her soft body warm in my hands, her living heart beating against my fingers.

"Huh. I never knew that." She smiled. "You're a good egg, Natalie Webb."

She asked me for paper and a pen and drew a map of Victor's poker room, which was also a movie screening room and billiard room and wet bar. I could have lived happily in that one room.

She added the poker table to her sketch and reminded me that we had to get Victor sitting between the two of us. "You'll only have a few minutes after we arrive to befriend him," she said. "To intrigue him so he'll want to sit next to you."

"You want me to flirt with him?"

"I don't even know if he likes women. But he likes being a good host. So you're going to be interested in everything he has to say, and stick close to him, and then you'll ask him to sit next to you."

We got Chinese takeout from the place down the street, and while we ate she told me more about the other players who'd be at the game: Ian McDonald, Jason Panella, and Danny Squire. "Danny's gonna seem intimidating," Ellen said, "but don't let him bother you. He's just brash and an aggressive bettor."

Ian McDonald, I learned, was a hedge fund manager, which was a familiar phrase that meant nothing to me.

"It means," Ellen said, "that he invests a lot of nothing and bets against the economy to make rich people richer."

"He sounds like a lovely man," I said.

Ellen smiled. "It's a better con than either of us will ever pull off."

And then there was Jason Panella, who made no secret about having inherited his money from his grandfather, who had started a pharmaceutical company that grew to a billion-dollar enterprise before he sold it to Johnson & Johnson.

"He sits on some boards," Ellen said, "though his main jobs seem to be skiing and scuba diving, depending on the season."

"How did they react to having a woman in their game?" I asked.

"I think they like it. They can show off a little, and I know how to play the part of a girl who's just *one of the guys*. The first time I went, I told them about the time I played against Michael Phelps and took his money. That sold them."

"Is it true?"

"About five years ago, in Atlantic City."

"I didn't think you liked A.C."

"I don't, but every so often I'll play in a casino to keep my poker chops up and do some intel—try to get new leads on home games. I was already at the table when he took the empty seat next to me. I thought he was reasonably attractive so I said something like, 'How's it going?' and he said, 'I just rescued the greatest dog.' It was cute."

"He'd get along well with my upstairs neighbor," I said.

"Huh?"

"She rescues dogs."

"Oh. I didn't even know who he was until he'd tipped the dealer some huge amount and left the table. Then everyone started going crazy." She took a bite of her egg roll. "How about you? You ever do magic for anyone big?"

I had told this story before many times. "Another Michael, actually. Maybe you've heard of him? Last name Jackson?"

Her eyes widened. "Get the fuck out."

I smiled.

"I can't believe you just beat out my Michael Phelps story. What was the occasion?"

"There wasn't one," I said. "Not one I knew of, anyway. This was back in '04." I told Ellen about how Michael had been in New York, recording. I was only seventeen—this was just a few months after my second-place finish at the WOM convention, during that astonishing year of touring. My mother drove me into the city from Jersey, then left me at the curb so I could walk into the recording studio alone. I was led to a small conference room just inside the entrance, and once I was set up a dozen or so people entered. I have no idea who they were. Studio staff or managers or whoever. I stood at the front of the room, and they sat around the conference table, turning their chairs to face me. Then

Michael came in and sat front and center and I did my twenty-minute show and left.

"What was he like?"

"He didn't say much. One of the tricks involved a signed playing card, and after the show he told me to keep it."

"Do you still have it?"

I shook my head. "Stupid me, I lost it in a move."

"Too bad," she said. "It's probably worth a lot of money."

What I omitted from my Michael Jackson story—this time, and every time I told it—was how, afterward, he had laid a hand, ungloved, on my arm and smiled at me and said, *I just know you're going to be a big star, Natalie.* And I omitted the part where, because I was seventeen, and because I had shows lined up in London and Lisbon, and because the prognostication had come from Michael Jackson himself, I believed him with every cell in my body.

"I've told you before," Ellen was saying, "your friend in A.C. did a fine job nullifying the cut. He really did."

"Not my friend," I reminded her.

We had cleared dinner from the table. Each of us now had a deck of cards out. "My point is, that's not gonna work here. These men aren't rubes. Victor's gonna cut the cards before I deal."

I was confused. Unless: "Victor's not in on it, is he?"

She watched my face, saw the gears churning.

"Nope," she said.

"He's really gonna cut the cards?" I asked. "Like a legit cut?"

"Yes."

"And then you'll be dealing the deck that I stacked?"

"Come on, Nat, you're the award-winning magician. Figure it out."

167

I didn't like knowing a method existed that I couldn't deduce right away. I considered Ellen's bar scam. The most direct path from A to B.

"Don't feel bad," Ellen said. "Though I must tell you, if you were a real card cheat, you'd think this was pretty easy."

"If it's so easy, then why isn't everyone doing it?"

"I meant easy to deduce. Hard to execute. That's a big clue, by the way."

Yes, it was. I was pretty sure I knew now, but I was still foggy on how it all fit together. "Some kind of pass," I said, and she smiled a little. All card magicians learned the classic pass—a very elegant, though difficult, secret cut used to move a card to the top or bottom of the deck—but many opted for other, easier methods. (In my experience, the classic pass was mainly useful for magicians to judge the technical abilities of other magicians.)

"How do you know where to get the break in the deck?"

Her half smile became a whole one. "Most of the time, you don't need one. The guy cutting the cards doesn't complete the cut. He leaves the two halves side by side on the table, and I can do a spin pass. It makes the age-old problem of the cut simply vanish."

None of this was intuitive for me because I performed standing up. I played to the audience, not to other people seated around a table. So the moves I used—they were different moves. But from somewhere in the back of my brain a move came to me: "The Charlie Miller table pass."

"What the hell's that?" Ellen asked.

I cut the deck and did a fairly poor version of the Charlie Miller, where under the guise of completing the cut and gathering the cards I reset the two halves in their original order, undoing the cut.

"That *is* a spin pass," she said. It was true. In doing the move, half the deck gets quickly spun 180 degrees.

"I learned it as the Charlie Miller table pass."

"Tomato, tom*ah*to," she said. "And you didn't learn it very well."

"It's not something I ever use," I said.

"Well, done right . . . here. Cut." She showed me the top card and handed me her deck. I lifted half the pack and set it beside the other half. She completed the cut and gathered the cards. Showed me the top card: it was the same card.

I'd had no idea the move was worth the effort. But it was. Now in addition to the Greek deal, here was another significant lapse in my training. I clapped softly for Ellen. She held up a hand: *no applause necessary.*

"What if he completes the cut?" I asked.

"What if who does?"

"You said the players usually don't complete the cut. But what if they do?"

"Just to be safe, the shuffler—you—will crimp the bottom card before handing over the deck to be cut."

Of course. After the cut, Ellen would feel the crimped card and do a more traditional pass so the deck would revert to how it was before the cut. Like she had said: simple. But difficult to do imperceptibly.

"The key," she said, "is to cover the small action with a bigger one. While doing the pass, I swing my body and arms toward the left to begin dealing to the first player. And like I said, these guys usually don't complete the cut. But just in case, this works, too."

I could see it in my mind—Ellen pivoting to her left, doing the move that appeared to be nothing more than a simple squaring up of the deck. Yet something wasn't sitting right.

"It *could* work, you mean," I said.

"I mean, it *does*. I tried it at a game where the dealer was also the shuffler, so I could crimp the card myself. But in Victor's game, the person to the right of the cutter shuffles. That means you'll crimp the card, Victor will cut, and I'll deal. And you'll create some kind of distraction at the moment when I swing my body. A cough. A stretch. Whatever. It's all we'll need."

"All right," I said, but maybe not enthusiastically enough.

"Relax," she said. "I've been practicing it for months. I'll be ready."

She'll *be* ready? That. That's what wasn't sitting right. "You said you already tried it in a game."

She waved my words away. "At a low-stakes game against a table of idiots."

I watched her closely. "You did the move before it was ready?"

"It *was* ready."

"Sounds to me like it wasn't."

She set her deck of cards on the table. "Don't lecture me, Natalie."

No one was smiling now. "Maybe you need a lecture." I took a breath to calm myself. "Listen, Ellen, you don't do a trick until it's ready."

"And I'm telling you it *was* ready. For them." She spoke slowly, enunciating each word. "For that particular game, for those particular idiots."

The Chinese food was feeling heavy in my stomach. "No. Either the move is performance ready or it isn't. Come on, this is like Magic 101."

"I'm not a magician."

No, and maybe that mattered. Maybe I was being unreasonable. Or maybe she was being cavalier. It seemed to me that in her profession, where a heckler wasn't the biggest threat, it was even more important for a new move to be flawless.

"I want to see it," I said. "Show me your classic pass." I held out the deck of cards.

"I'm not gonna audition for you, Natalie."

"You were pretty excited to show me your spin pass a minute ago," I said. "So why not this one?"

She glared at me.

"You already know what I think about your false deal," I told her. "It's amazing. World-class. But if I'm going to be part of this, I have to know that *all* the moves you might use are that good. It's only fair." I took the deck, crimped the bottom card, cut the deck so the crimped card was buried in the middle, and set the deck on the table. "So let's see it."

She watched me a moment longer. Then with a dramatic, teenage sigh she accepted the deck of cards and pivoted her body to the left. During this larger motion with her body and arms, she executed the pass.

It was fine.

Honestly, she did the move better than most magicians I knew. Done as a fast, hidden move during a card trick along with patter and misdirection, the move would have been more than serviceable.

But relative to her spin pass? Not in the same ballpark. And relative to her Greek deal? No. There was no comparing it to her Greek deal.

"You plan to steal a million dollars with that?" I said.

"Give me a break," she said. "My pass is damn good."

I took the deck from her, broke it in the middle, turned over the center card—five of hearts—turned it back over, and put the deck back together, burying the card in the center. Then under

171

the guise of squaring up the deck, I did the move: the bottom half of the deck became the top half. If she blinked, she missed it. If she didn't blink, she missed it anyway. No large action masking a smaller one. No misdirection. Just the classic pass done the way it's supposed to be done. A move I'd practiced for several thousand hours in my Plainfield bedroom as a teenager while the world spun on around me.

I turned over the top card.

"Huh," she said, staring at the five of hearts.

After Ellen left, I sat on the loveseat and worked late into the night on controlling the cards. I thought about all the things I used to tell myself about being a magician, things Jack had told me, things I'd read in books. How the magician *creates a mystery, an unbridgeable gap between cause and effect*. How with enough practice magic could be *a balm applied to the tyranny of the everyday*.

I actually wrote stuff like that myself in Jack Clarion's newsletter. I remember believing it. But at some point, or gradually over many points, I had lost the mystery, and a new tyranny had set in. Gig after gig. Rent check to rent check. Good technique, high heels, and a bowler hat, year after year.

I looked down at my hands. I took such care of them, filing the nails, constantly applying lotion I couldn't afford. People sometimes mistook me for younger than I was because of my face. They should've looked at my hands. The hands never lie. The veins were more visible now than they once were, the skin was looser. My hands were no longer the hands of a young woman.

These hands, and what I did with them. They were all I had. When I considered Cardini, Slydini, Dai Vernon, T. Nelson Downs, Harry Houdini—all those legends who made their

172

indelible impact on the art of conjuring—I had to wonder, who the hell was I?

Our time on this earth was so fucking limited. At some point we painted our last brushstroke on the Great Mural, and I had yet to make a single lasting mark.

I wanted to do something beautiful with these hands of mine.

10

♦

Ellen came over again later that week, and then early the following week. It was December 22. Her classic pass was
noticeably improving, and I was glad to learn that despite her
long experience and remarkable talent as a poker cheat, she was
willing to do her homework.

I was doing mine. Although I couldn't resist working on the
Greek deal and the Charlie Miller table pass, my card controlling
took center stage. It had always been good, but I knew that good
wasn't good enough.

We gave each other pointers—shifting a finger to reduce friction, tilting the deck to improve angles—the type of nuanced
criticism that can be given and received only by those who
already have a high level of mastery.

I was about to suggest Chinese takeout again when Ellen said,
"No way. I have a better idea, Nora."

"Huh?"

"Exactly," she said, frowning. "You need to practice being
Nora. Get your coat."

The festive atmosphere of the holidays was on full display in
the Gladewood Mall. We weaved through crowds and came

upon a junior high school band performing in front of a huge Christmas tree. They were trudging through a horn-cracking, reed-squeaking version of "Santa Claus Is Coming to Town." The band's conductor, brave woman, waved her arms in increasingly frantic circles.

Parents sat, rapt, on lawn chairs they must have brought with them. Others stood, tapping their toes, sucking on sodas, and snacking on Auntie Anne's pretzels while the band played on. When the song came to a stuttering, tentative conclusion, the audience, after waiting a moment to make sure it was truly over, erupted in cheers, conclusive proof that no creature on Earth has duller perception than a parent.

"They're so good!" Ellen said to the woman standing beside her.

"I know!" The woman beamed. "Is one of them yours?"

"Actually, no. I just couldn't help stopping to listen."

And suddenly the two of them were best friends, chatting about kids and music and last-minute shopping and the happy burden of the season.

"Tiffany, this is my friend Nora," Ellen said, drawing me in. "She's an event planner at some fancy hotels." She touched my shoulder. "Nora, maybe the kids could play at one of your hotels!"

"Wow," I said. "Yeah, that's such a great idea." The mother's eyes widened. "The thing is, our holidays are super busy. Our December calendar gets booked up by July."

"Oh." The mother's face fell. "But maybe next year?" She dug in her pocketbook for paper and a pen and wrote down Tiffany Wall, a phone number, and the name of the school. "Do you have a business card?" she asked.

"That's so funny—I just ran out," I said, taking the paper from her. "I'm heading over to Copy Lizard now to restock. But I'll call you." And then the band started playing "Jingle Bell Rock" and Ellen and I slipped away.

We really were headed to Copy Lizard in case Victor or any of the other men asked for my card. After all, what better potential clients would there be for an event planner than the rich men at the poker game?

As we walked, we practiced being Nora Thompson and Emily Ross some more, amid the lights and decorations, amid the shoppers in their bulky coats dragging along complaining kids, amid the teenagers shouting and showing off and hanging on to each other. I felt all of my years of entering this very mall during the holidays knocking against one another.

At Copy Lizard we mocked up a simple business card on parchment stock with *Nora Thompson* and *Professional Party/Event Planning* and a Gmail address we'd secured before leaving the house. For a contact phone number, Ellen told me to use the number she owned specifically so she could give it out when a weirdo at a card game asked for it. The outgoing message was a generic, "Please leave a message after the tone." We printed out a single sheet of twelve business cards.

I handed Ellen a card. "Should you ever find yourself throwing a big party, I hope you'll consider my services."

"Why, thank you, Nora." She narrowed her eyes. "You have experience, I hope?"

"I do," I said. "My family actually owns a couple of hotels, so you could say I grew up in the industry."

"Is that right? Which hotels?"

I rattled off the name of one actual, boutique Philadelphia hotel and two other names I had invented. "And you said you're a descendant of Smith? The gun maker?"

"That's right," Ellen said.

"You know, I hosted an event once for a group of mystery novelists, where a police officer demonstrated all sorts of weapons—guns and rifles and tasers. I can't remember if there were any Smith and Wessons. I'm not a gun person. But it was fascinating."

"It sounds it." We were approaching the center of the mall again, where the junior high musicians played on. "In fact, I sort of wish I had a taser right now." She grinned. "Want to get a drink?"

Champions, a sports bar, was overflowing with champions deeply in need of a break from shopping. The TVs over the bar and on the walls were tuned to various games, and the customers' loud conversations competed with the piped-in music—mercifully '90s hip-hop and not Christmas songs. We waited until two seats opened at the bar and wedged ourselves in. We ordered beer and a plate of nachos from a woman who had mastered the art of graceful multitasking. The beers were soon in front of us in frosted mugs.

"I actually watched a guy get tased once," I said.

"Are you still being Nora?"

"No," I said.

"Okay. Tell me."

I hadn't told this story in a long time. "A guy shoved his hand down my pants at a bachelor party. I told him he was an asshole and he hit me in the face. So I called the cops, and the guy got belligerent with the officer and ended up on the ground."

"Serves him right," Ellen said with more than a hint of bitterness, and I wondered if maybe I shouldn't have told that story. Why would I launch right into a depressing story like that? We had been having fun.

Making and keeping friends: not my forte.

"A guy hit me, too," Ellen said.

"At a poker game?"

"In my bedroom."

"Was it a break-in?" I asked.

She held my gaze a moment. "He was my boyfriend. Eight years." She drank from her beer. "But he only hit me for the last six. We were sort of engaged."

I sipped my drink and tried to figure out what the hell to say. "What happened to him?"

Ellen eyed me as if I were born this morning. "What happened to him? Jesus. Nothing happened to him. Nothing ever happens to anyone." She shook her head. "Fuck."

Only minutes earlier we were having a good time. Amazing, I thought, how quickly an evening can turn dark. Ah, the holidays.

At a table across the restaurant, some men and women were laughing up a storm. They probably weren't even trying to be funny. When their laughter died down, one of the women kept cackling. It was the kind of cackle you could hear a mile away.

"What are you doing for Christmas?" I asked Ellen.

"Going to my brother's."

"You have a brother?" I didn't know why this should surprise me, her offhand mention of family.

"He lives in Yardley. Wife, kids, the whole deal. He's a teacher, too. High school math. They always invite me over for Christmas brunch. It's nice."

"And these kids, they're real? Or are they the kind you show photos of at card games?"

Her expression was becoming more familiar to me. It meant I should have pieced something together but hadn't. "Those kids *are* the card-game kids," she said. "It's why the pictures are in my phone. That's the only time I ever do magic tricks, by the way. For the nephews."

I thought about my own plans for Christmas day: practicing the Greek deal. Calling my mother. Joy to the world.

"How late do you stay there?" I asked.

"Most of the day. Why?"

I told her about my Christmas evening tradition, going on five years: pizza delivery and *The Sting* on DVD.

"One of my favorites," she said.

"I know the poker scene isn't very realistic," I said, "but I don't care. It's just fun to watch. If you aren't doing anything later in the day, you should come over."

"Thanks," she said. "I'd like that." She brushed the hair out of her eyes. "But are you sure you wouldn't rather watch *Thelma and Louise*? I know what a feel-good movie you think it is."

I told her I was rescinding the invitation.

"Or maybe *Sophie's Choice*? That's a fun one."

After the nachos arrived, and once the bartender had placed second rounds of beer in front of us and walked away, Ellen said, "I'm sorry a guy did that to you at a gig."

"I'm sorry about your boyfriend," I said. "That must have really sucked."

"Sucks doesn't begin to describe it, Natalie." She took a long drink from her beer. "But thanks for saying it."

We ate and watched the crowd, all these people who'd taken a time-out from the bustle of the holidays to be with their friends. I felt almost like one of them.

J

On Christmas morning, I decided to wait until noon to call my mother since Reno was three hours behind. But at 11:30 she beat me to it.

When my phone started vibrating, I was doing something highly unusual. I was sliding a tray of cookies into the oven. Not the prefab kind, either, but the kind where you add eggs and flour and sugar and eye-popping amounts of butter. I figured cookies would make the apartment smell festive.

"Merry Christmas," I said into the phone. "I just put cookies in the oven."

"Oh, Natalie," she said, "we have such good news."

I was immediately on edge because of the manic tinge to her voice that she got whenever she was on the verge of making a terrible decision.

"What is it, Mom?"

"So you know how Chip is really good with people?"

I had no knowledge of this. "I guess," I said, and then stayed quiet while my mother told me about the plan they'd hatched.

It could have been worse. They had decided to become pawnbrokers.

"Our niche is going to be motorcycles!" she said.

"Pawnshops have a niche?"

"Oh, Natalie. In today's marketplace, you *have* to have a niche." I wondered what website she'd gotten that from. "And Reno's a great town for pawnbrokers," she added. That, I believed—all those casinos, all those people losing everything.

I pressed the phone a little closer to my ear. "Mom, they have you working on Christmas morning?" For the last few months she'd been serving drinks at Harrah's.

"No, I'm not working today," she said.

"Because I hear . . . you're in a casino, right?"

"No, I'm not."

"It sounds like you are."

The bells and whirs continued.

"We just have to raise a little more seed money, that's all." I didn't say anything. The background noise was saying it all. "Relax, Natalie. Chip's been on such a roll lately. I wouldn't even call it luck. He won two thousand a couple of weeks ago."

That did it. I couldn't resist. "How much did he lose winning that?"

"See? Now you're just being very negative. I called to wish you Merry Christmas and to tell you about this great new business we're both so excited about, and I hoped that my own daughter . . ." She sighed. "I'm sorry. I know you have your opinions, and that's good. That's how I raised you."

We talked a while longer about her pawn business. How Chip had found a great storefront location, "perfect for growing into." She was studying up on how to differentiate diamond from moissanite. Everything she said made me uneasy. Then she asked about me, and I'm sure I made her uneasy, too, with my vague and cagey replies. By the time we got off the phone I think we were both glad it was another four months until Easter.

And my apartment smelled like burnt cookies.

Ellen was due at five. She had proven to be habitually prompt, and it didn't surprise me when, at 4:50, there was a knock on my door. Only it was Calvin, not Ellen, standing on my stoop, in his blue jeans and gray shirt, looking as if he were in physical pain.

"Are you okay?" I asked, stepping outside and shutting the door behind me.

With the stores all closed, the street was quieter than usual. There was no trace of the wind that had rattled my bedroom window overnight and found its way into my tornadic dreams. Now the sky was blue and the air felt crisp and pollution-free, as if New Jersey had finally settled on an ideal autumn day now that it was winter.

"Here," Calvin mumbled, shoving a box at me. "Merry Christmas."

The box, which was crushed in one corner, contained a Christmas tree ornament visible behind a layer of clear plastic. Painted on the large silver ball was the face of Rudolph with his red nose. Beside the reindeer was the word *Joy*.

"Wow," I said, without overdoing it. I didn't want to condescend. This was a sweet gesture from a kid who didn't specialize in sweet gestures. "This is great. Thanks so much."

"You can hang it on your tree," he said.

"I sure will." He didn't need to know I had no tree. He might break into someone's home and steal one.

His mission done, Calvin now stood stiffly, hands in pockets, unsure what to do or say next. I asked him, "So what do you guys have planned for today?"

"Going to my cousins' in Kearny," he said.

"Is that good?"

He exhaled wearily. "It is what it is."

Calvin's sincere tree ornament, I realized, would be the only present I received this year. But even sadder was how many presents I had planned to give to others. A fat zero.

"Hey, can I ask you a question?" I said.

"You just—" He stopped himself.

"Nice catch," I said. "So you gave that girl some records, right? Which means you also like records? Like on vinyl?"

"Yeah," he said, "but not for some hipster bullshit reason. Vinyl just sounds better."

"Hang on a sec." I went back inside and returned a minute later. "Merry Christmas," I said, handing him the three remaining quarters of the hundred-dollar bill. "Go buy yourself some records. You'll have to tape the bill together first, obviously."

He stared down at the pieces of bill in his hands. I was afraid he might start to cry.

"What's the matter?" I asked.

"I'm so stupid."

"What?"

He shook his head angrily, as if trying to unloosen something. "I lost the other piece!"

Then I got to reveal that wonderful, little-known fact about American paper currency: more than half a bill and it's legal tender.

"Are you sure?" he asked.

"Positive." I warned him that a merchant would probably be suspicious when he handed over three-quarters of a taped-up hundred-dollar bill. "But the law's on your side," I said. "And you can always take it to a bank, where they'll exchange it for a clean one."

"Which bank?"

"Any bank."

He studied the torn pieces in his hands as if trying to master the idea of them being real. Then he looked at me and smirked.

"Sucker!" he said.

"What?"

"Now I don't have to shovel."

"Hey, man, a deal's a deal."

As he was waving the pieces of money in front of my face, Ellen's Prius pulled up behind my car on the street. Calvin stuffed the money into his pocket while we watched her get out of her car. She had on her trench coat, blue jeans, and a stylish wool brim hat.

Calvin's eyes widened. "Nice," he said, loud enough for her to hear. "You know her?"

"She's a friend of mine," I said.

When she got near, he said, "You two want to smoke up later?" He was Cool Calvin again, any trace of sadness or insecurity gone from his voice. "I can get us weed from my cousin in Kearny."

"Definitely not," I said.

Ellen gave him a quick once-over. "Good-bye, little boy." She flicked her fingers at him.

Calvin's face reddened.

"See ya, Calvin," I said. "Merry Christmas."

He gave Ellen an angry glance before turning toward the street and shuffling away, his mind full of tall mountains and weed, or vinyl records, or flaming excrement, or maybe nothing at all.

After calling in the pizza order, I opened a bottle of better-than-usual cabernet, poured two glasses, and told Ellen I wanted to show her something. She followed me over to the bistro table, where I dealt out four hands, using the Greek deal to give myself two aces.

"Not bad," she said.

"You know it's better than that," I said.

"Keep practicing with those oven-mitt hands of yours," she said, "and in another ten years you might really have something."

I knew Ellen was only ribbing me, but her words stung. Maybe because I'd been riding the high of impulsively giving Calvin a much larger gift than I could afford and he could have expected.

"What?" she said, reading my face. "I said it wasn't bad." She drank some wine. "Coming from me, those words are probably the best compliment you ever received."

"Because your own skills are so amazing, you mean."

"Actually, yes." She smiled. "That's exactly what I mean. This wine is good."

"You know Ace said the same thing about *his* skills."

Ellen raised an eyebrow. "Now that's a low blow. You saw me at the card table."

"I did. And you know how highly I think of your talent."

"Thank you," she said.

"But."

Her eyes narrowed. I couldn't tell if she was just playing anymore. "But what?"

I couldn't tell if I was either. "Nothing," I said. "Really."

"No, what?"

I hesitated a moment. "Your deal wasn't perfect. I'm just saying."

Ellen set down her wineglass. "My deal *is* perfect."

Maybe I'd overstepped, but false dealing was her livelihood. I hadn't meant to insult her—yet did it hurt to be honest? "At the poker table in Atlantic City?" The wine was helping with honesty. "It was a wonderful deal, don't get me wrong. I'd never seen the Greek deal before, and it caught me off guard. But don't forget: I saw something. I still caught you. So was it amazing? Yes. Perfect?" I shook my head. "Not quite."

She opened her mouth and then closed it again.

"Forget it," I said.

"It doesn't sound like you forget anything," she said.

I glanced out the window, wishing for the arrival of our pizza. "I just want us to be careful and prepared and not take anything for granted."

"No one's taking anything for granted, Natalie."

"All I'm saying is, if I can catch you, then someone else can, too."

"You want out? Is that what you're saying?"

"Ellen—"

"No, really," she said. "If I'm not up to your standards, maybe we should just forget the whole thing."

"I'm not saying anything like that."

"No one's forcing you to do this, you know."

"I know," I said. "It's just . . ." I supposed I wanted an assurance that she'd be as careful and prepared as I planned to be, but the last thing I wanted was to make her doubt herself. Walking into Victor Flowers's house, we would need confidence. Both of us.

186

Self-doubt could get us in deep trouble. I had thought Ellen was unflappable. Evidently, she was only as human as the rest of us. "This is pointless," I said. "Really. I don't even know what I'm talking about. I've seen countless card handlers, and you're at the very top. You know I mean that. And it's Christmas. Come on." I got up from the bistro table, went over to the loveseat. "We're supposed to be taking one lousy night off. So please—Ellen— come over here with your wine and let's watch this goddamn wonderful movie."

I gave her the gift of letting myself be glared at awhile longer. Then she came over.

December 29 was our last practice session. Three days later she would pick me up and we would drive together down the Garden State Parkway to Victor's house in the Highlands.

When I opened the door, Ellen thrust a bag at me.

"These beans are from Papua New Guinea," she said. "Fair trade, organic, and ridiculously expensive. Promise me you won't ever drink that mini-mart sludge again."

I thanked her.

"And don't store it in the freezer," she said. "It kills the taste."

"Duly noted," I said, and that was as close as either one of us came to addressing the tension of the other night.

Cooking for one all these years had stunted my culinary creativity, and we were back to spaghetti with sauce from a jar, doctored with fresh peppers and onions. Ellen offered to cut up the vegetables while I checked the weather on my computer in the living room. The extended forecast had been calling for snow on New Year's Day. Not a blizzard or anything, but still. It would have been devastating if after all the planning and practice, the poker game were to get canceled over weather. I was worrying about this particular devastating thing happening when another devastating thing happened.

I had typed the zip code for the Highlands into my computer, and the website was loading up the five-day forecast when Ellen swore from the kitchen. I went to check on her.

The kitchen faucet was on. Ellen was running her hand under it.

"What happened?" I asked.

"Nothing. I just . . . slicing the stupid onion. Ow."

"Are you okay?"

"Yeah. I think so. Hand me a paper towel."

I ripped a paper towel off the roll and handed it to her. She bunched it up and pressed it against her left thumb.

"It's not bad, is it?"

"God, that was so stupid. I should have . . . it's not a big cut. I sort of jabbed it. Do you have any Band-Aids?"

I didn't. I remembered that Harley had a first-aid kit but I'd heard her leave the apartment earlier. "I can run out . . ."

"No, the paper towel should be fine."

"Let me see." The last thing I wanted was to see her wound, but I knew I ought to. Ellen's fully operational thumb was a lot more critical than my queasiness around blood.

She was right: it wasn't a big cut. Still, the bleeding didn't seem to be stopping.

"I think it might be kind of deep," I said. Remembering how Harley had treated my dog bite, I said, "You have to clean it really well. So it won't get infected." Ellen had moved into the living room and was sitting on the sofa, head lowered. I knew we were thinking the same thing.

I tried to imagine our whole plan, all our preparation, coming to naught over an onion. She removed the paper towel and we studied the cut. "It's not going to close on its own," I said.

"It'll be fine," she said.

"You won't be able to deal the cards."

"Of course I will," she said.

"Ellen, I think you need stitches."

"You don't know that!" she said harshly, then bit her lip. "I don't even like onions. Why the fuck do you insist on putting fucking onions in your spaghetti sauce?"

"It classes it up."

"Oh, my god."

We sat awhile, not saying anything, Ellen keeping pressure on the wound.

"We can put it off," I said. "You said Victor hosts this game every year?"

"No way are we waiting another year."

There was a deck of cards right there on the table. She could have picked it up and proven right then and there that she could deal the cards, except that her right hand was holding the paper towel against her left thumb. "The thumb is really important for the deal," I said. "Is there any chance you could be the shuffler?"

"I'm the better dealer," she said.

"Not at the moment. And you said it yourself—all eyes will be on the dealer."

She winced. "I don't know. Maybe. I could probably still control the cards. I won't know until I try. But can you be ready to deal in three days?"

The truth was, I had ignored Ellen's advice, given to me on the night we first met up in my apartment. I had been obsessing on the Greek deal. And while it wasn't the same as if I'd been doing it for years or even months, I probably had dealt several thousand hands in the last week and a half. Over the next three days I could deal several thousand more.

But would I be ready?

"For a prize this big," I said, "maybe it's worth being patient."

"I've *been* patient, Natalie."

"I know another year sounds long. *I* don't want to wait, either. But—"

"You don't understand," she said. "I'm thirty-eight years old. You know better than anyone what I can do, and it's still taken me *twenty years* to get a quarter-million-dollar stake together. That's pretty sad. But I can't do any better. And now I have this one shot. I don't know what's gonna happen in a year. If Victor wins the election, will he still host a poker game? I doubt it. If he loses, will he keep the game going? I can't wait around to find out. January first is my exit plan. I'm not gonna change that."

"What do you mean, 'exit plan'?"

She shifted in her seat, took a deep breath, and shook her head. "Have you ever been to the U.S. Virgin Islands?" she asked. "Saint Thomas?"

I told her I hadn't.

"It's unbelievable down there. It's paradise. Warm weather, great seafood, all those rich tourists looking to throw away their money in the casinos. But you know what they don't have?"

"What's that?"

"Enough Montessori schools."

"I don't follow."

She removed the paper towel and inspected the cut again. Shook her head. Refolded the paper towel to a clean spot and reapplied it. "With a million dollars I can start up a first-rate Montessori school." She must have seen the confusion in my face. "What, you don't like kids?"

"No, not especially."

"That's because they end up like that idiot on your doorstep with the piercings everywhere. The little ones, though, they're all right. But the school where I teach, it's a travesty. It's not just my school. It's everywhere. It's the system. The teachers' hands are tied. The principals' hands are tied. All the creativity's gone. All the excitement. It's like that everywhere."

"I still don't get it. So no more poker?"

"The players who play forever do it because they love the action. I don't. And the cheats who cheat forever do it because they don't know anything else. But I do. I'm good with kids. I don't know. Maybe I'll still play some cards. Or I'll hook up with the local casinos, teach one of those 'how not to get cheated' classes. I really don't know. All I know is, I'm done with this—done with Jersey, done with grinding out wins, done with having to rely on low-life partners. Not you, Nat. You know I don't mean you. But no Band-Aids in your home? I'm just saying."

"Let me run out . . ."

"No, forget it. The thing is, I'm tired, you know? And I've checked it out. There's plenty of interest in Montessori schools down there. And with a million dollars, I could do it. I could get myself a nice place by the water, get the school going. I could have a life."

I wondered how many American daydreams ended with an epilogue set in Caribbean waters. Maybe Ellen would pull it off. Hell, maybe I would. The way she described it, I had to wonder what I was still doing in New Jersey when I could be soaking up the sun and performing for rich vacationers. Then again, I sunburned easily.

Something occurred to me. "You said you have a quarter million dollars saved, but we need twice that. There are two of us. Two buy-ins, right?"

Her face became a frown. "I've got it covered."

"How?"

"You don't need to know how."

"I'm your partner," I said. "I'm putting myself at risk. I need to know where the money's coming from."

She glanced down at her hands. "Let's say I'll be taking a cash advance on the cardsharp's credit card."

What did that even mean? "Are you talking about a loan shark?" She didn't answer. And then an even worse thought occurred to me. What if she was overstating the amount she'd saved? What if she was borrowing all of it?

"And what if you can't pay it back?"

"I'll pay it back. I'll pay it all back on January second. We're gonna win, Natalie."

I still wasn't sure how much she'd borrowed, but I knew I was no paragon of candor. I had yet to breathe a word about knowing Victor Flowers—about having been in his house all those years back, and about what he'd done to my father. At first I hadn't told her because I was afraid she'd ditch me as her partner. Now it was too late. We were too far along. And I told myself it didn't matter anyway, especially with more important things to consider, like Ellen's still-bleeding thumb.

"Let me take you to the ER," I said. "We have to know how bad it is."

"I told you, it's not bad," she said, and winced. "I really want to get out of Jersey. So help me, I do."

"Damn," I said.

"A fucking onion," she said. "A fucking fancy-sauce onion."

Online, I found an urgent care center that was on her way home and open late. I offered to drive, but she waved me off, told me I was better off using the time to practice my Greek deal. I found some masking tape and helped her tape a fresh wad of paper towel to her thumb, and when she left I fretted, passing time with a deck in my hand. It seemed cruel for a simple slip of the knife to upend all our planning and preparation. I put the TV on and found a show where ordinary people sang their hearts out trying to become famous. When it was over I shut off the TV and kept shuffling and dealing cards.

Finally, my cell phone buzzed.

"I just got home," Ellen said. "Four stitches and a tetanus shot. Could've been worse. I'm gonna get some sleep."

"But how is it?" She knew what I wanted to know.

Silence. Then: "I don't think I can deal the cards, Nat. Not the way I have to. Any other game, I swear I would just go ahead and take the chance. But not this game, you know?"

"And what about shuffling and controlling the cards?"

"My hand is still kind of numb right now." Her voice sounded flat from exhaustion and disappointment. "I think I can probably do it." Not the reassurance I had hoped for. "I have to see how it is tomorrow. I'll let you know."

Our decision to switch roles—for her to become the shuffler and me the dealer—happened gradually, over a series of phone calls during the next two days. There was plenty of incentive. Neither of us was ready to give up on the plan.

Ellen would still get the winning hand. Instead of her dealing it to herself, I'd be dealing it to her. But I wouldn't be throwing either one of us the occasional high card to rush the two worst players, Jason and Ian, out of the game prior to our prearranged hand. Ellen had planned to speed their loss along, same as she did every day as a cardsharp: pull an ace or king from the muck to improve her odds. But she didn't trust me to improvise, and I didn't trust myself. If Jason and Ian happened to lose quickly, so much the better. If not, that was okay. Maybe they'd get caught up in the excitement and go all in anyway. Maybe they'd fold. If they folded, Ellen would bleed them after the hand was over, once Victor and Danny were out of the game. She would have almost all the chips then and was the superior player. It wouldn't be hard.

But Victor and Danny, they could really play.

We focused on what we had total control over: the cards. Ellen didn't trust her deal, because the thumb was so important in holding the deck, but she promised that her shuffling and card controlling were relatively unaffected. I chose to believe her. And as for me, I'd been working on the Greek deal anyway, but now I worked on it as if nothing else mattered. My Charlie Miller pass was coming along, too, but I decided to shelve it. My classic pass was among the best in the business. If Victor didn't complete the cut, I would simply complete it for him, and then, locating the corner that Ellen would have bent at the end of her shuffle, I'd execute the classic pass.

We talked on the phone several times a day, and every conversation ended with one of us asking, "Are you sure you're going to be ready?" We always said we were. And with each call, our assurances became more assertive, more believable, and more true. Still. My Greek deal was performance ready, but performance ready, to my mind, wasn't gambling ready. It wasn't million-dollar ready. Or maybe it was. Maybe fear was clouding my judgment. I'd never done this before, and total perfection was perhaps an unreasonable goal. In the mirror, I fooled myself more often than not. But occasionally that second-from-the-bottom card seemed to drop at a different speed. Or it made a sound, a rustle, that to my ears was different from the other cards. Slightly louder. Slightly lower in pitch. I barely left my apartment. I barely did anything but deal cards. When the cards became too worn, I unsealed a new deck. I checked and rechecked finger positions, I slowed down the deal and went through the motions again and again.

From my teenage years I knew the benefits of repetitive practice—improved technique and, yes, avoidance. You could lock yourself in a room, shut everything and everyone out, and call it useful. But what I did in these last days of December was of a whole other magnitude. When I remembered to, I ate. When I remembered to, I slept. I always thought I knew what it meant to woodshed, but I was only learning it now. And yes, I was aware of the irony—how I was becoming the best magician I had ever been just as I had ceased to be one.

And on the afternoon of December 31, though I hesitated to put down the deck, I nevertheless drove to Edison, to Hār Salon, a business I'd driven past many times but never entered, where a chatty young woman named Celeste chopped off most of my hair—my hār—and bleached what remained.

New Jersey was a little more than an hour into the new year. Still punctuating the transition were random bottle rockets and M-80s and whatever other minor explosives teenage boys and former teenage boys preferred to ignite on their porches and in the street. *Pop. Pop-pop-pop.* Then quiet. Then more pops. The irregular rhythm sounded like gunfire, a minor massacre.

When the quiet returned and stuck around awhile, I knew I ought to sleep, but sleep felt as remote as another galaxy, so I slung a coat over my pajamas and left the apartment. For the first time ever, I wished I had a dog to walk.

The lights of most of the apartments across the way were off. The storefronts up and down the street were closed. There were no stars overhead and the air smelled of smoke. The cold felt good on my face. As I stood on the silent street a few flurries fell. It almost felt like winter. It almost felt like someplace else. Then the flurries stopped, and I returned to my apartment and removed my coat. I sat on the loveseat and picked up the deck of cards from the coffee table.

My parents loved your music, I said as I dealt. *They owned both your albums.*

Card, card, card, card.

My father worked for you.

Card, card, card, card.

But when he wouldn't break the law, you broke his ribs and then you broke him.

Card, card, card, card.

You broke my family.

Card, card, card, card.

The outer doorknob rattled, and I heard Harley enter the building. She shut the door louder than usual, humming a tune. She trudged up the stairs, and when she entered her apartment she said, "Jasmine, baby!" She laughed and said, "It's okay, baby." The two of them descended the stairs and went outside. I would never sleep. A glass of wine would help. I made myself drink water instead. Harley and her dog returned and went upstairs again. My phone said it was 1:38 a.m.

I turned on the TV, turned it off again.

I tolerated my own company for another ten minutes. Then I left my apartment and climbed the stairs. Knocked quietly on the door. I waited a minute and knocked a little louder, and the dog, Jasmine, came clicking across the floor toward the door followed by human footsteps. Harley opened the door.

"Natalie!" she said, stepping backward.

"I know. My hair's awful."

"No! It's cute. It's just a big change. But ring in the new year, right?" She was wearing sweatpants and a yellow T-shirt. She yawned. "I'm a little drunk."

In the year she'd lived upstairs I'd never seen the inside of Harley's place. "So could I come in for a minute?" I asked.

"Sure," she said. "Come in. Grab a seat."

It was hard to believe her apartment had the same bones as mine. Her living room looked like somewhere you'd willingly spend time. Soft lighting and a sofa that looked comfortable and modern, and throw pillows, and so much artwork on the walls, all that color.

Harley went over to the sofa. Jasmine jumped up and pressed her body against Harley's. There was a small patch on the dog's back where the fur was missing. "She's a little freaked out. I think because of the fireworks," Harley said. "Do you want a glass of wine? None for me—whoa!—I've had enough. Don't ever party with veterinarians. That's all I'm saying."

I faked a smile and sat on one of the cushioned chairs opposite the sofa. "No," I said. "Nothing, thanks." The wall to my left was covered in photographs—posed shots, candids, Harley and others on the beach, in the mountains, people in medical scrubs, people in dresses and suits . . . the scenes of her life, the people in her orbit, now and in the past.

"Is everything okay?" she asked.

We had each other's phone numbers. The week she moved in, she gave me a spare key for emergencies. I gave her mine. Then she asked me for my number and entered it into her contacts as if it were the most natural thing in the world. I'd done it, too, as if we would become fast pals, the gal upstairs and the gal downstairs, like in a sitcom from my childhood. Now a whole year had passed. I wondered why I'd done nothing to become her friend. Why I'd done nothing to become anyone's.

"I'm supposed to do something tomorrow," I said. "But I can't do it. I'm not ready."

"Do you mean a magic show?"

I didn't know if I was choosing her because I thought she was trustworthy, or because she had patched up my hurt leg with gentle hands, or because she was my neighbor and there was no one else. A lifelong allegiance to keeping secrets can take its toll. Do it long enough, and there's no one left to tell.

"Kind of," I said. She watched me, confused. "So I don't know you very well. That's my fault. But can you keep a secret?"

"Sure. Okay, Natalie. What is it?"

"That's a nice dog, isn't it?"

"Jasmine? She's the best."

"Do you think they're all the best?"

She smiled. "Yeah. Pretty much."

"This thing I have to do tomorrow. I want to do it, you know? But it's not an honest thing."

"And that's bothering you."

"No. Actually, it isn't. Maybe it should. But I want it. I want to do it. But I'm not good enough."

"Oh," she said, furrowing her brow.

I didn't mean the Greek deal, which was getting better all the time and might fool anyone even if it didn't always fool me. I meant the entirety of it: facing Victor Flowers and those other men, playing the role assigned to me, keeping my performance going all night long until the money was ours and we were safe. Ellen refused to admit that anything could go wrong. I lacked her confidence. Everything could go wrong. And if it did, what would I do? I'd assured Ellen I was all in, but was I? Would I crumble? Would I cry? Would I spill everything to save my own skin? I hoped not, but I didn't know. It was easy to keep a secret when the stakes of keeping it were nil. That was the thing: twenty-seven, and I still didn't know myself well enough to answer the most basic questions about honesty and loyalty and survival. If everything went right, I would walk out of Victor Flowers's house in less than twenty-four hours with two hundred thousand dollars and the knowledge that I had bested him. But if everything went wrong? I was afraid of what I might learn about myself.

"Is there anything I can do?" Harley asked, which seemed like a polite and perfunctory question, until I realized that, actually, yes, there was something she could do—that maybe this thing she could do for me was what had been itching the corners of my brain and driven me upstairs.

"My birds," I said. "If for some reason something . . . happens to me, would you take them?"

"What do you mean? What could happen to you?"

"Nothing. I'm just being—" I shook my head. "It doesn't matter. But I'd feel better knowing you'd take them. They're really easy. They're good birds."

Harley tilted her head, as if trying to see me from a different angle, and the motion reminded me of what the doves themselves often did. "Of course I will," she said, straightening her head again. "Listen, Natalie, I know it's not my business, but do you want to tell me what's going on?"

I almost did. The late hour, the intimacy of someone else's apartment, the fact that earlier I had sat and watched the ball drop over Times Square on TV, one more year of observing the thriving horde from my lonely sofa—it all made me want to reveal myself to her. But where would I start? I couldn't tell her about Ace, and meeting Ellen, and the poker game, and how what began as the prospect of a magazine article had become something else. I couldn't tell her about the Greek deal or the money Ellen and I planned to take. Whatever I said would require more, and then more still, filling in the gaps about who and why. But tomorrow the sun would rise, and I didn't want Harley—who was not my friend, because I had never taken the time to become hers—I didn't want her carrying around my burden. She had agreed to take my birds, and I was grateful.

"Thank you," I said, glancing away so she wouldn't see my eyes suddenly welling up.

"You don't have to thank me," she said. "They're animals. I take care of them. It's what I do."

"I think I'm going to go to bed," I said. I thanked her again and left her apartment for my own, which felt all the more stark. I returned to the loveseat and picked up a fresh pack of cards. The last one. I pierced the plastic wrapping with my fingernail and removed it, opened the top flap, and slid out the deck. If the magician was a good magician, the false deal was a near-silent, frictionless glide of card against card. A distant ice skater making wide circles over a frozen pond. A bird lifting itself into the sky. Card handling was softness, lightness. Without that, there was nothing.

I hoped I hadn't told Harley too much.

I looked up at the poster of Cardini. I watched him watching me. *Easy for you*, I thought, suddenly angry at the long-dead magician. *Your wife was your fucking assistant. You could tell her anything.*

The way to handle nerves was extreme preparation. My Greek deal wasn't quite there yet, not up to my standards, but I was getting closer all the time, and morning was still several hours away, and I was stone sober and a fast study and the owner of two remarkably capable hands.

I went to bed as dawn approached and tossed long enough for sleep to feel like a hopeless goal—though I must have slept because I dreamed of the house in Plainfield and awoke to the fading echoes of my father at the piano banging out a beer-induced, over-the-top version of "Band of Gold."

Ellen wasn't arriving until six that night. That left the whole day. Outside, it was gray and ordinary, with no indication that a new year had replaced the old one. I settled into routine activities: I cleaned the house, picked up a few groceries at the mini-mart. I practiced the Greek deal. I repeated the name I would be using until it sounded natural. *Hi, I'm Nora Thompson. I'm Nora Thompson. It's nice to meet you, Victor. I'm Nora Thompson.* And I repeated Ellen's, as well: *Emily Ross.* I practiced the Greek deal some more. I walked myself, step by step, through the evening, picturing the game table, where to sit, what to say and do.

Ellen arrived at my house precisely at six. It had been snowing lightly for the past hour. The forecast kept changing. Now they were saying we might get a few inches. But, crucially, Ellen had called me on the drive over and assured me that the game was on.

Her eyes widened, taking me in. "Wow, love the pixie cut."

"All in, right?" I said.

She smiled and came into the house. "I'd say you look exactly like a Nora Thompson."

Ellen's light brown hair had a stylish wave to it, and she had traded her trench coat for a denim coat bordered with faux fur the same color as her hair. It was unbuttoned, and underneath she had on a black turtleneck. She wore flowy batik print pants, and no jewelry, and little enough makeup and lipstick that most men would assume she wasn't wearing any. She truly was the embodiment of Emily Ross, hippie millionaire and rebellious heiress.

I had dressed in a classy but casual outfit of royal blue top, dark blue jeans, and tall black boots.

"Please," Ellen said, handing me a small canvas bag with palm trees on it, "don't lose this."

I unzipped the bag. Inside were two rubber-banded stacks of hundred-dollar bills and a third, smaller stack.

"My own bag is in the car," she said. "Not that I don't trust your neighborhood, but how about we get going?"

"What exactly are you implying about my neighborhood?" But I couldn't pull off the casual humor. My whole body was shaking. "I'll be right back," I said, and went to the bedroom for my purse and a last glimpse in the full-length mirror. I stuffed the stacks of bills into my purse and we left the apartment together.

The sun had already gone down, but the streets were lighter than usual because of the snow, which fell softly, no need for windshield wipers, and made even the ugly storefronts look like a painting. On the parkway, closer to the shore, the snow became a heavier sleet. As Ellen drove we both tried to stay calm, stay cool. We talked a bit, running through the plan we already knew so well. I listened to the rhythmic whip-whip of the windshield wipers. And then, so fast, we were exiting the parkway and getting closer to those rising, winding Highlands roads.

Ellen slowed the car and went just past Victor Flowers's driveway, where several other cars were already parked, stopping at the curb in front of his home, which, as it had all those years earlier, stood curtained behind a row of high hedges. She left the engine on, and together we sat in the dark, listening to the car's low idle and the irregular drumming of sleet against the windshield.

The dashboard clock said 8:22.

"Are we really going to wait another three minutes?" I asked, just as the clock changed to 8:23.

"Two more," she said.

I wanted to be calm and confident, but already I felt fear's insidious creep. It was the preshow jitters I hadn't felt in years, only magnified. Ellen placed her hand on my arm and said, "I'm gonna stack the cards, Victor's gonna cut the deck, and you're gonna reverse the cut and deal the cards. That's all there is to it. Easy peasy."

"Maybe."

"Not maybe. Definitely."

"Not definitely."

"Natalie, it's gonna work. We planned it right, and we practiced it. We're ready. Remember, cheating at cards is what I do."

"Not like this. Not for this kind of money."

"It's just another performance," she said, though I detected a slight hitch in her voice. "It's going to be fine," she said. "We're going to win all the money."

I tried to visualize the money, what it would be like to have it. "When this is over," I said, "I'm going to buy one expensive bottle of wine. We'll drink it together."

She smiled. "I love the thought. But when this is over, you and I will part ways and never cross paths again."

Maybe this shouldn't have come as a surprise. Still, I found myself resisting a twinge of betrayal.

"In twenty years," she said, "maybe we'll trade brief, nostalgic emails. I like you. I really do. This has all been . . . I don't know." She paused, finding the right word. "Nice." She shook her head. "You know what I mean. We can't be seen together after this."

I knew she was right. She and I were, in the end, partners in a risky endeavor, and while our business was about to conclude, the risk would last. No, we could not be seen together after this.

"The money's too big for it to be any other way," she said.

"Sure," I said. "I totally get it."

"Just focus on the cards and we've got this. Natalie?"

I was no longer in the passenger seat of Ellen's car. I was at my father's graveside on a hot August afternoon. The casket was being lowered into a hole. Winning tonight wouldn't get my father out of that hole. Everything could go exactly as planned, and my father would never know I'd gotten the better of Victor Flowers.

Victor would never know, either. I would have to live with that.

"Nat?"

"What?"

"Have faith in us."

She shut off the engine, and together we stepped out into the sleet. Sharing a single umbrella, we rounded the hedges and walked past several snow-ready vehicles parked in the driveway— two Mercedes SUVs, a Ford Bronco, a Jeep Wrangler—up to the path that led to Victor Flowers's front door.

The last time I had come here was a warm May afternoon with everybody in spring clothes, with music and sunshine. It took me a moment to square that image with the cold stone structure before me now, dim under the outdoor lights, the sleet striking the slate roof and the saturated, brown grass and the naked, skeletal trees. I shivered.

"Are you ready?" Ellen asked softly.

I nodded. "Yeah."

She gave my arm a gentle squeeze. "You're gonna do this, Natalie. You're a pro. You're the greatest card handler I ever saw. I'm lucky to be working with you."

I'll admit to loving Ellen in that moment in the dreary dark. She was a cheat through and through, everything Jack Clarion detested, yet she had made me work harder than anyone else ever had, including Jack. Just a few weeks earlier, I'd believed I was one of the best, but now I knew I hadn't been. I had needed Ellen. I had needed her fiercely honest assessment of who I was and what I was capable of becoming. Ellen was many things, but a flatterer wasn't one of them, and a compliment from her—here, now—meant more to me than if it had come from Cardini himself.

"Thanks, Emily," I said.

"You're welcome, Nora."

We walked up the path to the front door. With the eaves keeping us dry, Ellen closed the umbrella, took a deep breath, let it out, and rang the bell.

PART THREE

PART THREE

A

The man who opened the door must have been close to seventy. He looked not so different, though, from the person who'd been time-capsuled in my mind all these years—same razor-fine part of his now gray hair, same crystal blue eyes, same smile that said, *Relax—I've got it from here.* My memory failed to take note of his stature. Victor Flowers stood no more than five and a half feet tall. Towering over him, however, I didn't feel like a tower. I didn't feel powerful.

I felt like Big Bird.

But I had Ellen by my side, the arm of her coat grazing the arm of mine. She was stunning—unrecognizable as the frumpy and frenzied woman I'd met and quickly dismissed in Ethan Garret's bakery.

"I was starting to worry," Victor said.

Ellen's smile under the porch light was nothing I'd seen from her before, a dazzling blend of mild flirtation and major confidence. "Well, if it isn't the distinguished gentleman from New Jersey." Her voice, too, was alien to me—melodic, a few pitches deeper, a speck of gravel. She stepped into the house and pecked Victor on the cheek. "I would have thought a man like you could at least order up a drier evening."

I followed her into the house, into the heat.

Victor took Ellen's umbrella and placed it into an umbrella stand by the door. "I would have felt terrible if anything had happened." He turned to me. "I don't believe we've had the pleasure of meeting. I'm Victor."

I held out my hand. "I'm Nora Thompson," I said. We had met only that one time, at his Memorial Day party nearly two decades earlier. Now I was a grown woman. I had cut and colored my hair and doused my face with foundation, blush, cover-up, mascara. Even I didn't recognize me. Still, for a moment I felt certain he'd see through all that and know it was Dan Webb's daughter returning after all these years to steal his money.

"Emily speaks highly of you," he said, taking our coats and hanging them in a closet. "She says you're quite the player."

I thanked him, though I knew he was lying. When she had called up Victor to ask his permission for me to join their game this month, she hadn't said *quite the player*. She'd said *good, but not exceptional.*

"So you're an event planner?" he asked.

Ellen had also passed along the biography we'd made up: that I worked as an event planner, and that my family owned several hotels.

"I am."

"Then I hope you won't judge my hospitality too harshly—though at least the bar is fully stocked."

I could feel the tickle in my throat I got when I was nervous, but I made myself smile and say, "A fully stocked bar is pretty much the secret to event planning."

I was doing okay, even if my voice quavered a little. And why shouldn't it? This was a high-dollar game. The men were probably banking on these nerves of mine to make me a worse player tonight: less aggressive, or maybe more aggressive. They believed I was out of my element and my league.

"The other apes are in the kitchen," Victor said. "We'll collect them on the way to the game room."

I could fit at least five of my kitchens into this one. I had observed over the years that people with all the cabinet space in the world preferred to display their pots and pans and cutlery and appliances in plain view. A restaurant's worth of cookware sat on the counters and hung over Victor Flowers's large kitchen island, everything immaculate, the stainless steel on the pans so shiny I could have used any of them to pluck my eyebrows.

Three men stood by the island holding drinks. From our preparation, I knew each of them before being introduced. Danny Squire, car dealership mogul, with biceps big enough to stretch the sleeves of his black golf shirt; Ian McDonald, hedge fund manager, with the cowboy boots, razor stubble, and carefully messy hair; Jason Panella, thin and fit, surfer hair, closer to my age. I even knew Jason's drink: vodka tonic with a slice of lemon floating on top. Irrelevant, but Ellen had noticed. She noticed everything.

Victor introduced me to the men, and I endured handshakes that left my wrist sore. Ellen shook hands, touched arms, made references I didn't understand. They all seemed glad to see her. In the last year she had become a fully embedded member of their poker game, another Midnight Rider galloping home by midnight. Every month they got together, and every month Ellen sat at the poker table and cheated them, these staggeringly wealthy, competitive men, these winners in life, these ignorant, naive puppies.

Victor offered us drinks. Somewhere in this house, I felt sure, was the best Scotch I'd ever tasted. I longed for it to settle my nerves. Or a generous pour of wine. But I had agreed to nurse a single drink and no more. Ellen wasn't a fool. She saw I drank too much. I felt so revved and jittery, though, that I decided not to trust myself with even the one drink. I would drain it too fast and ask for more.

"Just a Coke, please," I said, "if you have it."

Ellen shot me a look.

"Keeping your wits about you," Jason said, and winked. "Smart!" To the room he said, "We'll have to keep an eye on the new one."

I smiled stupidly and clenched my teeth, furious at myself for going off script and vowing not to do it again.

Victor opened his refrigerator and dug around, coming out with a can. "Let me get you a glass," he said. I accepted the glass of soda over ice with hands that shook a little, and Victor led us all out of the kitchen and into a dining room whose walls displayed a number of large, vibrant paintings.

"I still say that's one ugly dog," Ellen said, touching Victor's arm. It was a marvel, her confidence, or her display of confidence.

"To be honest," Victor said, "the whole blue dog thing is starting to feel faddish to me." He nodded to the painting beside it. "Now *here's* one worth noting. You wouldn't normally think of Babcock as representational, but this is a very early work."

The paintings were all saturated in color. Who cared? This was suddenly real. I had prepared, but preparation and performance were never the same. The ice cubes in my glass were rattling. I had to calm down fast. We left the other side of the dining room and were back in the center of the house, near the front door and main foyer. Seeing the wide stairway on our left that rose and turned, leading to an upstairs hallway, I forced myself to say, with as much cheer as I could muster, "Looks like the British are coming."

On the wall above the staircase hung a tall painting of a frantic man riding an equally frantic horse through a narrow, dusty street. One of Paul Revere's hands clutched the reins; his other was keeping his hat from blowing off.

"I've always liked that one," Victor said, "even if it never happened that way."

"How do you mean?" I could do this. I could hold a conversation. And this was my job right now. To be interested in whatever Victor had to say. To make him enjoy talking to me, and then to make him want to sit beside me at the poker table.

"Paul Revere's mission depended on secrecy," Victor explained. "So it made no sense to shout, 'The British are coming' or anything else. That's just a legend. It's interesting, actually."

It wasn't interesting. I wiped my sweaty hands on my jeans and ran through the chain of events that needed to go perfectly: the seating arrangements, the game play and chip management. I needed to play tight and stay in the game long enough for Ellen's signal. Then came the stacking of cards followed by the Greek deal that would give Ellen the winning hand.

While everyone stood around with drinks listening to our host, I watched the men. They didn't seem so different from the men I performed for at corporate gigs. Yet each was ponying up a quarter million dollars for a few hours of entertainment. Each was confident enough to believe he could walk away the winner, and rich enough not to be deterred by the risk. Their money made them different, but what accounted for their money? Brilliance? Luck? Jason had been born into the right family: the ultimate luck. According to Ellen, he was a poor poker player. All this made me feel better about taking his money.

Ian and Danny didn't deserve to get taken, maybe, though they wouldn't miss their stakes. There was plenty more.

Everyone was still courteously listening to Victor's history lecture. "Take a guess how Paul Revere actually signaled the British advance?" he asked me. And to the other men, who'd clearly been through this lecture before, he added, "Don't give it away."

Jason glanced at me and fake-whispered: "He texted everyone."

"I'll give you a clue," Victor said. "Revere was a silversmith and engraver. No?" He smiled. "He made bells out of silver. Little ones, for himself and his fellow patriots William Dawes and Joseph Warren. The three of them rode on their horses and rang the bells to let people know about the British."

I was shifting my weight from foot to foot and trying to keep the ice from clinking in my glass when I glanced up at Ellen, who was staring at me, eyes wide. Right. Feign interest.

"Wow!" I said, a little too enthusiastically. Paul Revere's bell, Moses's staff, Santa Claus's beard. Who the hell cared? "So where are the bells now?" I asked, and with a wistful sigh Victor explained that none had survived the Revolutionary War: melted down, crumbled apart, lost in the Charles River. Suddenly, he brightened. "I recently acquired a Confederate army war drum from Texas. Come—let me show you."

I was desperate for the game to start—I needed the feeling of cards in my hands—but I followed the group into a room that smacked me with the hard force of memory. There was the black grand piano, there the trumpet on the wall, there the saxophone. After nineteen years, the instruments had multiplied. And I noticed printed cards mounted beside the instruments, explaining their origins. The saxophone had belonged to Julian "Cannonball" Adderley and had been used in the studio for Miles Davis's *Kind of Blue* album; the clarinet had belonged to Skip

Martin, who'd played in the Glenn Miller Orchestra. Each instrument had a story to go with it.

"This is what I want my own legacy to be, Nora," he told me. "I want to play a small part in American history." I realized that each person in the room must have been subjected—once, or quite likely many times—to Victor Flowers's musical tour through history.

"You want to be a part of history," Danny said, "then you gotta run attack ads. I'm telling you, Vic—"

"Yeah, yeah," Victor said.

"Yeah, nothing. It works."

"We all know it works," Victor said. "That isn't the point. I'm running a positive campaign."

"Then I'm *positive* you're gonna lose," Danny said, and laughed.

I was looking at the guitar on the wall. I remembered it from all those years ago, except that now I could decipher the sloppy signature on the instrument: Elvis Presley. The card said this was one of the guitars Elvis played during his final tour in 1977.

The army drum sat on a wooden stand in a corner of the room. It was painted red with the initials C.S.A. in gold and surrounded by painted gold fronds.

"What's the story here?" I asked.

Victor bent over the drum and tapped out a shave-and-a-haircut rhythm with his fingers. "The seller claims it belonged to the man who wrote 'Shiloh's Hill' and a number of other Civil War songs. My appraiser isn't so sure. The age checks out, though: mid–eighteen hundreds."

"You ever sing anymore, Vic?" Jason asked.

"Nah," said Victor. "Who has the time? And my pipes aren't what they were. Anyway, I'd rather keep taking your money."

217

This got a laugh out of Ian and a grunt out of Danny. "Come on"—he clapped twice—"let's play poker."

We walked down a hallway to the end of the house. Victor reached into his pocket and removed a key, which he used to open the door. He must have seen my expression. "Not even the housecleaners go into the cave without me," he explained. "Some of the wine in here, the liquor—it's obscene."

Entering the game room gave me a profound sense of déjà vu. Unlike with the music room and kitchen, I had never set foot in here, but I knew every inch of it. Ellen had mapped it out for me, and for the last two weeks this room had taken center stage in my mind. I could close my eyes and see the poker players at the table, hear their chatter, look over at the enormous video screen across the room that was tuned softly to whatever football or hockey or basketball game the men had settled on; I could watch the rise and glow of the silent flame in the gas fireplace along the wall opposite the windows, where the blinds would be shut for the evening.

Ellen hadn't mentioned the exposed wooden beams overhead or the soft carpet underfoot, but she had sketched out the wet bar along the wall before the row of windows. And just as she'd said— as she'd promised—our delayed arrival at Victor's home and subsequent tour of the house had taken long enough for the men to finish their drinks. While they went to the bar to replenish, I noted other aspects of the room: the chandelier with curved metal and black glass beads lighting up the poker table, which was made of gorgeous wood and brown velvet. The room seemed much more traditional than the rest of the house; I half expected an oil painting of hunting dogs running through a forest, but the artwork was all coastal—enlarged photographs of seagulls, terns, sanderlings. Above the fireplace was a picture of a blue heron, a nice touch even if herons knew better than to hang out in Jersey.

Victor approached me holding his refilled glass of whiskey. Softly, he said, "You sure you don't want a real drink? We've got stuff *above* top shelf here. I actually had to build a special shelf." He laughed at his own joke.

I told him I was sure.

"And you feel ready for . . . this?"

On the poker table, the chips were already divided and placed in front of each of the six positions. Also on the table were two decks of cards in their seals.

"Of course I'm ready," I said, forcing a smile. "Why do you ask?"

"I know you've come all this way in the weather, but I wonder if maybe you shouldn't play."

I frowned. "I don't understand."

"I just mean it's a lot of money."

"I know it is. That's why I'm here."

"No. I mean it's a *lot* of money. A quarter million dollars . . ."

"I know how much it is."

He nodded. "I have a beautiful home, don't I?"

I agreed that he did.

"The video screen, 4K projector, the Bose speakers and sound-proofing and seating . . . it's all top of the line. That's a fifty-thousand-dollar home theater. And this?" He rapped his knuckles on the game tabletop. "Nineteen thirty-five, genuine Cuban mahogany. You wouldn't believe me if I told you what it cost." He sighed. "I didn't always have all this." He gazed around the room, as if skeptical of what he'd just told me. "For a long time I had very little. My point being, I know how hard it is to accumulate—"

"Victor?"

"I'm not saying you aren't a good poker player. Emily says you're good, and I'm sure she's right. But you should protect your assets. You don't have to play tonight."

"Victor—"

"Please. Hear me out. It's never good to get in over your head. That's when you make poor decisions."

"Victor?" Finally, he stopped talking. "I'm starting to think your concern for me is an attempt to psych me out."

He examined me the way he'd probably examined that Civil War drum before deciding to call the deal final. "All right, Nora. Good luck. I hope everything goes well for you tonight."

"No, you don't," I said. "You hope I lose all my money." I let him watch me a moment, perhaps surprised by what I'd said. But I wasn't being rude, only blunt, and maybe a little flirtatious if he chose to think of this as banter. I reached out and touched his hand. "I'm sorry. I shouldn't have said that. Here." I patted the tabletop to my right. "Sit next to me."

He placed his drink in the recessed holder in the table. Immediately, Ellen appeared beside us and placed her own glass in the spot to Victor's right.

"We have him surrounded!" She laughed, and winked at me as if we were pretending to be in cahoots.

Ellen wouldn't begin to stack the deck for at least an hour. We wanted everyone to loosen up a little first—to become less attentive, more inebriated, and readier for the excitement of a big hand. That meant doing whatever we could to reduce any drama in the game before then. We would try to keep the wins and losses small. We would play tight poker. We would be careful.

The other men placed their drinks on the table, found seats, touched their poker chips. On the large video screen across the room, the Fiesta Bowl was on, the sound turned down. The men glanced at the game and made grunts of interest, and Jason explained that UCF wasn't supposed to be ahead. We all drew cards from the deck. Victor's was a jack, higher than anyone else's. He'd deal first.

As we began to play, I made a point to call small bets and fold prudently but not fearfully. I played my best poker. While we played the hands, chatter was sparse and perfunctory.

Been a solid winter without the snow. The BMW Seven Series is a hell of a car.

Heard you on the radio, Vic. Sounded real good.

I gotta get a new lawn guy.

How close, really, are we to self-driving cars we can buy?

I found myself tuning out the music and the chatter and focusing on my cards, on betting or not betting, on deducing what the other players might have in their hands. Gradually my heartbeat found its natural rhythm. Cards in my hands, cards in my thoughts. The cards brought me back to myself. But I knew that before long Ellen would need to make her move. Jason was already way down, just as Ellen had predicted. Danny was close to even. On the table were two decks of cards—blue-backed and red-backed, one to get shuffled while the other got dealt—and from the time Ellen first started controlling cards and palming them off to the time I dealt the fully prepared deck, there would be a minimum of eight hands played. That would take a while. We couldn't wait too long.

Whenever it was Ellen's turn to gather the played cards and shuffle the deck, I would glance at her in my periphery. It was after almost exactly an hour of play when she finally clasped her hands together and set them on the tabletop in front of her, an attentive pupil in school. That was our signal. When the hand ended, she gathered up the cards to shuffle.

And with so little fanfare, it began.

2

♦

We had another signal. There was no predicting exactly how many cards Ellen would be able to locate, control, and palm off the top of the deck during a single shuffle. She had to locate a total of nine cards: three jacks, three queens, and three additional hearts. We hoped she could find five of them during her first shuffle. Five would leave four more the next time the deck came around for her shuffle. But even if her injured thumb and Band-Aid didn't much hinder her card handling, several factors were beyond her control. If any of the cards happened to have been played during the prior hand, then Ellen would have an easier time locating them. If none got played, her job was harder. There was no predicting.

Our method was this: after Ellen was done shuffling and palming off as many cards as she could, she would set the deck down on the tabletop and lay one of her hands at the table's edge with the number of palmed cards indicated by the number of fingers pointing outward. Ideally, four. Three was less than optimal. Two would be deeply unfortunate: we'd almost certainly have to go through three entire rounds of Ellen palming cards. Not a total disaster, but the thought made us very uneasy.

It was Victor's deal, and while he began to lay out everyone's hole cards I forced my eyes away from Ellen while she shuffled the blue-backed deck. Eyes anyplace else. Create a small distraction, I told myself, and asked Danny where I could get a busted car window repaired.

He stared at me as if I'd just belched. "Try a windshield repair shop."

Victor finished dealing the hole cards and set the deck down.

"But does it have to be the dealer?" I asked. "Or can it be any repair shop?"

"I don't—it doesn't matter." Danny was playing with the chips in front of him, making his organized stacks more organized. "Just a place that does windshields."

My hole cards were terrible and I folded quickly. While the others continued betting, I watched the TV while keeping Ellen in my periphery. Her shuffle seemed to go on awhile. That was probably only because I was bothering to notice. Victor burned a card, and just after he laid the flop on the table, Ellen set down the shuffled blue deck. I casually glanced over, hoping to see four fingers. Dreading seeing only two. She adjusted herself in her chair, most likely moving her thigh on top of the palmed cards, and leaned forward.

Her entire left hand lay flat on the table.

I looked away, my heart lurching.

Five. She had stolen five cards from the deck.

She was so much better than I was.

Now I had to keep myself calm for an agonizing six more hands of poker before the blue deck would make its way back to Ellen to shuffle and—I prayed—position all the cards for my Greek deal.

I tried to play good poker, but the blinds were increasing and my palms were sweaty and I lost a couple of hands. By 10:15, when Ellen claimed the blue deck and began to shuffle once more, I was down fifty thousand. Ellen was up close to a hundred thousand. Whether that was from honest play or opportunistic cheating I had no idea. I made a point not to watch her when she had the deal. Ian was down a little, and Jason was down more than a quarter of his chips. Danny was about even when he made an aggressive move and lost what to my mind was an astonishing amount, fifty-two thousand dollars, to Ian on a hand he had no business being in. I wouldn't even call it a bluff. It was more as if Danny was foolishly trying to force his will onto the cards. When the hand was over and Danny had lost, he balled up his fists and I could see the tension in his forearms. He cracked his neck, stood up, and went to replenish his drink. Ian followed. When the game resumed, all the men were showing signs of becoming antsy— shifting in their seats, tapping on the table, checking the TV, where UCF was still beating Baylor. They were ready for something even if they didn't know what.

Victor dealt the red deck, and we began to play the hand while Ellen shuffled the blue deck. When she was done she set the deck down. She rested her hand on the table and softly scratched the tabletop with her fingertips. Our last signal. All the cards were now in position. She had done it.

She had found the last of the cards and returned to the deck the five she had taken six hands earlier. Without anyone noticing, the blue deck had just grown again to fifty-two cards. The evidence— our greatest risk—had just melted away. It was an incredible moment, a milestone I celebrated by not reacting at all.

The deck now sat in front of Victor. Though I couldn't see it, the bottom card was crimped, and the next cards were all in position. As soon as the current hand was over, Victor would cut the blue deck and I would execute the classic pass. Then I would deal the cards. My heart began to race faster, and I told myself to be calm, be still, but these were commands that my body would not obey. I had never been this nervous during a performance. I had never been this nervous.

I was banking on having a little longer to control my breathing and ready myself, but the hand went fast: Danny raised, Jason called, Danny raised some more on the flop, and everybody folded.

"Well, that was easy," Danny said, collecting the small pile of chips, and it was over.

I rubbed my hands on the thighs of my jeans to dry them off. Victor reached out for the blue deck, lifted half of it, and placed the top half on the table beside the bottom half. Two equal piles. Then he began to gather up the cards from the previously played hand so he could shuffle the red deck.

It was my turn. Complete the cut, do the pass, deal the cards. Quickly. Now. Don't think. Do not think. Do not.

It happened so fast.

One second I was completing the cut, and the next, it seemed, Victor was saying the words. He didn't sound menacing or angry. He sounded almost weary, as if he didn't want to be saying anything but had no choice. But he was saying it. He said it.

He said: "Wait."

Everybody's hole cards were dealt. I had just placed the remainder of the deck on the table in front of me.

"Hold it a second." He was staring at me.

I stared back. "What?"

He hesitated a moment. Then: "I saw something."

I fought the urge to glance over at Ellen.

225

"What are you talking about?" Danny said.

"I don't know," Victor said. "Something about the way she dealt the cards to herself. I can't"—he shook his head—"I'm just . . . I don't know."

"Speak English," Danny said.

"Something was different about it."

"You sure, Vic?" Jason said. "You were shuffling the other deck."

"Yeah, but still," Victor said. "I think I saw something."

"Did anyone else see it?" Danny asked, looking around the table.

"Ian?" Victor said.

"I wasn't really watching. I'm just not—"

"Hey!" I snapped, shutting Ian up. It was almost a bark, the result of a monumental effort to push sound from my throat. I'd been paralyzed for a few seconds, struck stupid and mute, until I finally produced from my befuddled brain the knowledge of what was happening, and what I was supposed to do about it.

Deny vehemently.

I struggled to transform my terror into something more useful, like anger, like deep offense. I looked right at Victor. "Exactly what the hell are you getting at?"

But Danny spoke next. "Did you just try to cheat?" His own struggle sounded like the opposite of mine. He was working to control his rage.

"This is so stupid," I said. "I didn't do anything."

"Guys," Ellen began, but Victor ignored her.

"I think you might have," he said, his voice remaining measured. "I think you were dealing from the bottom or something."

"That's total bullshit," I said. "You're being ridiculous and paranoid." I laid it on thick. I dared him to keep it up, knowing it

226

would lead nowhere because there was nowhere for it to lead. You deny vehemently, and then you stop cheating. The end. There was no evidence other than in the accuser's memory, and memory was a sieve that trapped nothing reliably, and everyone knew it. What had he seen? He thought he knew, maybe, but he didn't know, and he would become less certain with every one of my denials. That was how it went. There was no evidence. We hadn't used a cold deck. Ellen had already put the palmed cards back into the pack. No evidence. Not a shred.

"Well, was she or wasn't she?" Danny asked.

"I just told you I wasn't," I said.

Victor kept his gaze on me. "I think you're lying," he said.

"Then I think you're an idiot." I made myself keep up the terrible attitude. The sense of outrage. I made myself act as belligerent and sarcastic and nasty as I knew how. "So aren't we in a bind?"

He watched me a moment longer, then shook his head and said, softly, almost apologetically, "No. Not really." He stood up and, without a word, reached up to the black beads draped around the chandelier and tapped one of them. "There's one," he said.

The camera was so small that even if I'd had a reason to peer straight into the chandelier's wattage I never would have seen it.

Hidden in the patterned picture frame that held one of the gull paintings was a second camera. The third camera was mounted just under the lip of the bar.

"Do you always use those, Vic?" Jason asked.

"No," Victor said. "And I hope no one's offended. But there's a lot of money at stake tonight, and a new player I never met before. I thought it might be prudent."

"I'd say it's fucking prudent," Danny said. "Let's watch it. Let's watch this bitch trying to cheat us."

227

"Wait." I hated the weakness in my own voice, but I couldn't catch my breath, was having trouble processing what was happening. Only a minute ago I was dealing the cards. Now everything was moving too fast. "This is all . . . Let's just play the game."

"You need to play the game called shut the fuck up," Danny said. "Victor, how good are those cameras?"

I knew the answer without needing to be told. Everything would be top of the line. Those cameras would catch every pore on my hands.

"I don't feel good," I said, which was the absolute truth. "I'm gonna go. I'm gonna go now." The door was fifteen feet away. Beyond that was a hallway and another door and then the outside world. I went to stand.

Victor hadn't raised his voice. He still didn't, even as he reached out and gently held on to my arm to stop me from going anywhere. "You'll wait and watch the video with us. And Jason? Go find Russell for me. Ask him to come in here."

Russell?

Jason got up from the table and left the room, shutting the door behind him.

"What are we gonna do?" Ian asked. "This is crazy."

"We're gonna see," Victor said.

"Yeah, but then what?"

"First we see," Victor said. He had removed his hand, but I knew to stay where I was. When the door opened again a minute later, Jason was accompanied by another man. Seeing him, I was glad I was still seated, because my legs would have gone weak. I felt the sudden urge to urinate.

I had seen him once before, years ago. He was older now, but the years had brought no warmth to his eyes.

"It seems," Victor explained to this other man, "we have a situation."

He looked on, unsurprised, unconcerned. Situations were his business.

"I need to get something cued up on the screen," Victor said, "and I want to be sure that Nora—it is Nora, isn't it?"

"You want to see my business card?" I said.

"I want to be sure this young lady stays right here with us while we all watch."

Russell wrapped his hand around my upper arm and led me over to the screening area. His grip wasn't as soft as Victor's had been. I knew there'd be a mark.

Several soft leather seats faced the screen. The other men sat down but Russell stayed standing on my right side, behind the row of seats, his hand never letting go of my arm. Ellen, in a tacit show of solidarity, I supposed, stood beside me. The screen was immense, installed for football games and movies in high definition. Victor had spent a fortune on the setup, but he was no master at cuing up the file that had been recording, and we stood there for several agonizing minutes while he changed inputs and channels, the football game being replaced by a blank screen, then by static, then a blank screen again, and it all would have been comical—another old man bested by his technology—if Russell's fingers weren't digging into my arm.

Then I saw the poker table, the back of my body, my arms, my hands, and then it was us, our game, as viewed from behind me and slightly overhead.

What was higher than high definition? This. I couldn't believe how clear the visual was, and how large everything was on the screen. Victor had started playing the video, and we watched the prior hand unfold. He forwarded the video and we played the hand

229

at triple speed. He slowed the video again as Victor, on the screen, reached over to cut the blue deck for me. The men staring at the TV screen were motionless and unblinking. They were watching my hands on the screen. I watched myself reach out and complete the cut. I watched myself square up the deck and shift to my left. I began to deal.

Ian, Danny, Jason, Ellen, Victor, me.

Ian, Danny, Jason, Ellen, Victor, me.

No one had said anything during the deal, and I'd forgotten there was sound on the recording until I heard Victor utter that one, horrific word: *Wait*.

He pointed the remote control and the screen and the video paused.

"So?" he said.

"I saw it," Danny said.

"What did you see?" Victor asked.

"Something. I definitely saw something. Like you said—when she dealt the cards to herself. It was different."

"What about you guys?" Victor asked Ian and Jason.

"Maybe," Ian said.

Jason nodded. "I'm pretty sure I saw something. But I couldn't tell you what it was."

"Play it again," Ian said.

Victor rewound the video in play mode, and we watched the cards float away from the table and back into the deck of cards in my hand. I swung my body to the right, placed the deck on the table, uncut it into two halves. He pressed play again, and the men watched, transfixed, as I dealt the two hole cards to all six players. Victor paused the video again.

Jason said, "I can't tell you what she's doing, but it was something. It was like a—a blip."

"Victor, you saw it that time, didn't you?" Danny asked.

"I think I did." He turned his head to face Russell. "What about you?"

"Play it again," Russell said with no emotion. The pressure on my arm increased.

"Can't you do that in slow motion?" Danny asked. "Like frame by frame?"

"Yeah," Victor said. "That's a good idea." Once again the cards flew up from the table and inserted themselves into the deck, and I pivoted and placed the deck on the table. Time then moved forward again on the screen, but at a pulled-apart, glacial pace. The ten seconds of dealing must have taken well over a minute. The men in the room turned to statues, leaning forward in their seats, gazes fixed on the screen, determined to catch this new addition to their game, this stranger, this potential enemy among them. I couldn't blame them. Had I been them, I would have stared at the screen—at my long, high-def fingers—with the same ferocity. *I saw something*, Victor had said, and now they were all seeing it. And from where I stood, with Russell's eyes fixed on the screen and his fingers fixed to my arm, I could see myself deal the hand yet again, too—not that I needed to; I knew what I had done— and I could see them seeing their suspicions confirmed, and with only the smallest turn of my head I could see the bar with its top-shelf liquors and the poker table with its duplicitous chandelier and the seagull painting and the sanderling painting and the heron painting. I could see everything, and it all swirled around me, and my heart raced faster as the enormity of what was happening hit me with full force.

When the slowed-down deal was over and Victor paused the video again, it was Jason who broke the silence.

"I saw it that time," he said. "It was like a—"

"Like a hitch," Ian offered.

"Yeah," Jason said. "Like she was pulling her own cards out of a different place."

"So we all saw it?" Victor asked.

"You're damn right," Danny said.

"Russell?" Victor said, turning around again.

Russell said to his boss, "Doesn't sound to me like you need a tiebreaker."

"What about you, Emily?" Jason asked. "You're being awfully quiet."

Ellen was standing beside me, but not quite as close as before. "Hey, I . . ." She tried again. "I don't . . ."

"No one's blaming you," Victor said. "But I want to know what you saw."

She *had* to agree with them. To deny it—to be the sole denier in the room—would only implicate herself. We knew the plan going in. We knew the risks. We'd discussed them and agreed to them. If the plan went south, there would be no defending each other. Defending each other would only make us both look guilty.

"I'm really not very good at spotting that sort of thing," she said.

"You watched the tape three times," Victor said, any remaining patience having drained out of his voice. "I'm asking you what you saw."

She glanced over at me and then back at the screen even though the tape was paused, frozen on a shot of the cards already dealt, the two hole cards in front of each of us, simply another poker hand about to start, one of many, one that could be nothing special or that might contain the key to everything.

"I don't know," she said. "I think so? Maybe? I don't know. Maybe I did."

Such a timid assertion, and she even emphasized the word "maybe." But I felt the room darken.

"Damn it," Victor said, and got up from his seat. He sounded as if he'd been driving and had come upon a dead horse lying across the road. It was sad, and there was no going around it.

Following Victor's cue, the other men stood up as well.

"You can't get away with this kind of bullshit," Danny growled. "Victor, she can't."

"No, she can't," Ian said. "It's really fucked up." He shifted from foot to foot. They were all in motion now, wringing their hands, rubbing their arms. It was as if the anxious, angry energy of these men, forced to remain dormant while they'd watched the TV screen, now demanded release.

"She's gonna forfeit her chips, obviously." Victor faced me. "Damn it, why would you come here and do that? Huh? What kind of—"

"*Forfeit her chips?*" Danny looked around at the other men. "Victor, there's a fortune at stake here. You gotta do something. I mean, this is your home."

"One thing's for sure," Jason said, "we're gonna let people know about her. Let people know she's a cheat."

"*Wrong.*" Victor raised his voice for the first time. He stared down the other players. "Now I want you all to listen to me. I'm running for office. Do you understand what that means? It means this game doesn't exist. The Midnight Riders? Doesn't exist."

"Yeah, yeah, your sterling reputation," Ian said. "But Vic." He gestured all around him. "Danny's right. This is your home. It reflects on you. You let her get away with this, *that's* your reputation, too."

"No one's getting away with anything." Victor took a breath. "I'm only saying let's all calm down a second."

"Fuck you, Victor."

"Danny, come on—"

"No, really. You invite a cheat to your table and then you act like it's no big deal. If you kick her out, then she's no worse off than she'd be if she'd lost. What, are you involved in this somehow?"

Victor's eyes narrowed. "I think you want to watch what you say."

Russell, still holding on to my arm, stood up straighter.

When Danny spoke again, his voice was more measured. "She tried to cheat in a very high-stakes game, Vic. That ain't right. It's so far from right."

"So what do you want me to do about it?" The hair on the back of my neck stood on end a split second before I realized Victor had just referred to me as *it*.

"I want you to make it right," Danny said.

"She forfeits her buy-in," Victor said. "The rest of us split it up—a nice little payday—and we reschedule the game for another night."

"Says the guy who's down," Ian said. "I'm *up*. I have a good chance to win the thing."

"Or we can go back to playing if you want," Victor said. "We divide her stake and keep playing."

Danny was shaking his head. "The whole fucking night's ruined. Make it right."

Victor rubbed his temples and faced me. "Why'd you have to do that? Why'd you have to go and cheat and ruin the whole night?"

I wanted Ellen to say something, but she was being quiet. So quiet. I didn't know what to do or say, yet I knew I had to mount my own defense. "I already told you," I said. "I didn't—"

"Oh, shut up," Danny said.

I pretended to ignore him. "I'm gonna go," I said to Victor.

It couldn't hurt to try leaving again—but Russell wasn't lightening his grip, and Danny, who evidently didn't like being ignored, got right up in my face and barked out: "Bitch, you'll stay here."

"She'll forfeit her buy-in." Finally, Ellen was speaking up. "Won't you, Nora? She will. We drove here together, but I swear I'll take her out of your neighborhood and drop her off and never talk to her again. I'm so sorry, guys. I hate how this makes me look. I don't know much about Nora. I thought I knew her, but obviously I was wrong."

"Both of you get out of here," Jason said.

"Sure," Ellen said. "We'll get our coats and go. I don't know her well, but I know that a quarter million dollars can't come easily. Forfeiting the buy-in is gonna hurt her, probably forever. I get the sense she's not as wealthy as she says she is, and for all we know she could've borrowed her stake, and whoever loaned her the money is gonna come knocking when she can't repay. So forfeiting the buy-in isn't nothing. It's probably real bad for her." Unless it was my imagination, the temperature in the room warmed a degree. Ellen had found her voice, and it was a soothing one. I hoped it was persuasive. "So we're gonna go now," she said. "I'm gonna need to cash out, but we'll leave Nora's money, and that's the end of it. Okay?"

At first no one replied, as if everyone were waiting for someone else.

"Okay?" she said again.

Oh, Ellen, I thought.

You were doing so well. But when a door opens for you, you walk through it. You don't double-check whether it's really a door.

"Hold on a minute," Victor said. "Just wait a minute while I think."

I would have made a move for the exit, and maybe the other men would have let me go, but Russell was a trained dog waiting for his master's command to release. We were all frozen, just like on the TV screen. Everything was motionless and mute everywhere on the whole planet.

"Oh, fuck it," Danny said, shattering the stillness. "I'll do it myself. No one's gonna steal my hard-earned money."

Then he was on me.

A large man, he yanked me away from Russell and over to the bar. "Two hundred and fifty thousand dollars," he was muttering. "Try to take *my* money." Adrenaline and rage fueled him as he shoved me against the bar. "Hold her here!" he shouted, and Russell, after a quick glance at Victor, obeyed this other master. He held me while Danny reached for—oh, Jesus—the knife lying on the bar that Jason had used to cut the lemons for his vodka tonic. Danny had the knife in his hand, but I didn't know what he had in mind until he said, "You got to lay her hand flat against the bar," and Russell moved my hand as if it were made of paper so it was pinned there on the bar top, and I nearly screamed or fainted or vomited but before I could do any of those things, Victor said, "Stop this! Stop it immediately!"

Everyone froze.

"Danny, put the damn knife down," he said. "I said put it down."

Danny obeyed.

I could have hugged Victor Flowers.

He looked at me, and at the knife on the bar top, as if it had finally dawned on him that these men were about to do something horrific. As if realizing that it had gone too far too fast, but that it was still possible to step back from the brink, to rewind this unfolding moment just as he had rewound the video. It could all still be nothing other than a ruined poker night. A ruined evening, but not worse than that. I could still go home.

"I will not allow blood in this room," Victor said. And for one more blissful moment I continued to misunderstand. "Anyway, *that*," he said, pointing, "is the wrong kind of knife." The skin on my face lost its feeling. "I want everyone in the kitchen. *Now.*"

Russell was suddenly dragging me through the doorway, tugging me across the house toward the kitchen, the others trailing. The sounds I heard came from me, I think, though Ellen was saying things, too, she was shouting, and my blood was screaming in my ears, and someone—Jason?—said, *Hold on a minute, will you?* and then my body was being shoved against the kitchen island and I could smell Russell against me, his sweat and something else, something harsh and vulgar, and Danny was reaching up for something—What was it? What was he reaching for?—and I felt my arm being yanked outward, and one of my hands smacked the island countertop while the other arm was pinned against my body, and then I saw what Danny had reached for, big and awful, a meat cleaver that had been hanging above the island with all those other pots and pans and knives, and my vision scrambled for a second and finally found Victor, but he was facing the window—he was gone, checked out—and my legs went soft and I made a desperate jerk with my body, but Russell held on tight. He wasn't youthful anymore, but he still had strength and was steady and businesslike, and my eyes were fixed on the cleaver in Danny's hand.

"Here," he said, offering the cleaver to Ellen. "Take it."

She began to protest: "Please, you all need to—"

"You brought her here," he said. "Prove to us you weren't in on it."

Ellen watched the cleaver, eyes wide.

"She isn't in on it," Victor said, back with us again. "I know she isn't."

"You know? How do you know?" Danny put his face close to mine. "Was she in on it?"

I forced myself to shake my head.

"Is that a no?"

My tongue felt huge in my mouth. My voice was a curled-up insect. "N-no . . ."

"I vouch for her, okay?" Victor said.

"Yeah?" Danny nodded toward the cleaver. "Let's see you vouch for her."

Russell was crushing my hand. He had pulled the thumb and two fingers toward the edge of the island and down, leaving the exposed fourth and fifth fingers stretched out over the flat surface of the island.

"This is so wrong," Ian said, and I nearly wept with thanks, until he turned to me and said, "I mean, Nora, how could you do this to us?"

A whimper escaped my lungs, and I yanked my arm so hard I thought my shoulder would dislocate. But my hand didn't budge.

"Take it," Danny told Victor, still offering the cleaver. "This is *your* house, and it was *our* money. You have to show her that cheaters don't prosper."

"Just hold it a minute," Victor said. He took the cleaver and set it on the island. "We gotta slow this down."

"Man, this election is muddling your brain," Danny said. "I got news for you, Vic. She ain't voting for you."

"I don't want you joking right now," Victor said.

"Joking? No. I don't hear any jokes. And I'll tell you something else that isn't a joke. I place a couple of calls and it's over for you. I know how you use that foundation. How you cook your books."

Victor's eyes narrowed. "Like you're so clean."

"Me? Who cares? I'm a fucking car salesman," Danny said. "But you know me well enough to know I don't deal with bullshit, and this right here is the biggest bullshit I've come across in a long time."

"Come on, Danny."

"Come on, nothing. Nobody cheats me and gets away with it. Not for money like this. Now you're gonna make this right. Or by the time I'm done with you, the Flowers Corporation will be worthless and you won't get elected dog catcher."

"For Christ's sake, Danny—"

"Oh, just be a man, will you?"

Victor glared at Danny for another moment, then surveyed his kitchen—the men, Ellen, and me, with my hand still pinned to the kitchen island, the fourth and fifth fingers still fully exposed. Whatever calculation Victor was doing in his mind, whatever was tipping the scale in one direction or the other, didn't take long.

"I forgot something in the other room," he said. His voice seemed to hold no anger or aggression, seemed to hold nothing at all, and some remote lizard part of my brain sent an extra burst of panic that nearly shut me down completely.

"You sure, Vic?" Russell said.

Victor's reply was to turn his back on us and quietly leave the room.

The moment he was gone, Russell reached up lightning fast and with the flat part of his thick hand slapped the front of my face, connecting with my eyes and the bridge of my nose. Hard enough to shock and sting but nothing more. The slap wasn't meant to injure, only to misdirect. I squeezed my eyes shut and never saw him pick up the cleaver. But it was up and then down on my last two fingers so fast, I heard the bang and its echo against the kitchen's hard surfaces before I felt the pain.

Then came a second of stunned silence, and in that second there was no pain either. I forced my eyes open and saw a brightly lit room where four men and one other woman stood, frozen, a record stopped in mid-spin on its turntable, a planet stopped in mid-spin on its axis.

Or maybe it was only half a second.

Then everything revved again, too fast, and there came the obscene wave of pain and shouting and blood and pain and the drop of the cleaver on the island and the *Jesus* and the *My god* and the pain, and I was on the floor, crouched over my hand, clutching it with my other hand, and there was blood, so much blood, and I heard, *Someone get a dish towel!*

I heard: *This is what happens!*

I heard: *No, don't—Russell! No!*

I heard a machine's whir and grind.

I heard: *She needs to get to a hospital.*

I heard: *Not from here.*

I heard: *We need her gone.*

Ellen bent down and draped a dish towel over my bleeding hand, and my whole arm screamed, and I saw black, then Victor Flowers's kitchen, then black, then Victor Flowers's kitchen.

Ellen was cooing in my ear. I concentrated on her words, struggling to hear them above the roaring in my head.

" . . . get up, sweetie. You need to get up."

"No one breathes a word of this," said Victor, who had come back into the kitchen with our coats. "Not ever." Then time jumped ahead. Ellen was wearing her coat. She was laying mine over my shoulders. I was standing again, leaning against her.

Stay awake, I told myself. Stay awake. Everything depends on it.

"They're gonna go to the police," Jason said.

"No," Victor said. "Emily, you need to make sure she never talks. To anyone. Am I understood?"

"What's she supposed to tell the hospital?"

Blood spilled onto the floor. My blood. People were saying words to each other.

"No one can make her talk," Victor said. "And she's not gonna talk. Make sure she knows her life depends on it."

Mine. My life depends on it.

"I'll make sure," Ellen said.

"Not a word, Emily. I'm holding you responsible. You keep her from talking and I'll make sure you get your buy-in back."

"When?"

"No, you don't ask when. You just say okay."

I was up, barely, on my feet, Ellen's arm around me, supporting me.

Stay awake, I told myself.

Ian held open a door leading outside. Every step brought a fresh shock to my hand. We were outside. The door shut behind us.

The outside lights revealed a harsh, muted world. Snow in the trees, snow on the grass, snow falling and blowing and vanishing into the black bay far below. The frigid temperature kept me awake and moving. Ellen slowly guided me across the lawn, one foot on the snow-covered grass, then the next, around the side of the house, toward the front, and closer to the car on the street, the trees and shrubs and hedges around Victor Flowers's property making private our shameful, excruciating exodus. I fell. Ellen got down on her knees and helped me sit up, and then she helped me stand. Then we were moving again, moving across the surface of a new planet, frozen and harsh and windswept. I stumbled again and grabbed her coat tighter, nearly pulling us both down. She held on, keeping us up, and then we were trudging together once more, my good arm reaching around her waist, underneath her thick coat, and I held on as we cut a path through the fresh snow, leaving a wake of blood.

"We're a boat," I said.

"What?"

All I could manage was to repeat, "A boat."

She shushed me. "Come on, honey, we're almost at the car."

She led me to the passenger side. Sill holding on to me with one arm, she found her keys and unlocked the door, pulled it open, and eased me into the seat.

"I'll drive a mile and then call 911," she said.

"No!"

"What are you talking about?"

"Take me home." I had trouble catching a breath, forming words. "Don't argue." I could hear my words slur. "Hurry."

"No, Nat—that's crazy."

"Drive me home!"

"Honey, you need a hospital. They can't make you talk. Even if they call the police, the police can't make you say anything you don't—"

"Stop talking." With my good hand I had fished my phone out of my pocket. I held the home button and said, as clearly as I could, "Call Harley."

The phone echoed me—*Calling Harley*—and started to ring. Ellen's tires spun in place.

Harley answered. I would always consider this to be the miracle of my life. "Natalie?"

The tires caught traction. We pulled away from the curb.

"Are you home?" I asked.

"Yeah, I'm home. Natalie, what's—"

I interrupted her with all the words she needed to hear and not one extra. *First aid. It's bad. My fingers. Thirty minutes. My apartment. Don't tell anyone. Please. Do it.* I ended the call. When she called back a few seconds later I let it go to voicemail.

Elevate. I should elevate the wound.

"Natalie?" Ellen said.

Blood soaked the dish towel. Blood on the car seat. Direct pressure.

"Natalie, are you still with me?"

Stay awake. Elevate.

We passed the exit for the amphitheater where long ago I had seen Pearl Jam with my friend Jamie Carr and her older brother Lance, who'd been in college. The band had looked old. Lance had looked old. He kissed me by the bathrooms. His lips pressed hard. Direct pressure. Snow struck the windshield.

We passed the exit for Bayshore hospital.

Wipers pushed away the snow. Wipe. Wipe. Snow snow blood blood, blood in the snow, like a boat's wake—

"Another fifteen minutes. Okay? Natalie?"

—fourteen thirteen twelve eleven ten my fingers two were gone forever and God it hurt and all the blood elevate the wound—

"Hang on there, Nat. The roads are really bad. I wish I could drive faster. We'll be there soon."

—wipe wipe snow wipe wipe snow the cleaver echoed in the kitchen my bone was white I saw my own bone—

"We're here. Natalie? *Natalie.* We're here."

My apartment building. Ellen parked directly behind my car. She shut off the engine and left me in the seat. She went around to my side and Harley was there with us in the snow and they both held on to me. The snow was falling lighter, and there were no gusts, not like by the water. Harley and Ellen were dragging me toward the house like a drunk bride at her bachelorette party who should have known better but it was all okay and tomorrow morning I would be hungover but no worse and then we were stepping up onto the landing where the porch light was shining, waiting for me, and then we were going through the front doorway and into my apartment and I felt the heat and we were home.

4

♥

In my apartment, Harley lifted the coat from my shoulders and I fell to my knees on the carpet. Seeing the blood-soaked dish towel wrapped around my hand, she said, "Oh, Natalie, what happened to you?"

On the carpet beside the coffee table was an unzipped red canvas satchel. Covering the table were sealed packs of bandages and ointments and pills and tape.

"Her fourth and fifth fingers were severed," Ellen said.

"My god—where are they?" Harley asked. "Are they on ice?"

"They're gone," Ellen said.

Only then did I decode the meaning of the grinding sound in Victor's kitchen. Garbage disposal.

"She needs a hospital," Harley said.

"No," I managed.

"We have to call 911."

"*No!*" I struggled for more words. I needed an interpreter. "Ellen . . ."

"We got involved in something," she said. "Bad people did this. If we go to the hospital and the hospital calls the police . . . you have to patch her up."

"Are you crazy?" Harley said. "This isn't a patch—it's life-threatening!"

"Please," I said.

Harley pulled her eyes away from the bloody dish towel and knelt down to me. "Are you allergic to latex?"

I shook my head, and she pulled on a pair of gloves. "Help me get her over to the kitchen." She and Ellen dragged me there, and then Harley guided me down so I was sitting on the floor. The room got swimmy. The kitchen sink turned on. "Keep her from moving," Harley said. She unwrapped the dish towel. I turned my head away. "Now find a clean towel—dish towel, any kind of towel."

I heard the kitchen sprayer being pulled from its home. When the spray of water hit my hand, I screamed so loudly that Harley's dog started barking, and from my living room there came an intense flapping of wings against metal cage bars.

"Try to stay still," Harley said. "I know it hurts."

That word, "hurt," was a piece of cotton. It had nothing whatsoever to do with the fire bolt ripping up and down my arm.

"I found some towels," Ellen said.

"Put them in the other room by the table," Harley said, and went back to spraying my hand. I bit my lip to stop myself from screaming. When the spraying finally ended, she told Ellen to shut off the water. My shirt was wet. I was shivering. "I'm going to put some ointment on now," she said. I couldn't watch. The direct touch made me scream again but I did my best to hold still. More barking upstairs. More wings beating against the cage.

"I'm going to wrap it tightly in gauze," Harley said, "and we're going to hope the bleeding slows down."

After the initial contact, I felt my hand relax the tiniest bit as she continued to layer on the gauze, over the wound, around to the base of my hand, around my wrist, and back up, over and over. When I dared to look at my hand, blood was already darkening the gauze. She continued to add layers. "Help me get her over to the couch," she said, and with Ellen's help I was being lifted to my feet and guided over to the loveseat, then lowered again. My legs were lifted and placed over an armrest. Harley slid one of the back cushions to the side and underneath my head. She placed the other back cushion on my stomach and laid my arm on top. My birds, no longer frantic, started to coo—first one, then both of them. "You have to keep it elevated," Harley said. "Above your heart. That'll slow the bleeding and help with pain."

She wrapped one of my bathroom hand towels around the gauze.

"Can you keep pressure on it?" she asked me.

"I think so."

"Good girl." She covered me with the afghan. "Ellen, come with me a minute."

They didn't go far enough. Even with the birds cooing, I heard every word.

She needs a hospital. She needs sutures, specialists . . .

Can't you do it?

You can't just start sewing. I think the bone needs to be cut back to make a flap of skin. And she probably needs blood, and there's a huge risk of shock, and even if by some miracle she doesn't go into shock, she's gonna end up in the ER anyway when this gets infected.

She won't go.

Do you really think she should be making her own decisions right now? God, what did you two get involved in?

This wasn't supposed to happen. Pain slowed down time. An eternity passed before Ellen spoke again. *I have to leave. But I'll call for an ambulance from the road. Give me ten minutes. Okay?*

What do you mean, you're leaving?

But Ellen was already back beside the loveseat, crouched down. "Honey, Nat, I hope you understand, but we can't be in the same place. I'm gonna go. You're in good hands here."

"You can't leave," Harley said. She repositioned the afghan, which had slipped down from my legs.

"She has to," I said.

Ellen got her coat from the floor and came over to me again. She spoke softly. "I swear to God, Natalie, I thought your deal was great."

"It was perfect," I said. My teeth were chattering.

Her gaze moved to my bandaged hand resting on the pillow. "No. But it was the best I ever saw." She shut her eyes. "I'm so sorry."

She watched my face a moment and then left, shutting the inner door behind her and then the outer one.

"Open the blinds," I said to Harley. "Right away. Please."

She opened them, and from the loveseat I watched Ellen through the window, walking through the falling snow to her car.

"Unwrap the gauze," I said.

"*What?*"

"Harley, you have to do it." Each breath was getting harder. "Do it fast. Please."

I watched out the window again and then dug with my good hand beneath the afghan and into my front pants pocket. I had to shift a little to the side. The slightest movement sent my hand screaming.

Outside, Ellen's car door slammed shut.

I removed my hand from my pocket and looked. There had been no time earlier, when I stole it from Ellen, to do anything with it other than shove it into my pocket. There was no time now, either, to examine it, but I had to know what had been worth all this risk, all this deception, all this misery.

"What is that?" Harley asked.

It was a bell.

Silver and very small, it was about the length of a thumb. Engraved on it was a single word—REVERE—and a year: 1775. The clapper was stuck to the bell's side, silenced, with a Band-Aid.

"Wrap my hand up again," I told her, pressing the bell against the palm of my injured hand, "with this inside. Please. Hurry."

Harley glanced outside, where Ellen had gotten into her car but wasn't driving away, then back at me. For the first time, I think she understood that either she was going to do what I asked or she wasn't, but that logic and reason were not in play—that all this would be beyond her, at least for a while longer.

Rather than remove all the gauze from my fingers, she cut what was left and began to wrap the new gauze around the old, going over the wound, then up my hand to the wrist, back to the wound, again and again. I prayed that Ellen would drive away, but I wasn't surprised when her car's interior light came on. Of course she would want to touch the bell, hold it, remind herself it was hers finally, before leaving. And when she couldn't find it, there was going to be an explosion.

She got out of the car and climbed into the backseat. I couldn't see her any longer, but I knew she had to be searching under the seats, reaching into the car's crevices. She had to be frantic in that car. She had lost it. Everything she'd worked for this past year was unraveling. She left the backseat and got into the front passenger seat. More searching. Only a matter of time before she came back up the walkway.

The bell's shape was vanishing into the bulge of gauze when I heard a hissing sound through my thin living room windows. I couldn't place the sound until my beautiful, pathetic young neighbor came into view. He had on a leather jacket. No hat or gloves. The sound was the shovel dragging behind him across the top layer of snow.

He crossed to our side of the street, approached Ellen's car, and said something I couldn't make out. The passenger door was still open, and she turned around and looked up at him. I had no trouble hearing her response: "Get the hell out of here!"

Calvin watched her another moment, and without saying anything else he walked past the front of her car and began shoveling snow away from my rear tire. He dumped the snow by the curb. Shovel, dump. Shovel, dump.

"You're shivering," Harley said, tucking the afghan tighter around my legs. "You've lost a lot of blood. You're going into shock. You need a hospital."

I shook my head no and watched Ellen crawl across the center console to get into the driver's seat again. More searching. By the time she left her car again, my rear wheels were free from the snow, and Calvin was over by the passenger front tire. Ellen shut the driver-side door, went around and shut the passenger door, and headed back toward the apartment. My hand was fully bandaged again, the bell making only the slightest bulge at the palm. I covered my hand with the dish towel as Ellen came charging back into the building, then into my apartment.

My expression, pained and exhausted and frozen and light-headed, was no act.

Hers wasn't either: sheer panic.

Without a word, she crossed the living room toward the kitchen. I heard cabinets opening, items being thrown around. Then she was back in the living room. On her knees, she felt under the loveseat, looked under the coffee table. She slid her hand into the corners of the sofa, grazing my legs, my torso, as if I were an inanimate thing—a heavy duffel bag, a log—no longer of consequence. Every jostle sent a million volts through my hand.

"What are you doing?" Harley asked.

Ellen stood and leaned over me, examining the loveseat, and I noticed her exposed thumb, the neat stiches made with black thread, which the Band-Aid had been covering up until very recently.

"What are you looking for?" Harley asked. "Maybe I can help."

My neighbor wasn't going to win an Academy Award, but Ellen, scanning the living room, was too busy to notice. She went into the kitchen again. There were only so many places to search, but she had to keep at it because the alternative was too awful for her to consider: if it wasn't in her car or in my apartment, then the bell, whose theft she had planned and plotted with such precision and guts this past year, the bell she had successfully stolen from Victor Flowers's home without anyone knowing, had slipped out of her pocket back in the Highlands, somewhere in Victor's vast yard, in the deep snow, during our graceless trek to her car.

"It has to be here," she said, the queasiness in her voice having nothing to do with me or my injury. It was the thought that a search anyplace other than on Victor Flowers's property was probably fruitless.

"What does?" I made myself ask. She ignored me, but when one of the birds cooed again, Ellen glanced up at the birdcage. She kept watching it and went closer. Julius was pecking at a small silver object hanging from the top of the cage by a length of twine.

Not a bell. A small disco ball.

She muttered to herself and turned to me. "Where's a flashlight?"

252

"I don't think I have one."

She removed her phone from her pocket and was out the door and outside again. She began to search with the flashlight from her phone—first the stoop, then the walkway, slowly retracing her steps to the street.

"What's that, Natalie? I didn't hear you?"

Harley was kneeling down beside me. Time had skipped. I'd lost a couple of seconds. The afghan wasn't thick enough. My face felt clammy, but I was shivering hard. I didn't realize I'd said anything aloud.

"She never needed a partner," I said.

"What are you talking about?" Harley asked. "Tell me what happened."

It had all been misdirection. Every single moment since she drove me to that Flemington café. All our practice. All our planning.

"We were partners," I told Harley, "but she never planned to win the game."

The whole time, it was the bell she was after.

"I don't understand." Harley knelt down closer to me. "What happened to your hand?"

Ellen got them all watching the TV screen, staring at it at the exact same time. They wanted to see my false deal. They were dying to see it. No one would dare look away for even an instant. The bell was hidden in the room. While everyone stared at the TV screen, she stole it.

"She told Victor Flowers I was a cheater."

"Wait. *Victor Flowers*? She knows him?"

"She tipped him off, and he recorded me." I was her misdirection. Me. "She set me up."

"Listen to me, Natalie. I'm going to call—"

Her words got interrupted by the commotion outside: *"Son of a—what the fuck are you doing?"*

Even from in here I could see what Calvin was doing. He was dumping snow onto the wheels of Ellen's car. *Oh, Calvin, Calvin,* I thought. *She's dangerous. Let her go.* But he was blocking her in because he didn't like her and there was no readily available dog shit to set aflame in all that fresh powder.

"Stop fucking doing that!" Ellen spat.

He didn't even grace her with his gaze, just quietly scooped up another shovelful of snow and deposited it by her front tire. He turned the shovel over and patted the snow into place. Then he did it all again. Finally, she went over to him. "I said get the fuck away." She gave him a shove.

Still he said nothing. Just gave her a bored teenage half-glance and made a slow, shuffling retreat toward his own apartment building, dragging the snow shovel behind him on the unplowed road.

Ellen searched her car again—the back, the front, the seats, the floor, the dim beam from her phone's flashlight darting around the car. This time she was making sure, and she took her time about it. Then she froze. For ten, fifteen seconds, nothing happened. But everything was happening. It was all changing for her. Clicking into place. Then the flashlight beam moved again. I should have told Harley to lock the door, but I couldn't imagine it would have made a difference, and I was still hoping for Ellen to depart without ever thinking I knew anything. But in those quiet seconds, Ellen had decided that I knew more than I was letting on. And so while I couldn't see exactly what she was doing in the car when that flashlight's beam began to move again, she must have been opening and closing the glove box. That's where I assume she kept the gun, which she held in her hand when she stomped back into my apartment.

Her expression was different now. Or maybe it looked different because she was holding a gun. I saw less fear, more fury. She looked—and there is only one way to say this—murderous.

"You have it," she said, "so don't even bullshit me."

5

♠

Harley took several steps backward, nearly knocking into my bookshelf. "Is that real?" she asked.

"What are you doing?" I said.

"Where is it?" Ellen wasn't pointing the gun at me, but holding it was enough. The handle was black, the rest of it silver. It wasn't large—it could have been a kid's toy—but I knew it wasn't a toy, just as I knew the bell wasn't a toy, just as I knew that Ellen wasn't my friend and had never been my partner. My face was sweating, I was trembling, my hand screamed, and hovering above it all was the understanding that the world I thought I knew was an illusion. I had been fooled, and I had been a fool. But I wasn't a fool now, and the gun she carried wasn't a toy because one thing I knew for certain was that Ellen didn't play games.

I turned my head toward her. "Where is what?"

She told Harley to empty her pockets.

Harley turned her pockets inside out.

"Empty that bag," Ellen said.

Harley stayed frozen a moment, then took a tentative step toward the first-aid kit. She dumped everything out.

"Back up again," Ellen said. She reached down and felt around inside the bag. Then she pointed the gun at Harley, whose eyes widened. "What do you know about this?"

Ellen was losing it, and she held a gun. I didn't doubt for a second it was loaded, or that she would use it. To her, at that moment, everything was worth the risk. She turned and trained the gun on me.

"Tell me where the fucking bell is," she said. "Tell me right now or that hand injury is going to seem like a paper cut."

"I don't know what you're talking about," I said.

She approached Harley and with her free hand patted her down, feeling all over the outside of her clothes: her arms, breasts, stomach, inside her waistband. Outside her clothes she felt Harley's thighs, her crotch, her calves. "Take off your shoes."

Harley obeyed. Ellen felt inside each shoe. "Don't move," she repeated. "And don't test me." Then she turned to me. "Stand up."

No way could I stand up.

She grabbed the afghan and yanked it away from my body. "I said stand up!"

I tried. The room spun hard. I instinctively pressed my hands against the loveseat to steady myself, and my left hand screamed in pain and everything started to go black. I tried again to get up, turning my body until my feet were on the carpet. Then, slowly, I lifted myself off the loveseat. The moment I was standing, Ellen reached out and dug her hands into one of my pants pockets, then the other.

"You're acting crazy," I said, still believing that playing dumb was my best and only option. "I don't understand."

She started running her hand along my body, same as she'd done with Harley—my shoulders, my chest—but then she

257

stopped. She was eyeing my bandaged hand. Trying, maybe, to imagine the lengths a person might go in the name of misdirection. In the name of stealing something so valuable. And once she went down that road her conclusion came fast. She reached out and removed the dish towel. Stared some more at the mountain of gauze.

"Unwrap that," she said to Harley.

"What?" Harley said.

"You know what. Take all that off."

"No," I said. Gravity was pulling me back toward the loveseat but I remained standing. "I don't know what's happening, but you have to leave. Go. Get out. I'm going to call the police if you don't—"

She reached out with the gun and whacked the fingers of my hurt hand. My universe exploded.

I didn't think anything could be worse than the cutting itself, or the water Harley had sprayed over the wound, but I was wrong. I heard myself scream, and the birds started beating their wings again and the dog upstairs started barking again, and I teetered and fell hard against the wall, the windowsill jabbing into my hip.

Through the window, my eyes met Calvin's. He was standing in the snow at the far curb. Gone was the shovel. He was carrying something else, but I didn't know what.

"Unwrap it," Ellen told Harley. "Now."

Harley looked at me, and when I didn't protest—there was no protest left in me—she came over and slowly, carefully, began to undo the gauze wrapping. Around the wrist, around the hand, around the space where my fingers had been. Even with the gun trained on us she was a careful technician. Her animals were lucky. Her fingers did their slow, delicate work, as one layer came undone, then another. I felt unbelievably sad. Ellen would have the bell, and assuming she didn't kill me and Harley both, I would have nothing to show for any of this except for my wet, sickening crab's claw.

The next layer of the gauze came away blood-soaked, and Ellen looked away. I'll never know for sure what exactly caused her to divert her attention at that exact moment: the gore, or the sudden burst of light outside.

Ellen's car was on fire.

"My god," Harley said.

Gray smoke pumped itself into the air as the flames quickly overtook the hood. Ellen glanced back at my hand, the blood-soaked gauze partly unwound and dangling down. Maybe my willingness to let Harley unwrap it—gun notwithstanding—had satisfied her. Maybe she never fully believed I was hiding the bell behind all that wrapping, and in her heart of hearts she still believed it lay somewhere in the snow on Victor's lawn. And if she had any hope of making it back there, she had to be gone before the first responders arrived. And she needed a car.

"Give me your keys," she said.

This was the easiest request I'd ever granted. My key chain hung on a hook by the door. "There," I said, and she slid the key chain off the hook and gave my apartment a last fleeting glance.

"You breathe a word about any of this to the police," she said, "and you're gonna die."

The sweet parting words of a friend.

She ran from the apartment, made a wide arc around her car, which was engulfed in flames, and unlocked my door. From where she stood it must have been an oven. Much hotter than the spot where Calvin stood across the street, carrying what I now saw was a red plastic gas can.

Ellen got into my car and the headlights came on. Calvin had shoveled well. Ellen pulled my car away from the curb with no trouble at all, and then the BITCH car turned right at the corner and was gone.

I was still on my feet and desperate for the cold air. But not until Harley had unwrapped enough of the gauze to get the bell. She gave it a quick rinse in the kitchen sink and hung it in the birdcage beside the disco ball.

Then she rewrapped the gauze, and the two of us shuffled to the doorway. From the entryway I felt the heat from Ellen's burning car warm my face, but I also felt the cold, and the mix of temperatures reminded me of what a campfire had felt like on the one occasion, many ages ago, when my family had stayed at the beach long past sunset because you can't see many stars in Plainfield.

What for a moment felt like a cleansing mix of cold and heat quickly became a shivering sweat. I knew I couldn't stay standing any longer. "Calvin!" I called into the night. My voice sounded reedy and weak, but he heard me and came up the walkway. Close up, he looked petrified. "Listen to me," I told him. "You didn't do this. I did. Do you understand?"

He said, "You mean the fire? No, I did the fire." Always the literalist.

I coughed. "I'm *covering* for you. Now go home. That's an order. If you're my friend, you'll do it."

"I don't care who knows," he said.

I took a breath. "You and I are magicians," I said. "Magicians keep secrets. Now be a magician and keep your fucking mouth shut." I tried to smile, but it was a mistake, and I think I scared him. "I'm counting on you, Cool Calvin. Now go. And leave the gas can here."

He went.

As people across the way came out of their apartments, I was crouched down, Harley's arm around me, and I was telling her about the lawyer's business card in my wallet. "No one else," I told her. "Only him."

A siren grew louder, and then a patrol car pulled up to the curb across the street. The siren turned off but others blared in the distance. My door was still open and the birds were cooing.

"You'll watch my doves?" I asked.

"Of course," Harley said.

A woman in a police officer's uniform was coming across the lawn, making shoe prints in the fresh snow. "Is anyone in that car?" she called out.

The distant sirens were becoming louder.

"No!" Harley replied. "But she's hurt really bad."

Before it went dark, I noticed everything: the streetlights and the smoke and the bright fire and the snow on the rooftops across the way.

It was pretty.

The officer approached us. "What happened?"

6

♦

Until recently, I always thought mourning doves were *morning* doves. Certainly my own doves always began their call at sunrise. Once I learned the truth, I chose to disregard it. A dove's call is hardly one of grief. It's a wakeful, hopeful sound. It's the call of being alive, the call of camaraderie.

I couldn't see this particular dove in the branches overhead, but hearing it soothed me. I temporarily lacked its freedom and was glad to be the beneficiary of its call. Several times recently in the yard I'd seen cardinals land on branches, heard woodpeckers knocking against trees, watched geese pumping their way through the sky in vast V's, returning from their tropical vacation.

Such was the pastoral setting of the outdoor visiting area at the North Ridge State Correctional Facility. Inside the fence there was plenty of green lawn, and the trees this time of year were either in bloom or growing new leaves. The trees were tall but not wide. They were young, younger than the prison, and I liked knowing that people had been thoughtful enough to plant them for our pleasure.

In the center of the visiting area was a cement slab with rows of metal picnic tables and benches. Too many rows. Whoever planned out this spot had been overly optimistic about the menfolk coming to see their incarcerated women. I'd met too many inmates these past four months who never received a single visitor. It was a shame. Once the initial terror fades, prison is endlessly repetitive. Just knowing a visitor is coming can liven up an entire week.

I was waiting at a table all to myself. Besides breaking up the boredom, visitors gave me the chance to come out here, where there was a fine view of the rolling hills of Warren County, and where on a spring day like this, with the sky a deep blue and with only a few fair weather clouds and a soft breeze and the birds cooing and chirping, I could feel as if I were deep in nature. I could unfocus my eyes and make the fences and the razor wire and the guard towers disappear. I could temporarily rid my mind of the constant standing counts, the three a.m. sobbing that echoed down the cellblock, and the musty laundry room where I earned my nineteen cents an hour.

During my second month here my mother came to visit, bewildered Chip in tow. Jack Clarion came last month. They asked me, quite reasonably, why on earth I'd set someone's car on fire. I couldn't tell them the truth: "Because the teenager who saved my life didn't deserve juvie." Lacking a reasonable answer, I shrugged and said nothing, same as when the officers at my hospital bedside, and later at the police station, had asked me repeatedly and with increased tightening of the jaw to please just tell them what I knew.

I thought Brock McKnight performed well, given my refusal to elaborate on anything—no details, no motive, not a word about how I'd obtained my injury. He got the D.A. to reduce my charge from second- to third-degree arson. The D.A. probably figured I was covering for someone, but no one had been hurt in the fire, and here was an opportunity to close a case quickly.

At sentencing, a jowly man with a bald head and a "Judges Rule!" coffee mug sentenced me to two and a half years, with a chance of parole in 304 days. For handling my case, Brock charged me $1,800 plus the secret to the Four Queens trick. I thought it was a fair price.

And now on this pretty May afternoon my visitor was being escorted toward me by Simon, one of the kinder male guards. If I hadn't known she was coming, I might not have recognized her: hair shaved down to a buzz, no makeup, denim jacket, skin-tight jeans. Even her gait was unfamiliar, a cautious creeping that looked almost reptilian. When it came to Ellen, I had long since given up trying to construe what was real and what was an act. But she appeared pinched and angular and jittery, like an addict, and I found myself believing the desperation.

When she got near, she did what everyone did at first. Glanced at my hand, then away.

"I never knew they'd do that," she said. "I swear. You believe me, don't you?"

The wound looked a lot better now, but that's only because of how bad it had looked before.

"Sure," I said, and motioned for her to sit down across from me. "Does it still hurt?"

You can't visit a prisoner without getting invited first. For that to happen, she had to write to me. She wrote again and again. I ignored her notes for a while, but there were things I wanted cleared up, things I needed to know. Besides, as I said, prison was boring. And Ellen was many things but never boring.

"Sometimes it hurts," I said. "The scar tissue's still pretty sensitive."

Only a few other tables were occupied, nowhere near us, people in their intimate conversations. The guard had returned to the corner near the gate. He watched over us all but gave us our space.

"Tell me how you knew," she said.

Yes, the desperation was real. She had lost everything, and to make it worse she still didn't know how she had lost.

"This is a really good place to watch birds," I said, looking around. "I should get a birding book. I need to bone up."

"I assume you know by now what it's worth," she said.

I shrugged off her question. Of course I knew. While out on bail before my sentencing, I'd found a Rutgers anthropology professor willing to chat with me in his office long enough to refer me to a colleague in art history who moonlighted as an antiques appraiser. Rutgers is a vast university, and no one seemed to question my claim to be pursuing a master's degree in American history with a special interest in the Revolutionary War period.

"Honestly, there would be very little to compare it to," the art history professor told me once I had located her office deep within the windowless bowels of her department. Our conversation was all hypothetical, of course. The three Revere bells, after all, were all presumed destroyed or lost. But what if one of the bells were ever found?

"An object like that would shimmer with history," she said, her own eyes shimmering at the very idea.

She explained that Paul Revere was known as a silversmith and bell maker but was not known to have made bells from silver. There were rumors, though, of him making a few inkwell bells over the years—and for a bell that small he would have had to use a metal like silver. But all the known bells made by Paul Revere were large—for churches and schools—and made of copper and tin. "So this would be an extraordinary find," the professor said. "It would be the only confirmed silver bell that Paul

265

Revere made. Then add to it its historical significance. The Midnight Ride?" She reclined in her chair as if she'd just finished a satisfying meal. "Such a bell would be historical magic." I remained quiet, giving this appraiser time to appraise. "At a bare minimum, I would think five, maybe eight million dollars at auction." She sat up again. "But really the sky's the limit on this one." Then she shook her head as if erasing even the fantasy of coming across such a treasure.

"When did you decide to use me?" I asked Ellen now. I'd had plenty of time to reflect on this question and was no closer to an answer.

"Hey, don't forget—you found me. You chased me down. You came to my school. You couldn't be told no."

Maybe. Or maybe that had all been part of her plan. Had she recognized me in Atlantic City and done the Greek deal just badly enough for me to spot it but well enough for me to be amazed? Or had her plan started earlier? Had Ace tipped her off to our presence at that Atlantic City game? Had he and Ellen been working together to reel me in? Ethan, too? Late at night, in my cell, I entertained all possibilities—that Ace was smarter than he let on, even that Brock McKnight, my competent attorney, could have been behind the whole thing from the moment he first joined me in the elevator at that Newark reception. Had my desperation and loneliness been so apparent? Had I come across so much like a sucker? I wondered sometimes if Brock had been Ellen's connection for selling the Revere bell once it was stolen. My speculations would eventually circle back toward the probable, but prison gives you time to weave and reweave conspiracies of infinite design. And just when my theories would start to seem unreal and far-fetched, I would remember that the bell was real, and everything would seem possible once again.

"You have to tell me how you figured it out," she said.

"Figured what out?" I asked.

She scratched at her neck as if she had a bug bite. "Why weren't you watching the TV along with everyone else?" That was when she'd stolen the bell from the small safe hidden behind the painting of the blue heron. While everyone else was staring at the TV screen, watching me deal the cards in slow motion, she was stealing the bell. "How could you not watch the TV?" she asked. "You, more than anyone, should have wanted to see exactly where your Greek deal fell apart."

And here was the dilemma I'd been facing ever since granting Ellen her visit here. Some secrets are simply too good for the magician to reveal to anyone. But was I a magician any longer? Ever since that poker game in Atlantic City where I'd first laid eyes on Ellen, I felt myself becoming something else, something new, a butterfly emerging from its chrysalis. And now all I had to do was look around and I had my answer. I had only to remember where I was, in this temporary prison from which in just under two hundred days I would flutter away.

There was no need to keep my greatest secret from Ellen. As she herself once told me, the real suckers know they've been conned. So she might as well know how.

"I didn't cheat," I said.

"What?"

"I was still being a magician."

"What the hell are you talking about?"

"I told you," I said. "It's Magic 101. You don't do a trick until it's ready." I shrugged. "I wasn't ready." I watched her face as she tried to make sense of what I was saying. "I thought I was ready, but when the moment came . . . I didn't do it. I didn't false deal."

I had told myself I was ready, but once again my hands knew better and thought faster than my brain did. Or maybe not being fully satisfied with my technique was only part of it. Maybe I just wasn't ready to be a cheat yet. Or I knew that stealing all that money from Victor Flowers and his poker buddies wasn't going to bring my father back.

Maybe I was just afraid.

Ellen's face, already gaunt, was now drained of color. "And then Victor accused you."

The moment that happened, I knew I'd been set up. And the only explanation was the woman now sitting across from me. She had told Victor in advance that she was bringing a card cheat to the game. Who knew what reason she'd given? Maybe she told him I'd cheated her in the past and this was payback. Whatever the story, she had tipped him off to exactly when I would be false dealing the cards. Our weeks of preparation were nothing but a big con with me as the mark.

I was terrified, and so I had protested exactly as I'd been taught—loudly, vehemently, which helped me not at all—but I wasn't only terrified. I was also desperate for the secret. I wanted to know what was behind this wildly elaborate deception. To know what the prize was. So I didn't beg everyone to show their hole cards (not that it would've helped—even ordinary cards can become a winning hand, and a good cheat would avoid anything obvious). I didn't try to throw Ellen under the bus as the mastermind (not that they would have believed me). I protested, like we'd planned in the event of disaster, and then I shut up.

So Victor, stealth filmmaker, led everybody over to that giant TV screen to watch the recording of my deal. And this, too, was all part of Ellen's misdirection, a great big distraction to get everyone together, staring at that big screen as intently as jewelers in search of the flaw. Victor was told I had planned to cheat him, and so he convinced himself that I had. They all did. They watched my honest deal again and again. They watched, and rewatched, and watched in frame-by-frame slow-motion—slowly convincing themselves and one another that they were seeing me cheat—the subtle "hitch," in Ian's words. There was no hitch. They were searching for it, and so they found it. They worked themselves into a murderous froth, but it was all based on nothing other than Victor's accusation, which Ellen had forced on him just the way I forced playing cards on unsuspecting volunteers show after show.

And all this watching and rewatching of my deal on the TV screen, convincing themselves they were busting a card cheat, gave Ellen ample time to steal the Revere bell. No one saw her do it, because what was happening on the screen was probably the most compelling thing they had ever seen in their lives. They dared not miss a single frame, a chance to catch, red-handed, a cheat, their new guest, this woman with the short bleached hair who had waltzed into their high-stakes game and tried to rob them all, these men of strength and savvy, these self-described winners.

"You didn't cheat," Ellen said, as if trying out the words in her mouth.

"No. I didn't."

And because I hadn't, there'd been no reason for me to watch the TV. I knew I'd been set up, and I knew that the men were being distracted for a reason, so I watched Ellen step across the plush carpet to the fireplace and push aside the picture of the blue heron. It was a gas fireplace. There was no flue and plenty of space for the small safe that Ellen had opened in a few fast twists of her wrist.

"But you didn't rat me out," she said.

"No."

"You didn't cheat, but you"—she glanced at my hand—"you let them do that to you?"

I hadn't seen exactly what small object she had removed from the safe, but I saw her slip it into the pocket of her pants before shutting the safe again and sliding the picture back into place. And whatever it was, I knew it had to be worth a hell of a lot more than the million dollars she and I could have won together at the card table.

"I can't believe you dealt straight and let them do that to you. God, Natalie, you let them—"

"Yeah, I know," I said. "I was there." I'd had several months already to understand the implications of my own actions on that snowy January night. She had set me up and risked my life, and I was going to either take whatever it was she had slipped into her pocket or die trying.

I decided to put it into words she would understand. "I told you I was all in." When she didn't reply, I added, "And don't forget, you did the same thing in my kitchen."

That came to me only later—how cutting her own thumb had been part of the plan. She had needed me to deal the cards with just a couple of days of preparation so that when Victor accused me of cheating, I would have reason to second-guess my own performance.

She grimaced. "That isn't the same thing at all."

One small disappointment: Ellen had exaggerated her own injury. In my apartment, despite my own agony and the beginnings of shock, I remember seeing her exposed thumb as she helped lay me down on the loveseat. I took no notice of it at the time, but afterward I was sure of it. Two small knots of black thread on her thumb. Two stitches. Not four. I expected better of her. A stronger commitment.

"No, I guess it isn't the same," I said.

"When did you lift it from me?" she asked.

I was no expert pickpocket, but I had been bleeding everywhere and the snowstorm was gusty and Victor Flowers's yard was dark and Ellen was practically carrying me to her car. Distractions were everywhere. Our bodies were close. I knew which pocket to pick. It wasn't complicated.

"I lifted it from you exactly when I decided to." A smug reply, but I believed I had earned the right.

She didn't seem well. I wondered how much of our half-million buy-in she had borrowed, and at what interest rate. I wondered who might be after her, what sort of trouble she was in. "You don't understand," she said. "I had a buyer all lined up. He's probably still interested." Another neck scratch. "I can give you thirty percent. That's a huge amount of money, but we have to move on this. You have to tell me where it is. I'll take care of everything. But you've got to tell me where the bell is." When I didn't reply, she said, "All right, thirty-five percent."

"Take a good look at my left hand," I told her, "and say the words 'thirty-five percent' again."

"Forty percent," she said.

"You're getting closer," I said. "But first I want to know how it all started. How did you know what to steal? How did you know about the safe?"

"Come on," she said, "you think a man like Victor Flowers is going to keep that bell a secret from everyone? The greatest thing he ever owned?"

271

"How'd you know it would be in the safe?"

"Because the bell came first. The safe came second. The safe only existed because of the bell." She shook her head. "He showed it to the guy who installed the safe. Who happens to be a guy I work with from time to time."

She knew the safe guy. Of course she did. I'd forgotten what should have been ingrained: the secret was rarely as elegant as the trick.

And why would Victor Flowers agree to let his home be used as a place to catch a card cheat? That was the other thing I couldn't figure out. "Why would Victor invite this kind of trouble into his home?" I asked. "What was in it for him?"

She didn't answer right away. She surveyed the visiting area, fingers twitching, and I wondered if maybe she really had become an addict. Finally, she faced me again and said, "A 1695 Stradivarius."

"A violin?"

"A violin played at the premiere performance of the New York Philharmonic in 1842." She spoke flatly, as if reciting a memorized set of facts. "I promised a meeting with the current owner, who wanted to sell the instrument but didn't want to pay a big commission to an auction house. With my connection, Victor could have gotten a great deal on it."

"But the story was made up, I assume."

She was watching the trees, the yard. "A little creative thinking, a little Wikipedia." She scratched her neck. "But none of that matters. The bell. That's what matters. That's everything. And you need a buyer. Otherwise, it isn't worth anything. You know that, right? Forty-five percent. What do you say? Huh? I'll even pay the safe guy his points out of my share, but we have to do it now. People are following me. I don't know if it's Victor's people or the guy I borrowed the buy-in money from. I abandoned my apartment. I don't go to work anymore. We're both at risk until we sell the bell, get the money, and disappear. That's the only way to do it. I can get it done, but it's got to be now, Natalie. Please."

I listened to the mourning dove's familiar call.

"Fifty percent," she said. "Okay? Partners in the truest sense of the word. I'm so, so sorry about your fingers. Jesus, Natalie, I swear I never in a million years thought they would do something like that. If I'd thought for a minute they'd—I mean, they're just guys, you know? Guys with money. I'm so sorry, but let's do this, huh? Fifty percent. Partners."

I let her talk until the words trickled to a stop. Quietly, I said, "Fifty-one percent."

"Huh?"

"I want fifty-one percent."

"Are you being serious?"

"Fifty-one."

She sat, fuming and flummoxed, the player at the table with the losing hand and everyone knows it. Finally, she said, "And then you'll do it? We'll have a deal?"

"I don't know why you're making this so complicated," I said. "Fifty-one."

I clasped my hands together and set them on the tabletop, our old signal for the con to begin, only in reverse and minus two fingers. She looked away, then up at my eyes.

"Okay," she said. "You want fifty-one percent. You want that, then fifty-one it is. All right? That's over. Now where's the bell?"

I met her gaze, saw the hunger in it. I almost felt bad for her when I said, "I'm sorry, but I don't know what bell you're talking about." I stood up and waved the guard over. "Good-bye, Ellen."

"Wait—no, no, no—we just agreed—"

"Ma'am?" Simon was coming our way.

"We're done," I told him.

"No!"

"Ma'am, all right, let's go." Gently, he took her arm. She stiffened but knew better than to resist. I watched her go and listened to the birds.

I wished Ellen had come at two o'clock instead of three-thirty. Now there was very little time before dinner. In the white-walled dayroom I joined my regular poker game, already in progress. Today they were playing for small bags of Fritos and mini Snickers bars.

At North Ridge, the poker chips were a remarkably durable composite of toilet paper and soap. The game was Texas Hold'em with a couple of crazy house rules and strict limits on raising. Over the weeks, I was steadily improving my play. Yesterday we'd played for stamped envelopes, and I made sure to win one. I needed to write that letter to Bruce Steadman to apologize for never coming through with the *Men's Quarterly* article. *It turns out I couldn't find a good enough cheat*, I would explain.

I made sure not to win all the time. Then no one would want me in the game. But I won pretty much whenever I wanted to, because here was what I was learning: the ultimate misdirection? It was me. Whenever it became my turn to deal, everyone looked away from my hands. Even convicts had that much decorum.

I won't lie. I still woke up in a cold sweat. Still found myself reliving that excruciating night, especially those critical few seconds of Russell's smack to my face followed by the cleaver's invisible chop. In my waking hours I tried not to think about any of it and instead focused on getting the feeling and dexterity back in my hand. Some days the task felt monumental, but I couldn't imagine better physical therapy than card handling. My Greek deal was becoming smooth and silent. Friction is the enemy of the card handler, and all those two fingers ever did, I was discovering, was provide too much of it.

Not anymore. My false deal was becoming something to behold because there was nothing to behold. My hands were steadier than ever. My mind was sharper than it had been in a long time.

For the next six and a half months I planned to play a lot of poker. And I needed to continue to woodshed. In my cell were two decks of cards and a dozen poker books. As Ellen used to do—or as she'd claimed to do (futile as it was to separate the truths from the half-truths from the lies)—I would get to fantasizing about my own cabin by the water, days of snorkeling and nights of separating rich tourists from their money. But those were only passing thoughts. In the real world, my plans remained stateside. Upon release I would move to Reno, city of gamblers, city of my mother. She had somehow come up with the bail, ten percent of the $50,000 the judge had set, driving herself even further into debt.

I would have refused her bail bond, but I'd needed to be out of custody at least long enough to investigate the Revere bell's worth. And to rent a small safe-deposit box at my bank. No way would I be able to sell the bell anytime soon. Selling it seemed awfully complicated, and I would need help—but there was plenty of time to figure all that out, even if it took years. There was no rush. And I had to be sure to do it safely.

But I had the bell. That was the important part.

I hoped never to need the money, anyway. I was pretty sure I could earn a living as a poker cheat, enough for me and some extra for my mother. I knew I'd make more than I ever did as a magician. (Yes, Brock, so you were right all along.) And I knew what the upstanding citizens whose home games I planned to frequent would do when it was my turn to deal the cards. They would check their phones. Refill the chip bowl. They would look anywhere and everywhere other than at my hands.

When I was on the outside again, my two missing fingers would be my greatest asset. They would be my superpower.

Sasha, one of the game's regulars, dealt me in. "Where've you been?" she asked.

"I had a visitor," I said, and several of the women went, "Oooh," as if I'd just returned from a hot date.

The women checked their hole cards. I checked mine. There was less than half an hour until dinnertime. Today, I decided, would be a winning day.

To false deal in prison, I knew, was to flirt with suicide. These were not people who forgave. Yet I'll say this: never have I felt so alive as in those moments when the freshly cut deck was squared up and in my hand, and the playing cards began their soft skate across the metal dayroom table.

And so I played this game the best I could.

ACKNOWLEDGMENTS

My sincere thanks to Jody Kahn at Brandt & Hochman Literary Agents for her wisdom and kindness. I'm very grateful to Otto Penzler for his remarkable editorial insight and generosity, as well as to Deb Seager, Kaitlin Astrella, Allison Malecha, Roberto de Vicq de Cumptich, Gretchen Mergenthaler, and everyone at Mysterious Press/Grove Atlantic. For their willingness to help me with the details, lexicon, and milieu of poker at various levels, I would like to thank Paul Fabel, Jaclynn Moskow, Michael Blinder, Craig Gibian, and Owen Laukkanen. Thanks to Andrew Rabinowitz for guiding me on the legal details. And I'm very lucky to have the astonishing Joshua Jay as my magic guru and friend. I'm grateful to Christopher Coake, Becky Hagenston, Michelle Herman, Julie Kardos, Stephen Kardos, Michael Piafsky, and Catherine Pierce for their valuable comments on the manuscript at various stages.

Huge and hearty thanks to my family, both born-into and married-into, for their steadfast support and good humor. Thanks to my mother, Felice Kardos, who without ever meaning to made me a writer. This is the first book of mine she hasn't read. I like to think she would have enjoyed it.

One of the pleasures of working on this novel was returning to old hobbies and passions. The following books were especially helpful to me.

T. Nelson Downs, *The Art of Magic* (1921)

S. W. Erdnase, *The Expert at the Card Table: The Classic Treatise on Card Manipulation* (1995). Originally published as *Artifice, Ruse, and Subterfuge at the Card Table: A Treatise on the Science and Art of Manipulating Cards* (1905)

David Britland and Gazzo, *Phantoms of the Card Table: Confessions of a Cardsharp* (2003)

Karl Johnson, *The Magician and the Cardsharp: The Search for America's Greatest Sleight-of-Hand Artist* (2005)

Finally, a shout-out to the kiddos and another heartfelt thank-you to Catherine Pierce, aka Katie, for making my life (and my words—it helps to marry a poet) immeasurably better and more interesting.

All the magic in this novel is real.